Marcus rose from his machine

and headed for Christina with the swagger of a male tiger prowling after its mate. His eyes darkening in hunger, he quickened his stride, eating up the space between them.

"Did I do something wrong?" asked Christina.

Her reply came in the way of a rush of cool air when Marcus used his preternatural speed to cross the gym and scoop her up in his arms before pressing his lips to hers in a crushing kiss.

"That stretching was the sexiest thing I've ever seen," he managed to bite out before he kissed her again.

Marcus pinned her against the wall next to the sauna door, his body pressed into hers. Christina wrapped her arms around his neck and returned his kiss with equal urgency. His hunger fueled her desire. He built the lust between them, letting their passion mix in their mindlink until, like a tornado, their desire circulated between them, building until it became an unstoppable whirlwind.

Nicholai opened the door to the sauna and made a hasty exit. "Get a room, you two." Nicholai glanced at them quickly, a smile on his handsome face.

Marcus grabbed the open sauna door, catching it before it closed as he broke their kiss. "Sounds like a plan. I think this room will do."

Deadly Alpha

by

Brenda Sparks

*The Alpha Council Chronicles,
Book 2*

Deadly Alpha

Contact Information: info@thewildrosepress.com

Cover Art by *Rae Monet, Inc. Design*

The Wild Rose Press, Inc.
PO Box 708
Adams Basin, NY 14410-0708
Visit us at www.thewildrosepress.com

Publishing History
First Black Rose Edition, 2015
Print ISBN 978-1-5092-0271-3
Digital ISBN 978-1-5092-0272-0

The Alpha Council Chronicles, Book 2
Published in the United States of America

Dedication

To my readers, who mean so much to me!

Acknowledgments

First and foremost, my deep love and appreciation go out to Don, who is my rock when things get chaotic, and my good friends (as well as early readers) Barbara and Elizabeth. Their insights and feedback have been invaluable to me.

And last but most certainly not least, I owe my sincere gratitude to my amazing editor, Callie Lynn Wolfe, cover artist Rae Monet, and the wonderful staff at The Wild Rose Press for helping me share the Alphas with the world.

Chapter 1

Desperate to get home before sunrise, Marcus Botticelli tapped his foot on the steps of his friend's front stoop where he waited for his car. He glanced down at his watch and noted the time.

We need to get going. Now, he thought as the limo stopped in front of him.

A familiar wrinkled face emerged from the vehicle and greeted him with a smile. Payton opened the door to the limousine as Marcus approached.

"Thanks, my good man," Marcus greeted his trusted, faithful helper.

The two had been compatriots for the past forty years. The elderly gentleman, more friend than employee, did all the things Marcus could not do for himself, such as play designated driver and run errands in the daylight.

"Of course, sir. Where to?"

"Home." Marcus tucked into the vehicle.

The vampire settled into the soft leather interior. Home, a funny word. His house wasn't really a home. He'd left a real home to come live in Savannah.

Marcus loosened his tie and undid the top button of his black dress shirt while the limo pulled away from the spacious mansion. He missed Vegas, missed the life he'd had there, the woman he'd left behind. But she

1

belonged to his sire now, and he thought it best to leave her and Sin City to Stephan.

Through the darkened window of his limousine, Marcus watched the world speed past. With a weary sigh, he leaned his head back against the seat and closed his dark eyes. Exhaustion weighed heavily on his body, thanks in part to the twists his life had taken as of late.

"The sun will be up in forty-five minutes. We need to get home, Payton," Marcus, eyes still closed, instructed his driver. Although somewhat protected in the limo, thanks to special UV-proof window tint, it was still better to be safe in the protection of his home when dawn came.

"Have a nice evening, sir?"

Marcus gave a derisive chuckle. "I guess you could say that, if your idea of a nice evening out is attending a party that's sole purpose is for you to find your heartmate. I've been swarmed by beautiful women all night, all of whom hoped to be my one true love."

"I can think of worse ways to spend an evening," Payton bantered as he swung the limo left.

"I really shouldn't complain. These types of parties have their place, I guess. Too bad you never converted or you too could know the pleasure of a parade of women vying for your attention."

It was Payton's turn to laugh. "Even that could not tempt me to become a vampire."

"Don't knock it until you try it, my old friend. It's pretty good work, if you can get it."

"I'll take your word for it, sir," Payton said, while he slowed the limo. Marcus raised his head and looked out at the road. His eyes landed on a scene so gruesome it could have been part of a horror movie.

Cars and trucks piled the highway in crumpled heaps of color. A reddish orange glow from cars ablaze lit the scene. Marcus watched as people wandered around the site—some in a daze, others crying. A woman with wild eyes stood screaming at the horrendous scene, while a man and his child sat on the road holding their injuries.

"Where are the paramedics?" Marcus sat forward in his seat.

"I don't know, sir. Do you wish for me to call 9-1-1?"

"I'm sure someone has already done that, Payton. I'm going to go help."

Payton's gray brows drew down in concern when their eyes met in the rearview mirror. "But, sir, the time. It would be safer to stay in the limo."

Marcus glanced at his watch then shook off the warning. "I have forty minutes. I can help. I'll be back before the sun rises."

With that, Marcus took off his suit coat, slipped his necktie from around his neck, and rolled up his black silken sleeves, ready to work. Exiting his limo, he took off at a human-paced run for the scene.

As he approached, the odors in the air overwhelmed him. The pungent diesel fumes from an overturned dump truck burned his nostrils. The gasoline from the cars mingled with the smell of burnt rubber left on the road by the skidding tires. Another scent permeated the air, one that his brain identified with ardent fervor.

Blood—the crimson nectar that sustained his kind.

Luckily for him, he'd consumed enough blood

during the party to keep his fangs from extending in hunger. And yet still his mouth watered. Marcus swallowed.

He approached the first heap of metal with caution and noted the condition of the wreckage. The car, now a clump of twisted plastic and metal, was unrecognizable. Marcus saw a hand dangle lifelessly from a partially exposed arm that protruded from the steel square. Marcus reached for the wrist, wrapped his fingers around it, and touched the radial artery, confirming what the vampire already suspected, the occupant was dead.

A mass of metal burned next to the car, and flames licked the lifeless form inside, blackening it. With the person having no hope for survival, Marcus moved on, sending his senses out over the scene, in search of someone who needed help.

Suddenly Marcus saw movement out of the corner of his eye. His gaze swept the smoky scene, coming to rest on a figure barely visible through the haze. Given the slight build, he assumed the person to be a woman.

She must be injured, Marcus thought, noticing the river of red that ran from her head to pool on her shoulders. He carefully made his way toward her through the conflagration of distorted wreckage.

Chapter 2

White-hot pain tore through Christina Prescott's chest. Her hands ached fiercely. She forced her eyes open and looked around in a daze, while her vision blurred with tears caused by the white chemical smoke that enveloped her. She made out a blurry shape of a white pillow before her. Was she in the hospital?

As the powdery smoke cleared, so too did the fog in her mind. Her senses slowly came online, and she realized she sat in her car. With a quick look around, she realized she'd been in an accident, the deployed airbag causing the smoke in her car.

Her nurse's training kicked in, and she did a quick body assessment as she shifted each of her extremities one by one. Pain pulsed in her body from head to foot. No, make that head to toe, she decided, wiggling her ten little pigs. When she saw no bones protruded from her body, she palpated her abdomen, relieved to find it soft. *Good, no internal bleeding, no harm to organs there.*

With no sign of serious injuries, she unsnapped her seatbelt and tried to exit the car. She pulled the handle, but the door did not open with its usual ease. Christina gathered her available strength to push harder against the door, but it still wouldn't budge. Slamming her fist into the bent steering wheel in frustration sent a fresh round of fiery pain throughout her body, and a sorrowful moan pushed from between her lips.

Just as she thought to scream for help, she noticed a figure gliding toward her. Christina wiped at her eyes with fisted hands, trying to clear the image from her vision. The dark form, with no discernible features, closed in. A strangely beautiful orange and yellow glow surrounded it, the smoke and moonlight making it seem eerily translucent.

Awestruck by the sight before her, her brain struggled to make sense of what her eyes registered.

Wait, that glow is fire. A blast of heat poured over her pained body. Her eyes stung, probably from the black smoke that surrounded her.

This was like a scene from a horror movie—one where the poor heroine had been dragged into hell. It certainly couldn't be real. This must be a trick of her mind, or maybe…

No. It was too much for her mind to process. Surely it couldn't be, but what else could explain the flames, the smell of burnt flesh, the pain that wouldn't stop?

I died and went to hell, Christina thought while she tried to remember what she did in her life to deserve an eternity in purgatory.

As the shadowy figure closed in, its massive width blocked out the background from Christina's view until only the ominous form remained. Her heart felt as if it would beat from her chest, pounding against her ribs in a furious rhythm.

Wait. Did one's heart beat in hell?

Chapter 3

Marcus reached the woman in the car, relieved to discover the flash of red was the woman's hair and not a pool of blood. He quickly assessed the situation. The car had been hit on the driver's side, buckling the door inward. When he looked in the car to better see the passenger, his gaze locked with a pair of large emerald eyes.

"You're not the devil," the woman sighed with relief and leaned her head back against the headrest of her seat.

"Depends on who you ask, my dear," Marcus quipped as he grabbed onto the door and yanked it from its hinges. He threw it aside as if it weighed no more than a Frisbee.

Marcus' intense gaze raked her body, assessing her injuries with cold objectivity. "Are you all right, ma'am?"

"I think so, but for some reason I-I can't seem to move m-my legs." She ran her tiny hands over her thighs.

"That's because they are pinned by the steering wheel. Here, let me get you out." Marcus grabbed the wheel and, with little effort, pushed it back up to where the car's manufacturer intended it to be.

"What's your name?" He slipped an arm around

the human's back and the other under her thighs.

"Christina," she replied in a shaky voice as he lifted her out of the wreckage, her weight no more consequential to him than that of a child's. He carried her away from the other vehicles and placed her safely on the ground.

"You sure you're okay, Christina?" Marcus stood over her, his large body shielding her much smaller one from the view of the carnage behind him.

The redhead left a black streak across her forehead when she wiped a hand wearily across her brow. "Yeah, I'm fine."

Christina glanced around at the casualties. "We need to help these people. I'm a nurse. I can treat them, but I'll need your help."

The tiny woman futilely attempted to brush the dirt from her scrubs and assumed a nurse-like persona, looking surprisingly authoritative for one so small.

She stood, turning on her heels. Her first step landed on a wobbly leg. Marcus steadied her with a hand on her elbow when she swayed.

"You sure you're okay? Maybe you'd better sit down." He kept his voice low, calm.

It appeared to steel her determination like nothing else could. Christina locked her knees, as if willing them to support her.

"I'm fine," she reiterated, her voice strong with determination. "Really. People need me, I have to help. Now please move. I need to go see to that man over there."

Marcus dropped his hand and watched as she approached the first casualty she saw. A bone protruded from the man's right thigh. His blood bubbled on the surface of his jeans where the femur cut through the material.

"I need a pair of scissors," Christina mused, while she grabbed the bottom of the man's pant leg and tried to pull the material apart to gain access to the wound.

"Here, I can do that."

Marcus took the pant leg in both hands and ripped it up to the crotch. The coarse material tore as easily as a piece of stationery between his fingers.

"Thanks." Christina eyed him warily. "You sure made that look easy."

A look of suspicious disbelief passed over her face in a moment so fast Marcus almost missed it. Using the ripped material, the nurse made a tourniquet and tied it around the man's leg.

Eyeing the next patient, Christina ordered, "Come here, devil man, put pressure on this wound."

A troubling sound made Marcus' head snap up, his attention seeking the source. He turned his preternatural hearing toward the noise and easily recognized the keening tone over the wail of approaching sirens.

"I can't. There is a child over there who needs my help."

With one powerful leap, Marcus vaulted a car blocking his way. The child's mother stood by her car frantically pulling on the door in a futile attempt to open it. Marcus knew she'd never get it open, for another car and a concrete barrier pinned the vehicle.

He laid a large hand on the woman's shoulder. He made sure his baritone voice contained a calming compulsion when he spoke. "Excuse me, ma'am. Stand aside. I can get the child out."

Marcus gently guided the young mother out of his

way and, using his immense strength, pushed the car away from the concrete barrier. He opened the crushed door and extracted the screaming child, still strapped in his car seat. Just as he unbuckled the preschooler from the car seat, the sounds of screeching brakes and tires skidding along the road drew his attention. When he looked up, his eyes locked on a work truck.

The small truck, with a framework built onto the bed, carried typical handyman items, a ladder, basic tools, and buckets. But what pulled Marcus' gaze were the three metal pipes attached to the top of the frame. The vehicle skidded sideways and slammed into a stopped convertible, causing the work truck to rise up on two wheels. The metal poles on the truck dislodged. They flew through the air like missiles of death. The poles headed toward the nurse who busily compressed the man's thigh, completely unaware of the pipes careening toward her. Horror knotted his stomach.

He placed the preschooler safely in his mother's arms and quickly used his powers of persuasion to erase her memory of the feat he had performed. Marcus called on his preternatural speed and strength to go after the nurse. Tensing his thick thigh muscles, he launched himself off the asphalt and hoped like hell he would make it in time.

He flew through the air, his arms outstretched toward the woman. When he reached her, he engulfed her in his arms, his momentum taking her with him through the air. He encased her body with his own and rolled them over, so they would land on his back. As they began their roll, one of the pipes grazed Christina's forehead by a millimeter.

They landed hard on the hot asphalt, with Marcus

skidding on his back. His hold tightened around the nurse as the hard blacktop tore his shirt. Debris bit into the flesh of his back, and his strong jaw clenched in pain.

When they came to a stop, the nurse propped herself up using her elbows on his chest. Her green eyes wide, the human woman stared at him in awe.

The warmth from Christina's body seeped through their clothes, the sensation oddly comforting to him, like coming home. The feeling surrounded him, sank into his bones.

Lying together with her hair encircling his head, Marcus bathed in her scent. She smelled of jasmine and honey, a delicious combination. He drew the seductive scent deep into his lungs with several long breaths.

Christina shook her head, disbelief widening her eyes. "That was incredible! Are you okay? Did you break anything? Is your back okay?"

"I'll be fine. You're the one bleed—" Marcus' response died in his throat, his words stifled by the drop of blood that fell onto his tongue from the wound on Christina's forehead.

He swallowed the drop along with his words, immediately overcome. That one drop tasted unlike anything he had ever consumed before. It tasted like she smelled—like honey and jasmine—sweet in a way he'd never experienced. It warmed him to the core, made him come alive. His vision swam, and his body reacted like a school boy's, painfully hard and aroused.

Mine! The thought popped into his head without warning. *My heartmate!*

Acutely aware of his body's response to her, the vampire quickly rolled from beneath Christina before she felt his reaction. He leapt to his feet with the usual grace of his kind and extended his hand to Christina. She put her hand in his and allowed his strength to help her stand. Her petite fingers sent a wave of desire through his veins.

"The pole got you. You're bleeding." Marcus licked his thumb and reached for her forehead. As his thumb rubbed across the wound, his saliva sealed the small cut. He struggled to keep the thumb from going back into his mouth to taste her luscious blood once more. The howling sirens from emergency vehicles as more arrived saved him from the temptation.

"Thank…" Christina began, but one of the injured drivers moaned, and the nurse ran to help the next survivor without finishing her thought.

He watched her go. The world tunneled to her, taking his attention from the sting on his back. She was tenacious, merciful, and beautiful. His chest swelled with pride as he watched her help others, selflessly attending to their needs, while ignoring her own.

He'd found his heartmate at last. Someone he would love forever, care for, and protect. While he knew heartmates could be human, after all, his sire had a former human as his heartmate. He'd always assumed his would be a natural born vampire. He found it ironic that his mate turned out to be mortal. As the realization hit, so did the tingling sensation on his skin.

He looked down and saw his flesh beginning to blister from the rising sun. Dawn had come and brought the deadly rays that would burn him with their pink hues. His eyes burned and watered while he ran for the relative safety of his limo.

Once he was inside, Payton threw a blanket over

his smoldering body. "Close call, sir."

"Yeah, I kind of lost track of the time." Marcus wrapped the blanket around himself and tucked his long legs up under him to fit all six-foot-three inches of his body under the material. The UV tint on the windows would keep most of the rays off his skin, but he was glad for the extra layer of protection the blanket provided him. Still, he would be safest in his house. "Get me home as quickly as possible, Payton."

"Yes, sir, right away." Payton maneuvered the limo over to the shoulder of the road, hit reverse, and drove backwards down the highway until he came to an exit ramp. Taking the ramp, he headed for Marcus' home as fast as possible.

"It's times like these, Payton, that I wish I could dematerialize like other vampires. Just think myself home, and I'd be there."

"You'll be able to do it one day, sir. I'm sure of it. Every year your powers increase, as is the way of your kind."

"Yep, one day I'll be like Dorothy in the Wizard of Oz. I'll just tap my heels and think 'there's no place like home' and poof, I'll be there."

As Marcus huddled under the blanket, his thoughts returned to the nurse. *My Christina.*

After centuries alone, he'd found his mate. Ordained by the Fates, she was made for him, perfect for him. He would have to win her, of course, for being human she didn't understand what it meant to be a heartmate.

He would have to find out all about her, and he looked forward to the discovery. What was her favorite food? Animal? She was a nurse, but where did she work? What did she like to eat? What was her favorite restaurant? The questions bounced around his brain like a trivia game.

He would call her tomorrow evening and ask her out on a date. But wait, he didn't have her number.

He suddenly sat up. Panic twisted his stomach as he pulled the blanket tightly around his body. *Oh shit, I don't even know her last name.*

Chapter 4

Marcus sat on the couch, stretched out his legs, and crossed them at the ankles. He hadn't slept much. Thoughts of Christina kept him awake. Were it not for the pull of the day sleep, he would not have slept at all. He leaned back, closed his eyes, and her image flooded his mind.

With one hand resting on the back of the couch and the other holding a glass of wine, he saw a mental picture of them at the accident scene. He pictured her lying on top of him, her long red hair flowing down, pooling around his head onto the street below them. He brought the wine to his lips. As he consumed the contents of the glass, he realized he craved something stronger. He went to the bar and grabbed a bottle of two-hundred-year-old scotch. The date stamp on the bottle took his mind back to the time the Alpha Council formed, a little over two hundred years ago. The Alphas, considered the Special Forces of the vampire breed, dealt with those who became too violent or demented to remain in civilized society, and Marcus was proud to be a member of the elite group.

Payton's footsteps drew Marcus from his reverie.

"Excuse me, sir. I don't mean to disturb you, but I have the results of the search you asked me to perform."

Marcus poured the Lagavulin into a glass. After swirling the fiery liquid, he downed it in one smooth gulp.

"Let me see it." Marcus poured himself another glass of Lag before he made his way across the room to grab the stack of paper from Payton's hands. He flipped through it and looked at the human in horror.

"You've got to be kidding me. There can't be this many Christinas in the Savannah White Pages."

"I'm afraid so. That is everyone in the white pages with the name Christina, or C as their initial."

"How am I ever supposed to find her? There are tons of names here." Marcus asked rhetorically, waving the papers before Payton's face.

"Perhaps one of your fellow Alphas might be able to help you. I'm sure some of them have unique gifts."

Marcus' thoughts flashed to Demetri Romanoff. At over six hundred years old, the male had learned much in that time. Proficient in every type of combat with most types of weapons known to Marcus, Demetri was the Alpha Council's strongest fighter.

His skills were sharp but his mind sharper. He possessed knowledge few others did. He happened to have a home in Savannah, so he was familiar with the area. Perhaps he *could* help.

Marcus fished the cell from the pocket of his jeans, sat back down on the sofa, and balanced his glass on one knee. He hit the speed dial button. With each ring, his anxiety grew. Would Demetri think him a fool for not erasing Christina's memory? Would Demetri think him insane for thinking Christina is his heart—?

"Hello," Demetri answered, his voice deep and raspy, with just a hint of a Russian accent.

"Hey, man, this is Marcus."

"Hello, Marcus. What has you dialing my number tonight?"

"I have a bit of a situation here, and I could use your help."

"Do you need me to come over? I could be at your home in about fifteen."

"That's okay. No need. We can do this over the phone." Marcus wiped a nervous hand down his face and settled farther into the couch. *It will be easier if we aren't face to face anyway.*

"Whatever you want, comrade. So, what can I do for you?"

Marcus took a deep, steadying breath. "I kind of messed up last night. There was an accident on the highway."

"Yes, I read about it in today's paper."

"Yeah, so anyway, I helped people during the accident."

"You wiped their memories. Right?"

After a brief hesitation, Marcus answered, "All but one."

"What!" Demetri's voice roared from the phone, and Marcus pulled it from his ear. "What do you mean all but one?"

"There was a woman... Look, I know you are going to think I'm nuts, but she's my heartmate."

Now Demetri hesitated. "Why exactly do you think that? Please tell me you didn't drink her blood at the scene of the accident."

"I didn't exactly drink from her. She became injured and some of her blood fell into my mouth. I know she is my heartmate; all the signs were there. My entire body and mind reacted to her."

"Well, I guess etiquette dictates that congratulations are in order. It is understandable you didn't wipe her memory. I assume you told her she was your mate."

The ice clinked against the side of the glass when Marcus took a long swallow of his scotch before answering. "I didn't get the opportunity."

"So you will contact her this evening and share the news."

"That's the problem…I only know her first name. The sun rose before I got any other information from her."

An inelegant sound escaped Demetri. "That's no problem. I have the contact information for all the vampires in Savannah. If you tell me her first name, we can at least narrow down the possibilities."

"She isn't a vampi—"

"You idiot!" Demetri's shout rang from the phone, ending Marcus' reply. "You left the memory of a human intact! Are you dumb or just plain stupid? What are you going to do to clean this mess up?"

Marcus couldn't say his fellow Alpha's response surprised him. He'd expected it, really. But Demetri's ire did not help him with his problem. He slammed down the last of his drink before responding. "That's why I called you. I don't know how to find her. I tried to find her in the phonebook, but do you have any idea how many Christinas there are in the Savannah White Pages? It would take me years to call all of them."

As Marcus placed his emptied glass on the end table, he heard only silence on the other end of the line. Demetri's voice sounded calmer when he finally spoke.

"I have heard of vampires who can call people to them using their minds. It is supposed to work like a mindlink, only one-sided. You can't communicate with each other. One person is calling; the other is coming as commanded."

"I've manipulated others with my mind when I've been with them, but I've never done anything like that over a long distance. I didn't even know such a thing was possible." The surprise made his words flow quickly from his lips.

"I have not done it either. As I said, I heard of other vampires doing it. It's worth a try. Otherwise, you'll be spending the next several years calling numbers for every Christina in the phone book."

"No other ideas?" Marcus' brows narrowed in consternation. "Just in case that doesn't work."

"No, but if I think of anything I'll give you a call." Demetri's accent thickened, and a sense of foreboding flowed over Marcus. "For your sake as well as the sake of our kind, I hope you find her. The last male I knew who couldn't find his heartmate went insane and needed to be put down."

He didn't need the warning. More than once Marcus witnessed others losing their mates. In fact, just recently the Alphas took out a male who had gone crazy from the death of his mate, and Marcus had been forced to watch his own sire give up his heartmate. "I don't need the reminder, Demetri. I remember when we took out Lucio a few months ago."

"Then you recall how devastated the male was."

"What I remember more is Stephan's reaction to giving up Kat. And that was before he knew she was his heartmate."

Until a few months ago, Marcus lived in his sire's penthouse in Las Vegas. He enjoyed his Vegas playboy lifestyle—a different woman every night and no shortage of tourists with whom to bed or drink from, or both. Vegas was his kind of city, it came alive after dark and no one became suspicious if you slept all day. Oh yeah, he definitely enjoyed his Vegas life. That was until his sire, Stephan, came into town for a visit.

"When Stephan erased memories of us from Kat's mind and sent her away to keep her safe, it almost destroyed him. I've never seen my sire so distraught."

"Luckily, it all worked out in the end."

Marcus had to admit Demetri was correct. In the end, Stephan and Kat fell in love and set up house in the Vegas penthouse Marcus had once called home.

"I'm surprised you didn't stay in Vegas, Marcus."

"You know the saying, three's a crowd. Not to mention I didn't want to sit around the place watching Stephan and Kat make goo-goo eyes at each other."

"So that's why you came back to Savannah."

"I bought this plantation in the eighteen hundreds, thought it was about time I got some use out of it."

The southern plantation, though grand, no longer suited him. For him, it was simply a place to stay until he could sell it and move to a city more in line with his high-rolling lifestyle. He had to admit, however, he did enjoy listening to the southern drawl that slid through the lips of the women in Savannah, but that was the only appeal of his current abode.

Well, that and the fact that somewhere out there in the city his heartmate waited. He must find her, make her his. Anxiety crawled over his skin. The Alpha needed to know his mate was safe. He wanted to get off this damned phone and try the technique Demetri mentioned. It might be a long shot, but it seemed his only shot at this time.

Marcus ended their conversation in the traditional valediction of the Alpha Council, "Safe travels, Demetri. And thank you for your help."

"And safe travels to you as you try to find your heartmate. Remember it is imperative you do not fail."

With that directive, Marcus snapped the phone shut and tossed it on the cushion beside him.

There's no time like the present. Marcus closed his eyes in concentration, leaned back, and rested his head on the couch. *Man, I hope this works.*

After picturing the redhead with the big emerald eyes, he began repeating the same series of words over and over again aloud. "Christina, come to me. Come to me now, Christina."

****

When her favorite paranormal movie came to an end, Christina stretched her arms over her head. She ran through her list of To Do's for the next day: buy groceries, call insurance company, rent a car. As her thoughts turned to the accident, she contemplated her life.

I've been through so much lately. First, I lost my father six months ago to cancer, then I was offered a job, which would have been great, except when my boss found out about the offer she let me go immediately, and now I've been in a car accident. Well, that's three, so hopefully the old saying will be true:bad things come in threes, and I'll catch a break.

She needed a pick- me-up, and since the endorphin rush she got from running on the treadmill wasn't an option due to stiff and sore muscles, she went to her other vice, playing the piano. As she sat on the wooden bench, she lovingly caressed the lines of the wood trim. She had this one item left of the things her mother had given her before she left, an instrument through which she expressed herself, explored her talent.

Her fingers hovered over the keys. She closed her eyes and allowed her mind to drift. A face took form in her mind's eye. A face with a hard jaw and strong lines, which perfectly emphasized his dark eyes and short, chestnut hair. For a man, he boasted beautiful features. No, that wasn't quite right. The gentleman from the accident, the one who saved her, was not feminine in the slightest. All male, his broad shoulders and tall stature made her feel petite when he stood over her. His was a face chiseled by God, and it provided just the right inspiration.

Her fingers moved of their own accord, their muse the mystery man. Her music filled her one-bedroom apartment with minor chords and beautiful harmonies. She played a dark romantic melody, secretly dedicating it to him. Her fingers flew over the keys in Allegrissimo tempos, creating rich tones and long crescendos. When she finished the composition, a feeling akin to longing called to her. A need pulled her, and the man's face pushed again into her mind. For just a second, the rich tone of his voice seemed to whisper in her ear. She shook her head.

Okay girl, pull yourself together. He was just some guy. Get over it. You'll never see him again, so just get over it already. She put her head in her hands. *I need a distraction. Thinking about Mr. Tall, Dark, and, Handsome isn't going to do me any good.*

Lifting her face, she perused her selection of sheet music. Finding a piece difficult enough to require her full attention and distract her from her thoughts of the sensual stranger, she played, drowning out everything but the music from her soul.

Chapter 5

An achy edginess consumed Christina since she awoke that afternoon. At first, she thought it was a physical sensation left over from the accident, but upon rising she found it much easier to move. Her muscles still stiff, though not as sore, performed most movements pain-free.

After dressing, she grabbed a bite to eat and re-examined the edgy feeling. Her chest tightened and her heart pounded harder. Every cell seemed to be responding to something—a call, a pull toward...what? She didn't know.

The nurse within her looked for the explanation, demanded it. *Do I have Post-Traumatic Stress Disorder? Depression? Anxiety?*

Christina rifled through the symptoms and dismissed each diagnosis. No, this wasn't mental. Perhaps it was simply fatigue from too many stressful events, like the accident and the extra things she'd had to do as a result.

But my To-Do list is complete. So why do I feel like I could crawl out of my skin?

She pushed from the table and took her plate to the sink. The sun warmed her face through the window, but even that did nothing to ease the achiness.

"Maybe a workout will help," murmured Christina

to the house plants sitting on the windowsill. She dried her hands and went to her room to change into a black sports bra and matching athletic shorts. She laced her running shoes and grabbed a bottle of water, then went to get the one thing she never ran without—a book. Christina walked into her closet where a bookcase stood tall, containing a stash of her secret obsession—paranormal romance novels. She perused the titles one by one trying to decide which she could become lost in while she ran. Her fingers caressed the spines with a lover's touch, slowly and with reverence, until she found what she sought.

She took out one of her steamier novels and, after a stretch to wake her muscles, she mounted the treadmill. As she read, the book came to life, and Christina quickly lost herself to the fictional world of fantasy lovers. Her feet pounded the belt while her rhythm increased to a hard run, but Christina didn't notice. In her fictional world, she watched the lovers come together as one after fighting adversity. Her eyes flew along the words, eating up the pages.

Once she finished the steamy chapter, she became aware once again of her body and looked down at the sweat glistening on her arms. Her breath rasped from her lungs in hard puffs, and her pace slowed to a fast walk.

Is it the running or the book that has taken my breath away? Christina thought wryly. With a smile, she wiped the perspiration from her face and neck.

She stopped after completing four miles, her muscles tired but her spirit invigorated. While she cooled off in front of the open window, she noticed the sun had begun to set, leaving its pinkish-orange hues in the sky. The moon gave chase, so bright the glow of the setting sun did not diminish its light.

What a gorgeous full moon. Christina forced herself away from the beautiful sight and headed to her bathroom for a quick shower.

Her bathroom typified the rest of her apartment— small and efficient. Everything was neat and orderly in the white room that contained a tiny sink, toilet and shower-tub combo.

Christina slid the pink, flower-print shower curtain aside and turned on the water. While it heated, she rubbed her hands up and down her arms in a vain attempt to massage away the uncomfortable tingle under her skin. Her stomach knotted once more as the achiness and longing returned—the respite offered from her run now over.

She stepped into the shower, with hopes the water would wash the torment down the drain. But it only strengthened as the hot water rained down on her. And now the tingling brought a friend to the party in Christina's body. Her body came alive, hypersensitive. Her feminine channel throbbed between her legs. Heat pooled in her core. Moist heat ran down her thighs. She felt needy, wanton. The water touched her like a thousand tongues licking her sensitive body. It drove her wild. She turned, letting the spray hit her back, hoping to relieve the pressure on her breasts. She quickly soaped her body and shampooed her hair, each drop torture.

She turned off the water and began to dry off with a pink fluffy towel, the soft terrycloth not helping the building passion. The longing overwhelmed her. She needed a diversion.

Man, I am so uptight. A drive around the city might just do some good. Maybe I'll go get something to eat.

She chose her clothes carefully, though not exactly sure why it mattered. She tried on a pair of khaki Capri pants with a black shirt but quickly discarded them, when she realized they didn't seem special enough. Next she tried on a celebrity-endorsed sweatsuit, but she didn't want that either. As she put on her favorite pair of black skinny jeans and a green wraparound top, she knew she found her bliss. She twirled in front of the full-length mirror attached to the back of her bedroom door and approved of what she saw.

She brushed her thick hair, did her makeup, and checked herself one last time in the mirror before she grabbed the keys to her rental car. Exiting the front door, she turned the key in the dead bolt and went down the stairs to her nondescript Ford parked on the street where she'd left it.

The engine came to life, and Christina took off. Like a sailor drawn by the song of a siren, a compulsion drove her. Unsure where she headed, Christina darted through the city. Her stomach rumbled, but she pushed down the hunger, the need to continue driving foremost in her mind. A left turn here and a right there, seemingly lost in thought, she drove. Christina looked around in disbelief when she found herself on the outskirts of town.

Her gaze swept the sides of the street. Everything looked right, felt right for some inexplicable reason. She slowed the car when she came upon a wrought-iron fence. This place seemed special, as if something waited for her behind that fence. She knew it, *felt* it. She pulled over and parked the car. As she opened the door, the smells of the crisp night air, the combination of freshly cut grass, oak trees, and misty rain greeted her.

The houses were an impressive distance apart here, most of them mansions on large expanses of land. The dark street welcomed her, with a soft glow on the pavement created by the few streetlights that stood watch on either side. As Christina meandered down the deserted street, she felt strangely comforted, as if she found something she'd lost long ago. The need within softened, the ache soothed.

****

Marcus sat at the large mahogany desk in his office. Much as he had done throughout the day, the Alpha became still as stone and closed his eyes. He allowed his senses to flare outward, mentally visualizing the city as he did so. As his mind searched for the one he desired, he sent out a mental command. *Christina, I need you. You must come to me, tonight. You must find me. We belong together. I can wait for you no longer. Come to me.*

Sensing nothing, Marcus banged his fist on the desktop. As he glanced down on the paperwork for one of the many charities he had started, he thought only of Christina. His Christina. He had not had any luck summoning her, his desperation making it impossible for him to concentrate. He needed to come up with another way to find her.

I need some fresh air, he thought as he stood and crossed the room to the window. Opening it wide, Marcus took in the cool night with a deep breath. He placed his hands on the window ledge, letting the sill bear his weight. He hung his head low. His eyes closed.

Oh Christina, how am I ever going to find you? Marcus drew his fingers through his thick hair. The breeze carried the softness of jasmine and honey. His eyes snapped open as his head darted up. He drew in a super-sized breath, taking the amazing scent deep into his lungs. Marcus' dark brown eyes went wide as realization came to him.

It's impossible. It can't be. He drew another deep breath, filling his body with the allure of his heartmate. *It's got to be. Nothing else smells like her.*

Marcus grabbed his coat.

Chapter 6

Christina ran her hand along the iron fencing wondering why she'd been drawn here. Her gaze focused past the iron bars to the trees that lined a long gravel driveway. She imagined a beautiful house lay beyond those magnificent live oaks, which stood like sentries along the drive. An overwhelming need to enter the house pulled her.

Okay, Christina, get a grip woman. You don't know who lives here. Maybe I bumped my head in the accident. Christina pulled her thick hair back from her face. *Yeah, an MRI might not be a bad idea. I should get myself to the hospital, STAT.*

Christina turned to leave and ran into a mountain of immovable muscle. A small squeak of surprise escaped her throat. She looked up into the face of the mountain. His beautiful mouth turned into a smirk as he said, "Imagine running into you like this."

He's smooth. Christina stepped back. "What are you doing here?"

"I live here." He took in the expansive estate with a sweep of his arm. "What's your excuse?"

Waves of heat came off his body. They flowed around her, enveloping her like a blanket. Her stomach knotted, and her core clenched in response to his nearness. Christina stammered, "I-I was just out for a drive and… I don't know, felt compelled to stop."

"You were fondling my fence. Perhaps you'd like to come inside."

"I don't think so. I don't even know your name."

"I can fix that. My name is Marcus. Marcus Botticelli." His disarming smile took her breath away as he stuck out his hand.

Christina gave his hand a friendly shake. "I'm Christina Prescott," she said, before her fingers released their grip.

Marcus retained her hand in his, as if enjoying the feel of her skin against his. "I remember. So now that we have been properly introduced, would you like to come in?"

Christina hesitated. "Um…I'm not sure I should." She pulled her fingers from his grasp, unsure if she felt relieved or saddened by the fact he allowed their escape this time.

"Come on." Marcus lifted his arms, holding them out from his sides in a gesture to show he meant no harm. "What can it hurt? I saved your life, after all. Please come in. We could have a drink together. It could be your way of thanking me."

"You did save my life," Christina said, giving an insouciant shrug that sent her crimson hair flowing over her shoulders. Surely a man who had put his own life in danger saving others could be trusted. His kind, mesmerizing eyes captured hers, and she seemed to fall into his dark chocolate gaze. *Yummy.* "Okay…maybe just one drink, then I have to go."

He opened the tall iron gate for her. Its groan sent an involuntary shiver down Christina's spine.

Noticing her reaction, Marcus said, "Sorry about

that. It's a terrible sound, isn't it?"

"Yeah," Christina murmured not knowing if she trembled from the sound or from the sense she was walking into something that would change her life forever.

As they strolled up the gravel driveway, Christina took in the surroundings. She noticed the way the oak trees lined the drive like an archway. The branches stretched overhead, folding together as if they were Marines at a wedding, creating the military sword arch for a bride and groom. The Spanish moss hung from the branches and swayed in the breeze like veils of tulle. Overcome by the sentiment, Christina looped an arm through Marcus', then immediately chastised herself for the silly thoughts and brazen behavior.

"I can't believe I'm doing this." Christina glanced at Marcus, noticing how her five-foot-five-inch frame felt dwarfed by his size.

His hand closed over her fingers as he bent his elbow. The breeze carried his scent, wrapping her in its delicious smell. She wanted to get lost in him. *Whoa, where had that come from?* Christina's mind wandered in unusual directions as they walked. Swallowing hard, she forced her feet forward.

"What can't you believe you are doing? Coming to a stranger's house? That's the most sensible thing a person could do." Marcus looked at Christina and smiled, barely flashing his perfect teeth.

She shook her head. "My father would kill me for doing something like this. He always said I trusted people too easily."

"I must agree with your father." Marcus glanced at her. Her look of surprise brought a wry grin to his handsome face. "Usually I wouldn't advise you to go off with a stranger. But I know me, and I'm okay. I promise I won't bite."

Christina pulled her hand from his arm to wrap her arms around herself in a bracing hug. "I've always been a good judge of character. I listen to my instincts, and they've gotten me this far safe and sound."

His smile slipped from his face. "What do your instincts tell you about me?" Marcus removed his coat and draped it around Christina's shoulders, his eyes searching hers.

She grabbed the lapels then snuggled into it, drawing it closed not to ward off the chill in the air but to engulf herself in the masculine smell of Marcus. Christina examined her instincts about the man beside her before she replied.

"My instincts tell me that I don't need to worry about being around the man who saved my life."

A warm smile that reached the corners of his beautiful eyes rewarded her comment.

When they came upon Marcus' house, Christina's eyes widened. White wood siding enveloped the home, and green shutters framed each window. A wraparound porch, which matched the siding, housed several wicker rockers and settees. Six large columns supported a second floor balcony that ran the length of the front of the home. A set of wooden stairs led to the entry doors and completed the picturesque scene, adding to the charm of the plantation house.

Marcus ascended the stairs and grabbed one of the oak doors. As Christina stepped onto the porch from the top step, she noticed something out of the corner of her eye. Pivoting toward the sight, she glanced at the ceiling of the porch. The black winged creature let go of its perch and plunged into the night over Christina's head.

Startled by the animal, another small squeal of surprise sounded from her lips, and she stepped back. Her foot met air, sending her flying backward. Her arms flailed wildly in the air and sought purchase where there was none to be found. Suddenly two strong arms swept her up. Marcus' bulging biceps and large forearms encased her petite frame.

"You made that adorable noise again." He flashed a sexy, heart-melting smile.

He thinks my squeal is adorable. Christina lay pliant in his arms.

He lifted one eyebrow and the side of his mouth into a smirk. "I might just have to keep startling you, so I can keep hearing that cute noise."

"If I see another bat, you'll hear that noise again."

"Who, Barney? He's my attack bat."

"You keep bats?" Her eyes went wide, and Marcus chuckled.

"I'm just teasing. I do not keep bats. However, if one wants to visit and make a meal out of some of the insects around this place, I'm all for it. Let's get inside before he returns."

Marcus bounded up the stairs to his home and took her inside. The door closed behind them with a soft click. Christina felt a moment of unease but quickly pushed it aside. *Must be an automatic door.*

The sight greeting her eyes impressed her even more than the scene outside. They were in a grand foyer. To the right an opening invited people into a formal living room, while to the left a set of French doors beckoned friends to a sitting room. Crown molding encircled the top of the white plaster walls. Mirroring each other, on opposite walls, were two original Mort Kunstler paintings of the Civil War. Dark hardwood flooring, covered with an oriental rug, led straight toward a large staircase that wound its way up to the second floor.

It took Christina several minutes to take in all the beautiful sights the home offered.

And this is just the foyer. The thought pulled her from her perusal, and she realized Marcus still held her in his strong arms. The heat from his body sent a flare of desire coursing through her blood.

Color crept up her neck to heat her cheeks as she discovered he had been intently watching her. The hungry look in those eyes stole her breath.

"Um…you can put me down now," Christina whispered with a smile. "Or do you plan on holding me all night?"

"The thought crossed my mind." Returning her smile, Marcus released her legs so her body slowly slid down his. Her heartbeat raced in her chest and her breathing increased, causing her breasts to gently graze his chest with each inhale as they stood toe to toe.

"Thank you." Christina turned out of his grasp. He seemed reluctant to let her go as he slid his hands from her shoulders, down her arms and over her hands.

His long gait took him past her as they walked. He opened the partially closed French doors to his sitting room with a gallant sweep of his arm. *"Entrez, mademoiselle."*

"Parlez-vous français, monsieur?"

"Yes, I speak French. *Et vous?"*

Walking into the impressive room, Christina answered, "Me? No, I took a couple of years of high school French, but that was it. *Merci beaucoup* and *voulez-vous coucher avec moi ce soir* is about all I remember now." She giggled then placed her hand demurely over her mouth.

Coming up behind her, Marcus whispered into her ear in a low, husky voice. "Those are the only two phrases I need to hear."

Without looking at him, she stepped away before her body took control and turned her into his warmth. Acutely aware of him, she felt his gaze on her while she crossed the room. Christina blushed and feigned interest in the wet bar she saw in the corner. "How about that drink you offered?"

Marcus licked his lips. The act sent a shiver through her body to her core. "You have no idea how much I'd like a good drink right now. Something red."

"How about this Merlot?" Christina picked up a bottle and held it for his inspection.

"Sticking with the French theme, I see. That's a perfect choice. I'll get the glasses."

While Marcus busied himself getting their drinks, Christina took in the room. In the large sitting area, the parquet floor was partially covered by another oriental rug and a set of matching, striped Louis XIV chairs faced the fireplace whose mantel was adorned with gold leaf.

Marcus hoped Christina approved of his home. She certainly seemed to be taking it all in. Of course, if she found anything lacking, he would see to it that it was fixed to her liking immediately. He had spent a small fortune renovating the place and kept it well-stocked in the event visitors dropped by.

Thankfully for him, vampires were able to ingest food as well as blood. In fact, Marcus found most human foods delectable. He especially enjoyed indulging in sugary sweets and many alcoholic drinks. It was one of the few human customs he still regularly partook of even after two hundred and fifty years of existence as a vampire. It helped him assimilate with his human friends.

While Marcus poured the dark red wine into two glasses, discreetly adding blood to his, Christina settled onto the couch. The Alpha sauntered across the room to join her, a wineglass in each hand.

After handing one of the glasses to Christina, he lifted his in her direction. "Here's to…" he hesitated, his mind going blank as he watched her tongue dart out to lick her red lips. The sight hardened his most masculine part, and his heart race with desire.

Christina saved him by raising her glass in a toast. "Here's to thanking the man who saved my life."

They clinked goblets. His gaze tracked her lips as they closed around the rim of the delicate crystal, then lowered to follow the fluid movement of her throat when she swallowed. His hand tightened around the stem of his glass.

"Here's to what I hope will be a beautiful evening with an even more beautiful woman." He loved the way her cheeks blushed at his compliment. He smiled into his glass.

By the third bottle of wine, Marcus knew much about Christina. The more she consumed, the freer the information about her flowed. He now knew she was, for all intents and purposes, an orphan. She was off from work for the next seven weeks, thanks to her current employer letting her go when she'd given them notice about taking a new job. She lived alone and planned on moving to Atlanta to start her new job at St. Joseph's Hospital. And, oh yeah, she was a virgin. That last bit of information had been especially revealing. Apparently, she was saving herself for marriage.

"You know, I think I've been talking about myself all evening." Christina's Southern accent slurred. "Tell me more about you."

Looking down into the glass of red he'd been nursing, Marcus replied, "There's not much to tell, really. I'm just your typical male who goes around rescuing damsels in distress." Marcus flashed his best smile, careful not to expose the tips of his fangs. The longer she remained in his presence, the more his baser instincts pushed their way to the surface. He struggled to rein in the biological need to claim his heartmate.

He wanted to taste more of her blood. No, he more than wanted it, he craved it, needed it desperately. His hunger rose, even though his appetite should have been sated by the blood he'd consumed with his wine. Marcus realized the hunger wasn't for sustenance but a hunger for his mate. His body recognized Christina as his, and it wanted her body and blood.

"I know you speak French and English. Do you speak any other languages?"

"I actually speak Italian, too. Italian is my first language."

"You were born in Italy?"

"Yes, I grew up there." Marcus grabbed the nearly empty wine bottle. "May I top off your glass?"

Christina leaned slightly across his lap while

holding the stemware under the bottle. As he poured the last drop of wine into her glass, she swayed. Marcus quickly set down the bottle and pulled her back against him with his free arm to steady her, tucking her against his side. Where Christina leaned into him, her warmth seeped into his skin.

The sigh escaping through her parted lips made him push into her mind to glean her thoughts. The combination of the wine and his warmth had a tranquil effect on her. Her eyes closed, and she yawned, placing her hand over her mouth. Her head felt heavy, too much for her neck to support.

She lowered her head onto Marcus' chest over his heart, sending a tingling sensation throughout his body. Marcus sensed her exhaustion, and the Alpha's protective instincts flared to life. He wanted to provide for her, take care of her. She struggled to keep her eyes open, and he could do no other than provide what she needed.

He lowered his head and whispered against the top of her head, "You're so tired, Christina. Sleep now, my dear. Sleep and don't awake until I command it."

He punctuated his directive with a gentle mental push, assuring she would stay asleep until he awakened her. After he slipped from the couch and located her purse, he pulled her driver's license from her wallet to obtain her address.

A smile tugged at his cheeks when he turned back and looked down on Christina's pretty face while he tucked the wallet back in the pocketbook. He plucked his car keys from his pants.

"Let's get you home and into bed, Red," the Alpha whispered. A wicked smile took his face.

Chapter 7

After opening the car door, Marcus kissed the top of Christina's head and scooped her into his arms. Her head lolled back against his shoulder. Looking down at her peaceful expression, Marcus felt his heart clench. Never had he seen anything more beautiful than the sight of her lying in his arms. The most beautiful woman in the world and she would be his.

He climbed the stairs two at a time to the second floor. He easily found the door number that matched her license and opened the door with his mind. Marcus carried Christina into her home. Another mental command shut the door, sealing them into darkness. With his preternatural vision, Marcus had no trouble seeing.

He stood in Christina's tiny one-bedroom apartment. The place looked spotless, white-glove-inspection ready. He expected no less from Christina; even injured, she had seemed organized, her car neat inside.

His long gait quickly ate away at the length of the hallway until he came to a bedroom at the end. Toeing the door open, he carried Christina into the room. A soft glow from the streetlight below illuminated the room. Using his mind to turn down the pink, ruffled bedspread, Marcus laid his heartmate gently onto the soft cotton sheets. He gazed down at her as he ran the back of his hand over her cheek. She nestled instinctually into the touch, turning her face slightly toward him.

"You are so beautiful," he whispered.

Marcus removed her shoes then lifted her legs and tucked them under the sheets. He brought the comforter up under her chin, swaddling her before he bent down to brush a soft kiss on her forehead and whispered, "Sleep well, my heartmate, until morning."

Marcus pushed into her mind to reaffirm the compulsion would wear off by dawn, which was just enough time for him to examine the apartment and get to know his heartmate a little better.

His eyes traveled to the nightstand. On it sat an alarm clock and a small lamp that partially hid a book from his view. He reached for the paperback, noting the title with a raised eyebrow before flipping it over. It was about vampires. *"A stunning story about a woman and the dark lover who will go through the fires of hell to save her,"* said the quote on the back of the book.

His eyes continued their journey about the room, absorbing every nuance. A flower print hung on the wall across from her bed, but he noticed no other pictures in the room, save for the framed photo of Christina and an older man with their arms around each other. Marcus presumed the man in the picture must be the father she'd spoken of.

His survey of the room garnered him more information about Christina, but his appetite for knowledge about his heartmate wasn't sated. He made his way to her closet to see if his hunger might be appeased. Opening the door, he found it much bigger than he expected, given the size of the apartment. The large walk-in closet, lined with wooden slats, held an aromatic scent of pine. Against one wall stood a wooden bookcase with five shelves. Marcus ran his eyes over the pictures on the spines of the books. *Christina has a collection of romance novels. That little minx.*

A quirky smile pulled at one corner of his mouth upon the discovery. He carefully examined the books, reading each title. Every last one of them happened to be about vampire lovers. *Unbelievable!* He pulled one of the stories from its resting place and turned it over to see the cover. *No freakin way!* He replaced the book. *What is the chance I'd find a kinky, vampire-loving human?*

He stifled a deep belly laugh and made his way back to the living room. This time he allowed himself the luxury of taking in the surroundings.

Upon the walls hung more framed prints of flowers. In the living room sat all the basic necessities—a couch, a wooden coffee table, a television.

And her upright piano. *Well, hello there.* Another piece of the Christina puzzle. She must play piano. Or maybe someone simply gave her the thing. Marcus made a mental note to discover all her hidden talents as he ran a finger up the keys.

What have we here? Fingering her collection of DVDs, he noticed a pattern. Every third or fourth title was about vampires.

We are meant to be, he thought, flicking through the cases.

He walked through the living room and reached for

the door. The thought he needed to lock the door behind him stilled his hand on the knob and made him stop. A simple thing really—locking the door—hardly worth thinking about. But when he realized the deadbolt was her only protection, he found himself wishing she had an alarm system for added security. Luckily, soon enough she'd be living with him at the plantation, if all went according to plan.

And didn't that just bring a whole new round of wishing to his brain. The plantation wasn't overly secure, either. It had special shutters on timers and every day, minutes before dawn, they automatically closed, sealing off the rooms from the sun's rays. When closed, the shutters encased every window on the home, but they would not be enough protection, not once Christina came to live with him.

For the first time, something in his home would be irreplaceable to him.

His heartmate.

Marcus stepped out of the apartment, then closed and locked the door with a thought. At the top of the stairs, he paused, sparing a moment to glance over his shoulder. He nodded in satisfaction, knowing the apartment was locked up tight. On his trek to the car, he made a mental note to ask Payton to arrange for an alarm system to be installed at the plantation immediately. The Alpha just hoped, given the evil that surrounded him, it would be enough to keep her safe, for he already loved her and knew he'd never live without her.

Upon arriving back at the estate, Marcus leaned against the front door and scrubbed a hand down his face. His willpower teetered.

He longed to taste her sweet blood again. His body craved it like a smoker yearned for a cigarette. Marcus wasn't sure he would be able to stop once he started to drink. Maybe if he drank other blood first, maybe if he could sate his physical hunger, he might be able to control himself when he took her vein. Until then, he wouldn't risk it. The draw of her blood might be too strong.

Calling on all the willpower he had carefully honed over the years, the vampire pushed away from the door. He needed a distraction, and the sound of Payton milling around the kitchen gave him just that.

Marcus made his way into the kitchen. The room had been remodeled to accommodate modern appliances, most of which were disguised as cabinets. The ovens, dishwasher, and refrigerator all had faux doors which blended seamlessly with the white wooden cabinets hanging on three walls of the room. The only appliance easily identifiable was the stove top.

"Where is the blood? I'm starving." Marcus opened the refrigerator for a look.

"I'm sorry, sir, it would seem you finished it last night, and we are out. I will get you some from your supplier tomorrow." Payton placed some fruit on the table.

"Dammit, I really needed some." Marcus slammed the door shut with more force than he intended, causing the items in the fridge to shake. Vampires were able to go days without blood, if needed, and he could wait, but he wasn't sure he should be around Christina while the hunger took him. The way her blood called to him, it would be difficult to resist her.

In the middle of the kitchen stood a granite island,

on one side a second sink and cutting station beckoned to the chef, while on the other side a bar called to eaters to come and sit a spell. Above the island, copper pots hung, ready for use, which Marcus tapped, sending the pans clanging into one another before he sat at the island.

"Payton, what are your plans for today?"

"Nothing in particular, sir."

"I need you to add something to your list."

"Certainly." Payton began to clean the counter, as if they needed it.

"I need you to hire a contractor to install an alarm system. I want a security system installed ASAP—like today. I want it to have all the bells and whistles, motion detectors, emergency locks—the works."

"Of course, sir. I'll make it my priority. May I ask why the sudden need for such a system? Is there a threat I need to be aware of?"

"No, there's no threat, but there is something I wish to protect."

"Should I have a safe built too?"

Marcus considered the question. The only thing in this house he wanted protected was his mate. Quite frankly, he believed a pedestal to be more appropriate of a place for her than a safe. "No safe, but a panic room might be a good idea. You can't be too careful, you know."

The older man raised a questioning gray brow. "Now I'm really curious. If I may ask, what exactly are you protecting?"

"Payton, my friend, I have found her. I found my heartmate. "

Payton smiled amicably, looking genuinely happy.

"Congratulations! When will I get to meet her?"

"Hmmmmmm." Marcus pondered the question. "Well, considering I left a note at her place about her car being parked in front of the house, I'm guessing she will come by later today to pick it up."

"Will she be staying for a meal?"

"We'll invite her for dinner and dessert." Marcus wagged his brows. "And if I'm very lucky, maybe breakfast tomorrow."

Marcus watched a curious look cross Payton's wrinkled face. Unable to stop himself, he pushed into the butler's mind to discover what troubled the man. Marcus struggled to keep the smile from his face when he found the man worried about whether or not Marcus had honorable intentions toward the woman. Payton's old-fashioned notions were one of the things the Alpha enjoyed about the man.

"I'm heading down to my quarters to get some shuteye. Please work on that security system for me, will you? I'd like it in place as soon as possible."

"Of course, sir."

After a congratulatory handshake, Marcus left his companion and walked downstairs to his suite. The master bedroom occupied what used to be the basement. He had it specially renovated when he'd bought the house. The door to the suite opened into a spacious sitting room. Two fireplaces in the room stood proudly, located on opposite walls. In front of one fireplace, a pair of leather chairs flanked a small round table which held a chess set. Across the room a dark blue couch, with a table nestling its back, welcomed a sit. As he made his way through the sitting room, he paused to admire the original Peter Paul Rubens painting on the wall, appreciating the art with new eyes. He wondered if Christina would like it. Hoping she would, he opened the oversized cherry door to his sleeping chamber, feeling light of heart with happiness.

In his room, his four-poster, California king bed, adorned with black silk sheets and a matching comforter, was the focal point of the room. The cherry wood bedroom set included a wardrobe, long dresser with ten drawers, and two end tables that sandwiched the bed. At the end of the bed sat a couch with a marble coffee table, perfect for resting one's legs on. Two columns stretched from floor to ceiling supporting an ornamental arch. A seventy-inch flat-screen TV in a cherry media armoire completed the set.

Marcus crawled into bed exhausted from a lack of sleep the past two nights. As the lethargy of the day crept upon him, he thought of his heartmate. Excitement to see her again welled in his chest, and he welcomed the sleep that would take him to Christina in his dreams.

Chapter 8

Reality came to Christina slowly as she fought her way through the induced sleepy haze. She remembered the wine, remembered feeling tipsy, but she didn't remember anything else. Panic made her skin tingle. Christina clutched the sheets to her neck while her eyes swept the room, and she was much relieved to discover she lay in her own bed.

"How did I get here?" she wondered aloud.

She didn't have to wait long for an answer. She reached for the folded paper with the words *read me* on the top. Christina rubbed the last of the sleep from her eyes and read.

Dear Red,

You passed out on me tonight. Hope you didn't find me that boring. *wink* I brought you home and tucked you into bed.

Christina's cheeks flushed with heat. She lifted the sheets and peered beneath. Relief flooded her when she realized her clothes from the previous night were still on her body. Her eyes darted back to the note.

Don't worry, I was a perfect gentleman...this time. But no promises for next time.

Marcus' face formed in her mind's eye, and her heart beat in rapid succession. The grin on his sensual lips stretched to his eyes—eyes that sparkled with an unnamed emotion. Possession. Lust. Hunger? Another blush heated her cheeks.

Speaking of the next time, I'd like to see you again.

Your car remains parked in front of my estate. Should you be so inclined, I wish you'd drop in to say hello when you come to pick it up. Or you could simply call me, and I'll come to get you tonight. Either way, I hope we are together again soon.

Did she want to see him again? Yes! Christina felt oddly unsettled, as if her body craved something she couldn't quite explain. She normally enjoyed the peace of a moment alone; tonight she wanted nothing more than to be with someone.

"Not someone. Marcus," she murmured aloud as she glanced down at the phone number and address written at the bottom of the paper.

She clutched the paper to her chest and glanced out the window, shocked to discover it was almost sunset. She'd slept the day away!

"Must have had more to drink than I thought." She smacked her lips in a desperate attempt to rid herself of the bad taste in her mouth.

"Yuck. Cottonmouth. I need a toothbrush and a shower. STAT."

Thirty minutes later, Christina exited the shower and wrapped a towel around her body, tucking it in at her breast, while she crossed the space to the vanity. She wiped the fog from the mirror with a hand towel and put her hair up in a simple French braid, then applied her makeup. Once she looked presentable, she left the bathroom to get dressed.

Christina chose a loose-fitting white shirt. In contrast, the navy pants were a little tight but not bad.

Her stomach rumbled with hunger as she donned her shoes.

"I really need to eat something, but first I should get my car back."

After a short cab ride, Christina found herself with a dilemma. Should she retrieve her car and go home or take the welcome offered by the open gates to the plantation? Her feet seemed to move up the gravel drive of their own volition. The delicious aroma of freshly cut grass mixed with honeysuckle to tickle her nose as the night air flowed over her skin. The thought of seeing Marcus again made her pace quicken.

When she arrived at the home, Marcus stood on the porch, looking down at her with hungry eyes. Christina pulled nervously at the tight-fitting pants, conscious of the way he watched her movement. She rolled the sleeves on the shirt, drawing his heated gaze.

"I'd hoped I'd see you tonight." His voice sounded thick and raspy.

"I needed to get my car."

"When you didn't call me for a ride, I was afraid you'd pick up your car and drive away without stopping in to say hello."

"I wanted to thank you…for taking me home."

"It was my pleasure." A sexy smile took Marcus' full lips. "I'm always happy to help a damsel in distress."

"I don't know how much distress I was in, but I do appreciate the ride home."

"Why don't you come in for a bite?" A mischievous smile spread across Marcus' face, and Christina wondered if he had something planned.

"I wouldn't want to put you to any trouble. I'm not

all that hungry." Her stomach grumbled its disagreement.

Marcus smiled and made his way down the stairs. "It's no trouble. Payton would be quite upset if you didn't stay for dinner. He's been cooking all afternoon."

"Who's Payton?"

"Let's go find out." Marcus extended his arm when he approached the last step, and Christina allowed him to lead her through the house to the kitchen.

The wonderful aroma of ginger filled her nose, making her stomach growl. After a quick introduction to his valet, Marcus helped her into a seat at the table.

While they enjoyed the Thai feast prepared by Payton, Christina became enraptured with Marcus. She sat across from him, her full attention on every word he spoke. It wasn't until Payton approached their table with a cordless phone in his hand that she registered the thing had rung.

Without taking his eyes from Christina, Marcus asked, "Who is it, Payton?"

"It's Mr. Romanoff, sir. He wishes to speak with you."

"I have to take this call." Marcus grabbed the phone. "Please excuse me."

He left the room quickly. Christina heard the deep timbre of his voice trail off as he put distance between the two of them. She wondered just who this Mr. Romanoff was. Marcus seemed to take on a different persona when he answered the phone. His shoulders tensed, his face tightened. If she had to guess, she would bet they had a working relationship. Maybe Mr. Romanoff was his boss.

Payton did not give her much time to ponder their

relationship.

"Did you prepare all this?" Christina swept her arms around the table to indicate the meal before her.

Payton nodded his head. "I did, ma'am."

She looked over at the older gentleman and smiled her appreciation. "It was amazing. Thank you so much for preparing it. Can I help you clean up?"

Payton looked appalled. "No, ma'am. I will be the one to clean up, not you."

"Are you sure I can't help? I don't mind."

Payton adamantly shook his head. "I'm positive."

Christina cocked her head to one side, sending the stray wisps of her hair flowing over her shoulder. "You remind me of someone, but I can't think of whom."

"Master Marcus has mentioned that I resemble Michael Gouch."

"Who's that?"

Payton blew out a heavy sigh. "He was the actor who played the part of Alfred Pennyworth."

Christina gave him a questioning look, then shook her head indicating that she did not recognize the name.

"Batman's butler on the TV show in the sixties," Payton clarified.

Christina's eyes widened. "Of course. You look exactly like him."

A rosy flush took the valet's face. "Not exactly," he murmured.

"Well, no, but close enough to be related. That's so cool. I always thought he was the brains behind the bat in that show. I bet you are a lot like his character."

Payton's eyes met hers. He straightened ever so slightly under her compliment, a smile reaching the lines by his eyes. "Do you watch much TV? We have a media room that you might like."

Christina allowed Payton to take her plate. "I really don't watch that much TV, but I love to read."

"If you are finished, you might want to wait for Master Marcus in the library. There are some wonderful books in there you could pass the time with while you wait for him."

"That's a great idea." As Christina got up to go to the library, she paused. When Payton turned to look questionably at her, she smiled shyly and asked, "Can you tell me how to get to the library?"

A few twists and turns later, Christina opened the doors to the library and strolled into the room.

"This is amazing," she whispered in awe.

The ceiling of the room stood as tall as the house, extending up to the third floor. On three walls were built-in bookcases, each two stories in height. On rails, a mahogany ladder slid between the cases filled to capacity with leather-bound editions. In the middle of the room, a settee adjacent to two wingback chairs, all covered in a thin-striped material, encouraged people to relax and read. A round marble topped table with a Tiffany-style lamp separated the two chairs. The glow of the lamp flowed softly over the small table, spilling over onto the arms of the chairs.

As she fingered some of the bindings, Christina murmured to herself, "William Shakespeare, Walt Whitman, Mark Twain—these must be originals. They look so old." Realizing more treasures probably resided higher, she climbed the ladder all the way to the top to search. Not finding anything she wanted, she pushed the ladder to the next part of the bookcase. After her fourth push, she found Bram Stoker's *Dracula*.

"This will do," she commented aloud, hooking the book's spine with her fingers.

"What will do?" Marcus' deep voice boomed in the quiet room.

Not expecting company, Christina's body jerked in surprise, causing her to lose her footing. One hand held the book she pulled from the shelf. The other grabbed at the air trying to find a rung on the ladder.

Christina fell, closed her eyes and let out a scream as her stomach seemed to drop to her toes. She realized Marcus was too far away to help, and her mind barely registered that the landing would hurt before she felt a pair of strong arms cradle her. She looked up, meeting Marcus' eyes with a wide gaze. "How did you get to me so fast?"

Ignoring her question, Marcus replied, "You know, for someone so beautiful, you certainly fall down a lot."

"You think I'm beautiful?"

In answer to her question, Marcus slowly lowered his head and captured her lips. His gentle kiss barely brushed her mouth. When he started to pull back, Christina parted her lips in invitation. It was an offer he did not resist. Marcus deepened the kiss, sweeping his tongue into her mouth. Their tongues danced together in perfect harmony to a song as old as time.

Christina may have been virginal, but she'd been kissed before, or so she thought until Marcus touched her lips. His searing kiss branded her, making her his. His tongue masterfully stroked her inner passion, creating a raging fire in her blood. Lost in his kiss, she felt time stood still. She wanted to remain in his arms, kissing him forever.

Chapter 9

Marcus was...drowning. The feel of Christina in his arms, responding to his kiss with all the intensity and passion he felt, pulled him under as his inner beast rose to claim its mate. He wanted her. Wanted to be inside her. Take her.

Here.

Now.

He struggled for breath, worked to maintain control, but quickly realized that would be an impossible task as long as they were joined. He warred with the beast within, struggled to rein it in. Christina deserved to be courted, not taken like a common whore. She deserved all the love he could give. He wanted to make love, not have sex with her. The thought gave him the strength he needed to dampen the fiery heat of passion coursing through his body. He called on years of honed self-control to break the kiss.

When he pulled away, his raspy breath escaped from his lungs. He needed to find a way to distract himself from the feel of her lips on his. His eyes flowed over her body, landing on the book she still held in her hand.

"What did you find?" Marcus nodded toward the book as he slowly released her to the floor. The feel of her body sliding down his did not help his tenuous control.

"Huh?" Christina brought her hand to her kiss-swollen lips. She lifted the book to read the title. "Um...*Dracula*."

"Interesting choice." Marcus held his arms tightly against his sides, afraid where touching her might lead.

"I've read it before, but it's good enough to read again. Plus I've always kind of had this thing for vampires. I like the lore."

Seeing an opportunity, Marcus gestured to the settee. "There's something we need to talk about, Christina. Please sit down."

He joined her on the couch, taking most of the space with his broad shoulders and muscular thighs. He sat with his legs wide, leaning his forearms on his knees. Clasping his fingers together, he turned his head and looked at her. "Tell me what exactly about the vampire lore you like."

"I like the idea of a being with super strength and speed. I think it is kind of cool how they can do things with their minds. They tend to be written as sex symbols. I even like the dominance of most vampire characters, not in an abusive way of course. But most women like the idea of being 'taken' not just made love to every now and then."

Duly noted. A wry grin lifted one corner of his mouth. "What would you do if you found out vampires are real?"

"Ummmm..." Christina tilted her head to one side and looked thoughtfully into his eyes. "I'd be very curious. I'd want to ask them all sorts of questions."

"Like what?" He pinned her with his dark stare. Anticipation knotted his stomach.

"Like I'd want to know what parts of the lore are real. What the authors got right."

As she spoke, Marcus remembered the last time he told a human about his true nature. Just a few years ago, he'd met a young dancer in Vegas named Katrina. Once Kat believed he was a vampire, she attacked him. Fearing for her life, she kicked and punched him, tearing at his face with her nails. He needed to restrain her to keep her from hurting herself more than him, and that only increased her panic and fear. Eventually things had worked out, and they were now fast friends, but Marcus didn't look forward to reliving that experience.

"And if you found out someone you knew was a vampire, how do you think you would react?"

"I don't know." Christina shrugged her shoulders extraneously. "I guess I'd be okay with it because if I'd known them for a while and they hadn't hurt me, I'd assume they were fine. I'd hope I'd be cool about it."

"What if I told you I know a vampire? What if I told you I know several of them?"

"I'd say, can you introduce me?" Christina giggled.

Marcus let an undemonstrative, stoic smile pull his full lips into a taut line. *Here goes nothing.* The warrior took a deep, fortifying breath. "What if I told you I am a vampire?"

"Yeah, right. Sure you are." The svelte human reached over and gave his thigh a patronizing pat.

Marcus took another deep breath and let it out slowly through his nose. "Christina, I *am* a vampire." He paused, allowing her time to absorb the confession, and noted the look of skepticism on her face. "Seriously, I'm telling you the truth. Think about it.

Think back to the night we first met, the accident. Remember what I did that night, vaulting cars, pulling car doors off their hinges?"

The smile slipped from Christina's pretty face. "That was just an adrenaline rush. You hear all the time how a mother will lift a car off her baby."

"Well, what about the times you have fallen? When you fell off the porch and just now when you fell off the ladder. Think. Where was I?" He paused a moment to allow her to consider his question. "I was nowhere near you as you started to fall, but I still caught you before you hit the ground. How do you explain that?"

"Okay, so you are very strong and very fast, but that doesn't make you a vampire. I mean, I've seen you eat food."

"Vampires can eat food. That's one of the myths that isn't true."

"I've seen you drink. You and I drank three bottles of wine."

Marcus noticed a slight tremor to Christina's voice. His preternatural hearing took in the increase of her heartbeat. "Think back to last night. You saw me drink something red, but it wasn't just wine."

She shook her head adamantly, sending the wisps of escaped tendrils swirling around her face. "But I drank it too. It *was* wine."

He kept his voice low, the timbre soothing. "Your glass contained wine, mine contained wine and…blood."

The silence was deafening while Christina considered what Marcus told her. Unable to read the play of emotions on her face, he pushed into her mind, needing to discover her thoughts. Like a movie, she played their conversation in her head, inserting the inhuman things she witnessed him do.

Christina's eyes went wide as she put her hand over her mouth. "You are either a vampire or an insane psychopath."

She truly wondered if he'd gone crazy. Well, that was almost insulting. "I assure you I am not a psychopath."

The silence stretched out between them like a bungee stretched to its limit, threatening to snap and send them into opposite directions. He watched the emotions flash over her face, listened to her heart race. She struggled fruitlessly to keep the emotions from her face. From what he gleaned from her mind, he knew she fought to come to terms with his admission.

Christina crossed her legs. She wondered if he might be telling her the truth. All the years spent reading paranormal romance novels had left her wanting a vampire for a lover, lucky for him. The authors made vampires seem sexy and mysterious to her. Dangerous but sinfully wanton. The stories always ended in a happily ever after where the vampire vowed to love the woman for eternity. Which happened to be exactly how Marcus wanted to spend their life together.

Breaking the silence, Marcus ran his fingers through his hair. "You okay? Is there something I can do to help you deal with this? Can I get you some water? You want to go for a walk and get some fresh air or something? You name it, anything."

Christina looked at him skeptically. "Okay, prove you are a vampire."

"How?" Marcus cautiously asked, raising one eyebrow.

"Bite me."

"Excuse me?" The warrior did not keep the incredulousness from his voice.

Christina brought her hand down from her mouth to her throat. "You said anything. If you are a vampire, bite my neck and drink from me."

"I don't know if I can do that." *It would be too hard to stop.*

Christina rose from the settee to pace the room. "I want to believe you. You seem so sincere. So why can't you bite me?"

"Because I don't drink from people." *Much.* "Technology has helped vampires as much as it has helped humans. We no longer have to drink from the vein. We have blood suppliers and can keep it fresh for long periods of time. The only drawback is we are slightly weaker."

Marcus clasped his hands together and sighed. He needed to make her understand. He wanted her badly. It took all his willpower not to throw her down on the settee and rip the clothes from her body. If he drank her blood, his inner beast would want more, and he wasn't sure he possessed the strength to rein it in a second time. "You don't understand, Christina, drinking from a vein has become a very intimate thing. It's like sex for me."

Christina crossed the room, turning her back to him, so he could not see the emotion on her face. "So that's why you won't drink from me, you don't want to be intimate?"

Good God! Being attacked would have been better than this, Marcus thought, hearing the pain in her voice. By refusing to drink from her, he'd hurt her. This was going all wrong. He shook his head. "It's not that I don't *want* to drink from you. I'm just afraid I wouldn't um…stop if I started." *I swear to the heavens above, I will never again tell a human what I am. It never goes well.*

"Oh." Christina's eyes clouded as she crossed her arms over her chest. *Hold it together, girl. Don't you let him see you cry. You are insane*, she mentally chastised herself. *Getting upset because he won't bite you. Geez. I must be the one who needs the psych ward.*

Though he heard her thoughts, Marcus found himself unsure of what to do. He hated to see a woman cry, and instinct told him Christina would turn on the waterworks at any minute. She needed reassurance. She'd misunderstood what kept him from doing what she asked.

The Alpha stood slowly and approached her with his hands at his sides. As he came up behind her, he made his footsteps heard. Putting his hands on her shoulders, Marcus leaned down to her ear. He whispered in a thick, raspy voice, and his lips brushed her lobe as he spoke, "If I was going to drink from a vein, it would be yours, *cara*."

He leaned down to test her resolve, surprised when she leaned her head to the side and gave him better access to her neck. He put his lips on her neck and inhaled her scent deeply into his body. The fragrance of jasmine and honey filled his lungs.

She trembled slightly in his hold but bravely stood her ground.Christina took a deep breath, and Marcus knew she braced for the sting of his teeth, but all she felt were his lips as he slowly kissed his way up her neck to suckle her earlobe. Releasing her lobe, he turned her around so she faced him. He looked into her eyes and slowly bent to capture her lips. Her hands slid up his forearms, tracing his flexing biceps to land on his thick shoulders. She gripped him tightly, no doubt feeling the muscle and sinew under the pads of her fingers as she tried to pull him toward her.

He deepened the kiss, parting his lips to invite her tongue for a dance. She eagerly swept her tongue into his mouth, tasting the spicy flavor within. His fangs lengthened from his gums. Marcus moaned into her mouth, the sound low and sensual.

Christina's body hummed with an excitement Marcus sensed as she eagerly explored his mouth. Her tongue swept from one side to the other, probing each thoroughly. She ran the tip of her tongue around one of his fangs causing an electric surge of lust to course through his body. Her tongue brushed his fang once more.

She went stiff in his arms and quickly withdrew, scraping her tongue on his fang. When she pulled away, she made the little sound Marcus found adorable.

He recognized the sweet taste of her blood and realized what happened. Knew the sound that escaped her mouth meant she was shocked, scared. In the blink of her eye, Marcus sat across the room in one of the chairs to put some space between them.

"You really are a vampire?" It was as much a question as a statement.

"Yes," he answered slowly, in order not to startle her.

"You have fangs." Christina tapped her own teeth and made her way to the settee next to Marcus' chair.

The Alpha noted the ease with which she closed

the gap between them. Perhaps surprise more than fear caused the noise. Marcus smiled wide, allowing his fangs to show. "They kind of come with being a vampire."

The look of wonder on her face made him push into her mind to garner her thoughts. Relief flooded his body when he realized she finally believed his claim. Seeing *was* believing. If the speed at which he crossed the room hadn't been enough, seeing the fangs in his mouth would have been. He could tell she found them definitely too big to be human.

Other parts of him were larger than most humans as well, and he couldn't wait to show her those.

He obviously piqued her curiosity. "Can I ask you some questions about being a vampire?"

He placed his elbows on the armrests and steepled his fingers. "Sure, go ahead."

Marcus hadn't realized by saying those three words he opened the door of higher education to Christina with him acting as her professor. The first thing the nurse in her wanted to know about was vampire biology.

"What causes people to become vampires?"

"As best vampiric scientists can tell, the original vampires were created when the virus that caused the Bubonic Plague mutated, producing the vampiric symptoms. The scientists hypothesized the virus caused their hormones to increase, which in turn made their muscles enlarge, giving them increased speed and strength. Their hearts and lungs grew larger to accommodate the amount of blood and oxygen needed for the preternatural skills. Because of the increase to the size of their hearts and lungs, more room in their chest cavity was needed so their stomachs and intestines began to shrink." Marcus crossed his legs, resting one ankle on the opposite knee. "Our scientists also think the mutated virus is the reason we are immune to all human diseases."

"That actually makes sense." Christina nodded in understanding. "Did you know some humans are naturally immune to the HIV virus? Researchers have traced their ancestry back and believe they are decedents of people who survived the Bubonic Plague. If the plague virus can keep people from getting HIV, then a mutation of the virus might very well be the reason why vampires are immune to other diseases."

Marcus leaned back in his chair. "MRI technology allowed our scientists to discover that the vampire brain is more active than a human's. They believed this accounts for vampires being able to have special abilities such as reading minds and telekinesis."

Christina leaned forward. "You know, the mutated virus theory would also explain why most vampire stories were written after the 1400s."

Marcus' chest expanded in pride at his heartmate. Her logical brain and understanding of physiology not only helped her to understand vampirism, but her natural fascination with the breed made her accepting of the idea.

Many of his kind believed that there was a reason some people seemed more intrigued with the idea of vampires than others. Perhaps humans who had been bitten experienced the ecstasy of their bite and would subconsciously crave the breed even though they did not consciously remember the event.

Marcus could not help but wonder if Christina had

been bitten by one of his kind. The thought sent a wave of jealousy down his spine that knotted his stomach. If he ever found another taking her blood, he would kill the bastard.

Her biologic curiosity apparently sated, Christina drew him from his deadly thoughts by asking about the myths.

Marcus inclined toward her, leaning on the arm of his chair. "There are some really cool things that come with being a vampire. For instance, our powers increase as we age. Some vampires can dematerialize from one place and materialize in another."

A wide grin swept her pretty face. "Now that would come in handy. Let me see you do it."

Marcus sat back in his chair. "I can't do it yet. But I did discover that I could command people with my mind from far away."

"That would be amazing." Christina's eyes went wide with excitement.

"Yeah, it is." Marcus stared sightlessly ahead, remembering how he had drawn Christina to him. A smile spread across his face.

Christina prodded on. "What other things can vampires do?"

"Some can manipulate minds. Some can hover off the ground, while others can heal with their auras. I even know one who can control animals." Marcus uncrossed his legs.

"How do people become vampires? How is the virus transmitted?" Christina twirled a lock of her red hair.

Marcus tracked her movements with his steady gaze, wishing it were his fingers in her hair. "A vampire exchanges blood with a human by taking from the human while the human takes from him. It takes a while. They form a blood circle until their blood mixes thoroughly. Then the virus does its thing."

"Does it hurt?"

"Hell, yeah. A lot. I mean all your organs, brain, heck, even your cells change, so yeah it hurts."

Christina's voice lowered. "Do people ever die going through the change?"

Fear streaked down his spine from the question. He wanted Christina to become a vampire. Now that he had found his heartmate, he wanted an eternity to love her. He'd seen his sire, Stephan, almost lose his mate because of her human frailties, and he would not repeat the same mistakes. He didn't want to scare her away from making the conversion, but he also did not want to lie to his mate. Marcus forced an insouciant shrug. "Usually not, but I suppose it could happen."

"How can vampires die?"

"Why? You planning on killing me, Red?" Marcus chuckled.

"No, just curious." Christina's smile made his heart beat faster in his chest.

"Well, we can heal really fast if we are at full strength, so it's not easy to kill a vampire. The two best ways are either something like a dagger through the heart or cut off the head. Of course, fire and lengthy exposure to sunlight works too. But don't be getting any ideas," Marcus quipped as Christina joined him in a chuckle.

"Oh, I have lots of ideas, Marcus, but killing you isn't one of them." She flashed him a mischievous grin that sent a wave of desire through his veins.

Chapter 10

"Excuse the interruption, sir." Payton stood in the doorway of Marcus' game room. Following through with his stroke, Marcus hit the cue ball, leaving a blue chalk kiss on the white ball. With a loud crack, it hit the eight ball, sending it ricocheting off three sides of the burgundy felt table before it fell into its resting place in the corner pocket.

"You're not interrupting. What's up?" Marcus straightened and leaned his cue stick against the table.

"You have a visitor. Mr. Romanoff is here."

"Demetri? Send him in," Marcus instructed, placing his cue stick back in its holder on the wall as Demetri's six-foot-six-inch frame filled the doorway.

Demetri Romanoff was a brutishly built male, his neck and face thickened by years of pumping iron. His square-jawed, hard face possessed high cheekbones and a broad forehead. His steel-gray eyes were wise from centuries of experience, with slight lines etched into the corners by his six hundred years of life.

Marcus crossed to greet his friend and smiled.

"Hey, Demetri. It's good to see you." The Alphas grasped forearms in the way of the warrior. "What brings you to my home?"

"It is good to lay eyes on you too, comrade. You look well." Demetri's slight Russian accent rolled his

R's.

"Yeah, I am well. I'm better than well actually. I feel amazing." Marcus led Demetri into the room. "Wanna play a game? Perhaps billiards?"

"Actually I'm eyeing the foosball table over there." Demetri gestured with a nod of his head that sent his long black hair waving across his shoulders.

The two Alphas began their game, strong hands sending the rows of little wooden men spinning. Marcus cleared his throat. "I thought you had gone to your place out west. What brings you back to the east coast?"

"I contracted to have some work done on my Savannah townhome, and I wanted to come down to supervise the work personally. I thought while I'm in the neighborhood I'd come by and see you. It's been a little over a week since we spoke on the phone, and I wanted to see how things were going." Demetri spun his men and sent the ball into Marcus' goal. "Score!"

Marcus fished the ball from the holding area and dropped it back into play. "It's going pretty good. I've seen Christina every night for the past week. She is really something. She's fun and bright. I love her mind. She is so curious."

"Curious about what?" With a flick of Demetri's wrist, the ball again crossed the table and found the opening on the other side. "Score!"

"She can't learn enough about our kind. She is always asking me questions."

"Where is she? I'd like to meet her."

"She is at her apartment getting ready for our date tonight."

A look of surprise crossed Demetri's face, and he

locked eyes with the younger vampire. "Your heartmate isn't living with you? You are allowing her to remain in her own apartment?"

Marcus took advantage of the distraction and sent the small ball flying into Demetri's goal before responding. "Look, she's human, not vampire. She doesn't know she is my heartmate yet. I have to take it slow. I can't scare her off."

"Don't wait too long, comrade. You are just putting off the inevitable. The sooner you bring her here and convert her, the better."

"It's not that simple. I want her to come here on her terms. I will not force her to move in or convert!"

Demetri lowered his arms to his sides. Marcus watched the muscle of his jaw twitch. "Marcus, you and I go way back, so take some advice from your old friend. There will soon come a time when her wishes will be irrelevant. You are a strong male who needs, both physically and mentally, to be with his heartmate. We both know what can happen when a male doesn't have his female. You need to speed things up and claim her as yours soon, for both your sakes."

With a twist of his hand, Marcus made the ball careen across the table into the goal. He marched around the end of the table, his purposeful stride closing the gap between him and Demetri. His hands clenched into fists at his sides as his teeth clamped down tightly. "First, there will never be a time when Christina's wishes are irrelevant to me. And second, you do not need to remind me what can happen when a vampire doesn't have his heartmate. I have hunted enough of them with you when they went insane."

Anger at Demetri's edict furrowed his brows. "I

will have Christina as my heartmate. I will claim my female, and she will live with me. But I will do it my way, in my time. I do not need your advice. Clear?"

Demetri looked down slightly on Marcus. He seemed to be measuring Marcus' resolve, and the warrior stood his ground more than happy to be measured. The Alpha knew his resolve was solid.

Apparently satisfied with what he saw, Demetri cocked one side of his mouth. "Okay, comrade. I feel you. I'll back off and let you do things your way." The older vampire crossed his thick arms over his massive chest. "Now get back over there so I can finish kicking your ass at foosball."

Marcus smiled a cocky grin and relaxed his hands. He returned to his side of the table as he quipped, "I believe if you check the score we are tied, friend. You're hardly kicking my butt."

Marcus deliberately changed the subject as Demetri dropped the ball into the center of the table. "Did you happen to catch the news tonight? Did you see the story about that woman who went missing?" Marcus launched the ball across the table with blinding speed.

Demetri deflected it and directed the ball back. "Yeah, I saw it. The reporter said police didn't have any clues, just video surveillance that showed her leaving a café. Another good reason to get your heartmate in your home and under your protection."

Marcus shot Demetri an *are-you-really-going-there-again* look, and Demetri dropped the subject. As the game continued, the two vampires exchanged manly insults and ribbed one another about their skills. By the end of the game, Marcus found himself behind by two goals.

"That was fun," Demetri commented. "Interested in me kicking your butt on one of your arcade games? Mortal Conflict perhaps?"

"No can do. I have to go. It's almost time for me to pick up Christina for our date."

"Well in that case, I'll take my leave. Oh, by the way, Michael is in town. We should all meet sometime soon for a beer."

"Sounds like a plan. Call me, I'll be there."

Demetri nodded. "Thanks for the game."

"Anytime, my man, anytime. Safe travels."

Demetri dematerialized as Marcus left the game room, heading for his date with his heartmate.

****

Christina carefully applied her lip gloss for the third time that evening then gave her hair one last look-see. With everything to her liking, she clicked off the bathroom light and sauntered across the bedroom to don the dress she'd chosen for tonight.

She'd been out with Marcus every night since she found out vampires really existed. Her heart raced, stomach knotted, and she wondered if it was from anticipation of being with Marcus or the anticipation of being with a vampire that caused her condition.

She enjoyed Marcus. What woman wouldn't? He was easy on the eyes, handsome with his dark chestnut hair worn short and feathered back from his masculine face. She loved his attractive features with his straight nose, strong cheekbones and deep brown eyes, which sparkled in a way that made her feel special when he looked at her.

A perfect gentleman, he treated her with respect

and kindness, always attentive to her every need. But inevitably at some point in every evening with him, she remembered he was a vampire, and her heart would race from a combination of excitement mixed with a small dose of self-preservative fear.

She checked her reflection in the mirror one last time, noting the way her long-sleeved dress flowed over her curves, and silently admonished herself for her fear of him. The man had done nothing but been kind to her. Christina believed she could trust him. She had good instincts about people, and her instincts told her she was safe with him. The sound of the doorbell drew her from her thoughts.

****

Marcus stood outside the door to Christina's apartment. His nature tempted him to will it open, but he knew that would be rude, so he restrained himself and rang the bell. The vision that greeted him rewarded his self-control. The door opened wide to reveal a beautiful woman dressed in a dark-green satin dress that made her eyes resemble emeralds. Her long, auburn hair flowed over her shoulder like a river of blood, causing Marcus to crave her all the more.

Fates above, how he desired this woman. She was his first thought upon rising each night. His desire for her tested his self-restraint at every turn, but her virtue remained intact. Though if he were to give into the temptation and drink from her again, it probably would not remain so.

"You look amazing, *cara*." Marcus took her hands in his and stretched their arms wide. He twirled her like a ballerina, so the dress flared out, exposing her lithe legs to his heated gaze.

"Thank you. What does *cara* mean?" Christina asked.

"It's an Italian term of endearment. Loosely translated it means beloved."

He called me beloved. I hope he truly feels that way because I am starting to really like him. If I am honest with myself, I have to admit my feelings are quickly progressing from like to love, and if he doesn't feel the same, I am in for a heart break the size of Texas. Christina's eyes locked with his. *I hope he isn't reading my mind.*

Marcus worked to keep the smile from his face. Of course, he was in her mind. He found it impossible to stay out of it, wanting to know her better.

She gave him a shy smile and glanced down at her attire. "I'm not sure where we are going, so I hope this dress will do."

"That dress is perfect. I wouldn't want you to change. If it wasn't appropriate for what I planned, I would come up with something that would allow you to wear it." Marcus brought the hand he still held to his mouth and placed a kiss in her palm. He allowed his passion to show in his eyes, telling her he wanted more. Much more. "Shall we go, my dear?"

Christina grabbed her coat and took the arm Marcus offered, letting him escort her to his car.

"Where *are* we going?" she asked as Marcus opened the passenger door to his Italian sports car, then handed her inside to melt into the buttery leather seat.

"What, don't you trust me?" Marcus feigned a hurt expression, for just a moment, before allowing it to morph into a genuine smile. "Just sit back, relax, and let me take you."

Marcus winked when Christina smiled in understanding of his double entendre.

Chapter 11

The vehicle purred under Marcus' expert skills. They caught a red light, and Marcus seized the opportunity. "This is for you," he said, plucking a single white rose from the center console.

As Christina wrapped her fingers around the stem, she felt the bite of a thorn. Still seated in her mind, he felt the pain even as she did.

"Ouch!"

Marcus smelled the blood before Christina even registered the pain. *Damn that florist. I said no thorns.*

Christina looked at the drop of blood forming on her finger and started to bring it to her lips. Instinct took over and Marcus' hand shot out of its own volition. His fingers were a vise around her wrist, tight but not painful.

He slowly brought her hand toward his mouth. A fast movement would have brought out his predatory instincts to strike, but doing this slowly had its repercussions too, giving the blood time to drip down Christina's finger.

He heard her draw a deep breath when he brought the finger to his mouth. His tongue started down low and licked up the line of blood toward the origin. He sucked the finger into his mouth. His tongue twirled around the tip, sealing the wound. A small moan escaped Christina's throat in response to the heat generated by his touch, sending his senses into overdrive. He closed his eyes and savored the experience of her essence on his tongue. She tasted like ambrosia, making him want more, so much more. He wanted to take her right here, in his car. Pin her between his body and the leather seat.

She would be exquisite. The warmth of her inner heat surrounding him. The image of her legs wrapped around his waist made his mouth draw hard around her finger.

The honk of a horn brought him back to the present. He released Christina's wrist, gunned the gas and sent the car off like a rocket. The ponies under the hood pushed them back into the soft leather.

That was close, thought Marcus as he slowed the car to the speed limit, forcing deep, calming breaths into his lungs. *Her blood drives me crazy.*

Christina sat clasping her rose with both hands in her lap. Concerned by her silence, Marcus gleaned her thoughts. She sensed the tension in the car and knew Marcus seemed upset but was unsure as to why. Apparently, he wasn't as good at hiding his desires as he thought.

She opened her mouth to speak, then closed it with an audible click of her teeth. The tiny sound seemed to echo in the car. They rode in silence until Christina commented nervously to end the screaming silence, "So, you never said where we are going."

"You'll see." Those two words were all Marcus managed to say, his voice having been left back at the stoplight. He white-knuckled the black and silver steering wheel in an attempt to wring out his desire.

His heart galloped a furious pace in his chest. Hot blood coursed through his veins, heating his passion. His inner beast roared in need—for his mate, for her delicious nectar. Marcus cursed the preternatural senses that allowed him to hear the pounding of her steady heartbeat. His eyes found her pulse, beating under the soft flesh of her neck for just a second before they returned to the road.

Marcus planned a picnic in the park, but now he doubted the prudence of that idea. Being alone with Christina might not be the best idea at the moment, at least until he tightened the reins on his lust and brought it back under his control.

Marcus decided to drive for a while, needing the distraction. He opened the sunroof, grateful for the cool evening breeze. The smell of the oak trees that lined the street mixed with her amazing scent. As he drove, the warrior took in the soothing night air. It calmed his desire until he finally locked it away once more.

When they arrived at the park, they found it desolate as a desert on a hot summer day. Walking hand in hand, they looked for a perfect spot for the blanket. Marcus carried the picnic basket while Christina carried her rose. Marcus found a small clearing in the middle of a group of pine trees by a manmade pond. He flipped the blanket, spreading it on the ground with a courtly gesture, like a lord laying his coat over a mud puddle to help a damsel.

The grass and pine needles crushed beneath him when they sat on the wool blanket. The meal Payton prepared for them tasted superb. The veal was tender and the pasta *al dente*, but he looked forward to dessert the most.

"That was delicious," proclaimed Christina after she finished the last of her veal.

Marcus nodded. "Payton is an excellent cook. I'll let him know you appreciated his effort. Now for the *pièce de résistance*." The vampire pulled a white china plate from the wicker basket and presented it to Christina. Her little pink tongue licked her lips delicately as she looked upon the ten red strawberries dipped in white and dark chocolate. They looked like they wore tiny delicious tuxedoes.

"Try one." Marcus lifted one of the strawberries and brought it to Christina's mouth. Her lips curled around the berry when she brought her teeth down to bite through it. The movement pinned his gaze.

"Ummmm." Christina's sound of approval came out somewhere between a moan and a sigh, heating Marcus' blood once again. He leaned forward and captured her lips, shifting his weight gently to push her down beside his body. As their tongues twirled together, he brought one hand to her knee and found the hem of her dress. His hand raised it tantalizingly slowly, his desire for her sliding it higher. His fingers gripped her thigh before they moved even higher toward their prize.

Christina shifted her leg slightly under his touch, opening for him. A thought pressed at the back of his mind. He should stop this now, before it went too far. But he couldn't. He wanted this, needed this, and Christina seemed to be in agreement.

He shifted his hold, moved his hand farther up her leg. He drew circles on her inner thigh, then the back of his hand brushed her moist channel through her delicate lace panties. Her heart raced. The scent of her arousal flooded the air.

She wrapped her arms around his shoulders and pulled him closer while their kiss deepened, growing more intense and passionate. His tongue swept between her lips, ran seductively over her mouth, claiming her for his own. He pushed his chest against her breasts, needing to feel the soft curves of her body against his hard lines. His mind became a haze of sensual desire, fed by his consuming passion for her.

Marcus suddenly stopped and pulled away, leaving Christina gasping for air. He went marble-still, his gaze looking out into the dark park. Christina regarded him, easily reading his alert stance to know something must be wrong. She released her grip on his shoulders immediately and brought her fingers to her kiss-swollen lips.

"What's wrong?" she whispered, looking around nervously.

Marcus rose to his knees, his intense gaze focused on the surrounding tree line. "I heard something. We're not alone."

He sat back on his heels, his head jerked toward the woods, then he disappeared into the trees.

Christina propped herself up on her elbows and looked in the direction Marcus had gone. Unsure what to think, she got to her feet and packed the basket just in case they needed to make a hasty exit. After a few anxious moments, during which Christina paced the clearing, Marcus emerged from the forest carrying a small object.

She narrowed her eyes in an attempt to bring them into focus. Cradled in Marcus' arms lay a small child. He placed the toddler before her on the blanket.

"Who's this?" Christina bent down beside the child.

Marcus wiped the boy's long bangs from his eyes. "I don't know. I didn't sense anyone other than him. I'm guessing he wandered off from his parents."

Christina looked down on the sweet face. By his facial features, she knew he had Down syndrome. The boy, small in stature, looked to be about three years old, Christina guessed. The nurse did a quick medical assessment of the child.

"He seems all right, Marcus. He has a few scratches, probably from traipsing around in the woods, and a few bug bites but nothing serious. He doesn't have any signs of dehydration. He couldn't have been in the woods too long." Christina pulled the child's shirt down after checking his abdomen. Thank goodness it seemed normal, no signs of injury.

"What's your name, sweetie?"

Silence was her only answer.

"Maybe he can't talk," suggested Marcus.

"That's possible. Often children with Down syndrome have delayed communication skills."

"Perhaps he is hungry."

Marcus reached into the picnic basket and plucked a strawberry from it. The boy took it, then graced them with a sweet smile. He ate it hungrily, so Marcus brought out the entire plate. The boy ate the berries two fisted, putting them into his tiny mouth as fast as he could. When he finished, Marcus and Christina laughed. Chocolate and strawberry juice poured from his mouth like red and black lava from a volcano. A coating of the sticky lava encompassed each tiny finger as well.

"I wish I had a camera," Christina mused, chuckling.

"Your wish is my command, milady."

Marcus pulled his cell phone from his pocket. After he set it on a nearby rock, he angled it toward the child. The couple sat on each side of the boy seconds before the flash ignited.

When Marcus showed her the picture of the three of them, her throat tightened with unshed tears. They looked like a family. A question came to her mind.

"Can vampires have babies?"

"Technically, yes, but there are complications."

Marcus lifted the child onto his lap, and Christina quelled the instinct to tell him not to, due to the sticky hands. Instead she pulled a napkin from the basket, impressed that he appeared oblivious to the mess in his lap.

"What complications?" She used a napkin to wipe the little mouth and fingers of their new friend.

"Well, first of all, only two vampires can conceive, so there is no cross breeding with humans, which limits our potential to parent. Second, the virus that changes us affects all of our organs, including the reproductive ones. It is difficult for some vampires to conceive after the virus changes the organs. It's almost like nature is working against our kind. I guess it's nature's way of keeping a balance." Marcus mussed the child's hair. "When vampires do have a child, it is treasured by all for the miracle it is."

Christina looked at the little face smiling up at her, then back at Marcus. "I'm sure his mother thinks he is a miracle too. Can't you do something to figure out who he belongs to?"

"I can try to read his thoughts. They might give me a clue as to where his parents might be."

Watching the intensity in Marcus' eyes, Christina wondered what he was finding in the young brain. She didn't have to wait long.

"His name is Dillon. I have an image of a house and several memories of a blonde woman caring for the boy."

"Probably his mother."

"Agreed."

"Could you get his address?"

"No. But I have an idea." Marcus stood. "There's no way he wandered far from home with those tiny legs. His clothes are in good shape, so he hasn't been out too long. Let's get in the car and drive to nearby neighborhoods. Maybe we'll get lucky, and I'll spot something from his memories."

Christina nodded. "Good idea." She made her way toward the picnic basket.

Marcus wrapped the toddler in the blanket as Christina picked up the wicker basket. He carried the child in one arm and tucked Christina under the other, pulling her against his chest as they walked. The gentle sway of his body made the boy snuggle into Marcus and close his eyes. He fell asleep quickly, obviously tired from his great adventure. Marcus seemed like a natural with the child. He would be a great caring father one day. The thought brought a smile to her lips while they made the short trip to the car.

When they arrived at the vehicle, Marcus placed the child delicately into Christina's lap, careful not to wake him.

They drove through the nearby neighborhoods. The

third neighborhood they turned into was a gated community. The gate opened for them, probably from Marcus willing the thing open with his mind, Christina supposed as they drove into the subdivision.

"There," Marcus whispered, pointing toward a group of people. "I recognize the blonde from his memories. I think she is his mother."

Marcus pulled to the curb and helped Christina exit the car with Dillon cradled in her arms. She appeared so natural with the sleeping child. She would make an amazing mother to his children. His chest ached with joy as he let himself believe this could be what having his own family would be like. The thought brought a sad smile to his lips.

The woman he believed to be the boy's mother turned and watched the trio come toward the group of searchers gathered on the sidewalk. Christina pulled the blanket away from Dillon's face, revealing him to his mother. The sight of her son made his mother cry out in relief before she ran toward them.

Marcus bristled from instinct when the woman approached his heartmate. Surprise took him at the intensity of the need to protect his mate and the child. The fierceness of the instinct staggered him; the knowledge that he would do anything to keep his mate safe was shocking. He fought the compulsion to put himself between Christina and the human running toward them, for he knew that the human woman presented no real threat. She simply tried to reach her baby. Pushing down his nature, he allowed the reunion between mother and child.

After explanations were made and the two of them tearfully thanked, the mother turned with Dillon, hugging him to her chest in a loving embrace as she made her way along the sidewalk.

Dillon, awakened by the commotion, looked over his mother's shoulder and smiled at Marcus and Christina. His tiny wave goodbye tugged at Marcus' heart.

Christina looked up into his eyes. "That was the best date I have ever had. Thank you!"

She wove her arms around his waist and squeezed tight. Marcus wrapped his arms around her, pressing her closer to him. He kissed the top of her head and placed his cheek there to rest with a sigh.

"I agree, *cara*."

****

The vampire walked along the Savannah street. His boring companion made him feel twitchy. His palms itched, mouth watered in anticipation while wicked thoughts flowed through his mind. He needed some action. Now! "I'm outta here, man. I need a little F and L."

"F and L?" asked his cohort.

With an evil, fang-baring grin, the vampire answered, "Yeah, food and a lay. I'll see you tomorrow."

The vampire turned on his heels and strode away from his associate. The woman he'd taken the night before hadn't been enough to sate his sadistic appetite. An iniquitous plan formed in his mind while he walked. He needed two girls, wanted them innocent, not seasoned. He didn't want someone from his usual BDSM haunt. Tonight, he wanted to smell the fear and anxiety, wanted it rolling off the females to fuel his sinful lust.

He worked the plan in his mind until he spied two women across the street casually making their way along the sidewalk. He crossed the road and quickened his gait to easily catch up to the women. Remaining several feet behind them, he listened to their trite conversation, waiting for his chance to pounce. Anticipation boiled in his blood. All senses heightened. The smell of car exhaust mixed with the scent of the various cuisines coming from the restaurants. His vision narrowed to the females. He loved this, the thrill of the chase. The hunt called to him. His fangs lengthened in eagerness of what was to come. He allowed his predatory instincts to rise to the surface as he stalked his prey.

"Hey, sis, I'm so bored. There's nothing to do in this town. Let's see if we can find a bar," suggested the woman with short brown hair and a stick-thin body. The vampire didn't care for short hair. He preferred long hair he could wrap his hand around and wrench, but he would make do.

"I know. This vacation sucks," whined her sister.

Her long brown hair, swept up into a ponytail, and curvy hips were much more to his liking. His tongue jutted out to lick his lips in anticipation as he imagined what that hair would feel like in his fingers when he forced her to fulfill his dark fantasies.

I'll call her Lay and her sister Food, he thought, referencing his earlier "F" and "L" comment.

"I wish something exciting would happen." Lay twirled a strand of her ponytail with her finger.

"I wish we could find a little adventure," whined Food.

"You found it," he announced as he willed the

muscles in their larynges to stop working so they couldn't scream, then grabbed them both about their waists and carried them into the alley. They struggled, flailing their arms and legs in a useless attempt to escape. He laughed.

The vampire could have frozen their bodies by taking over their minds, but he liked it when his prey fought. They both kicked at him and scratched his arms futilely. However, the victims could not throw off his bruising grip as he pulled them deeper into the dark alley.

Lay turned in his arm and pushed against his chest in a fruitless endeavor to free herself. He turned toward the curvy sister. Capturing her eyes with his nefarious stare, he gave her a mental command to be still. Her body went rigid, not even a finger twitched. As she stood silently by and watched, the vampire sliced her sister's neck with his fangs. With her blood pouring down her shirt, the vampire turned his attention back on Lay.

"If you do as I command, I won't kill her." *Yet.* "Nod if you understand." He released his mental hold on the muscles of her neck. Lay nodded her head slowly, unable to command her mouth.

"That's a good girl."

The vampire turned back to the skinny one and lowered his head to her neck as she continued to fight him. He subdued her by pinning her against the rough wall of the alley with his body. His draws deepened, became more insistent as his excitement increased. He sucked Food until her heartbeat stuttered, and she fell limply against him. When unconsciousness took her, he sealed the wound on her neck with a swipe of his tongue and callously let her fall to the alley floor in a heap. As he rounded on Lay, he wiped her sister's blood from his mouth with the back of his hand. He ran the hand down the girl's face, leaving a red trail on her cheek, and released her from his mental hold.

The curvy female looked down where her sister lay and stammered in a frail voice, "You k-killed her,"

"I didn't kill her, you twit. She still breathes. Her heart still beats. Feel." The cruel vampire grabbed Lay's hand and placed it over the right breast of her sister. The sight made his groin thicken in perverted pleasure.

"Now if you want her to live, you'll do as I command. Come here!"

Tears streamed down Lay's face. Her hands shook, and she tried to back away.

Fates above, this is going to be fun, he thought, licking his lips as he reached for her.

An hour and a short drive later, the vampire took the sister he called Food out of his car and flung her over his shoulder. The woman lay unconscious, still weak from her earlier blood loss. As he walked, he grumbled about what transpired in the alley.

After he'd taken Lay up to a fire escape three floors above the alley for a quickie, she'd carelessly fallen over the railing and tumbled to her death. Her neck made an audible cracking sound when she landed head first on the concrete below. Knowing he had a backup, he jumped down, landing easily on the balls of his feet and grabbed Food, muttering, "Home sweet home."

And that was precisely where he was. Home. Or at least a place he thought of as his true home. The place he'd designed to accommodate the real him. He put on a front for the world, but here he let the facade drop, allowed his deep, dark desires to come out and play. He carried Food behind his garage to a specially designed building that stood in quiet depravity.

"Luuuucy, I'm home," he called out as he walked through the door to the chamber of horrors he referred to as his playroom. The sound of muted crying met his ears.

"What, not glad to see me, my dears?" The sarcasm dripped from his words.

Glancing around the room, he did a quick inventory. Everything sat where he'd left it. To the left there were cabinets that housed his instruments, knives, gags, restraints and such. In the middle of the room, stood a table with leg and arm restraints attached to it. It had holes speckling the surface and a water spigot for easy clean up. Along the concrete walls were shackles, five of which currently held muted occupants.

He dropped Food on the dirt floor, bringing down the curtain on his opening act for this evening. He moistened his lips, amped up and ready for act two to begin. He dragged his latest toy by the ankle over to a vacated spot on the wall and shackled her wrists. When he snapped the cuffs shut, the hostages' whimpering increased. No doubt they knew he was ready to play. He bared his fangs then cracked his neck to each side. Spreading his arms out wide, he glided toward the group of women shackled to the opposite wall.

"Now, now. If I didn't know better, I'd think you girls didn't love me." He bared his fangs. "Now come give Daddy some sugar."

Chapter 12

Marcus donned his riding gloves and jumped on his motorcycle. With a kick of his boot, the engine roared to life, all one-hundred-ninety-eight horses ready to go. He gunned the throttle, enjoying the rumble he felt reverberating through his body. With a tap of his foot, he put the sleek black bike in gear then took off down the drive, spitting gravel behind him.

The warrior loved this bike, loved how the night air flowed over him, bringing with it the smells of the city. He inhaled deeply, scenting the life around him: the woodland and river creatures, the lush vegetation in the marshes, the sea itself. The faster he went, the more his senses heightened from adrenaline, allowing him to take in more of the city.

Marcus parked the bike in front of his favorite restaurant, First Bite. Standing three stories tall, the brick building in Savannah's historic district boasted matching bay windows stacked on top of each other, one on each floor. Carved columns supported the roof of the porch sheltering the wooden rocking chairs that beckoned patrons to sit and talk a spell.

The first floor contained a restaurant for humans. It served typical southern cuisine and a variety of beverages. Conversely, the second floor was strictly for vampires. It offered the same items available on the first floor, but also provided its patrons blood either in a bag or, for the right price, served at a perfect 98.6 degrees from the vein. Being vampires themselves, the owners of First Bite knew how to provide what their kind wanted. The third floor promised a different type of satisfaction—one not mollified by food or blood. For a price, the patron could get whatever they desired. Both vamps and humans alike worked there, leaving no one's sexual appetite unsated.

Marcus walked through the front door. The smell of food assailed his senses. Humans sat before him at round tables whose floor-length tablecloths added to the restaurant's elegance. The walls, adorned with Victorian period wallpaper, boasted electric lights in iron sconces that bathed the room in a soft glow.

Marcus maneuvered through the dining area to the staircase located in the back of the room where a big, burly vampire stood at a red velvet rope allowing only vampires access to the second floor. As Marcus approached, the bouncer nodded once in acknowledgement and unchained the rope, allowing Marcus to pass.

"Thanks, Jason." Marcus discreetly placed a fifty in the bouncer's free hand.

At the top of the stairs, the Alpha entered a mirrored glass door into a foyer. A hostess greeted him from behind a podium. "Hello, sir, may I show you to a table?"

Marcus flashed her a wide smile. "I'm meeting a friend. Is Mr. Romanoff here yet?"

After checking her list, she replied, "I believe he is. Right this way."

Marcus followed her into the dining room, his gaze

sweeping around the room rather than letting it fall to her bottom. As a mated male, there was only one rump he wanted to watch.

His eyes spied Demetri sitting in a booth across from the bar.

"Here you go, sir."

The hostess gestured toward the booth and handed Marcus a menu, while he slid in smoothly.

Demetri followed the Alpha's movement with his eyes. "Hello, comrade. I'm glad you came."

"Wouldn't miss it. Is Michael coming?"

"I don't know. I left him a voicemail. We'll see if he shows."

A pretty vampire came over to their table. Evident by her youthful face, she'd been converted in her early twenties, but there was no telling how old she was. She bent at the waist and leaned her forearms on the table, giving the males a nice view of the bosom peeking out of her low-cut shirt.

"How may I help you this evening? Would you like to start with a drink?" She flashed a demure smile that showed the tips of her fangs.

Demetri leaned forward, placed his hands over the server's and looked deep into her eyes. "I am in the mood for something special tonight. Do you happen to have any AB negative?"

"Our last bag just went to the lady over there. I'm sorry."

Demetri and Marcus watched as the lady the waitress referenced raised her glass in Demetri's direction and smiled. Dressed in a pair of black jeans that hugged her long legs and a sweater that swelled over her ample bosom, the woman seemed to revel in

Demetri ogling her. Her porcelain skin and beautiful face was surrounded by a wealth of long, blonde hair. As she took a sip from her glass, Demetri nodded in acknowledgment, then turned his attention back to the waitress.

"I guess I'll have some AB positive instead. Marcus what do you want?"

"I'll take a glass of A positive mixed with Vodka."

"One AB Pos and one Truly Bloody Mary. Got it," the waitress repeated, then sauntered toward the bar.

The older vampire leaned over the table toward Marcus. "Now that's what I call a yummy dish." Demetri gestured with his thumb toward the waitress. "I wonder what she is doing after her shift."

The Russian licked his lips, earning a raised brow from Marcus.

"You'd have better luck with Miss AB negative over there. The waitresses in this place have a strict rule about fraternizing with the customers. Fraternizing is left for the people up on the third floor."

An affronted look crossed Demetri's face. "I've never had to pay for company, and I'm not about to start tonight, comrade."

"It looks like you won't have to." Marcus gestured with a sideways nod of his head. "Those two females at the table over there seem to be interested."

Demetri glanced in the direction Marcus gestured. Shadows from the candle flickering on the table danced upon the faces of two dark-haired female vampires. When they made eye contact, they smiled and wiggled their fingers in invitation. Demetri turned back to Marcus without acknowledging the females.

"They're not my type. I'll be right back." Demetri

slipped from the booth and glided over to the woman sipping his AB negative. "Excuse me. Pardon the interruption. Are you dining alone this evening?"

The woman glanced up meeting his gaze. "Yes, I came in for a little peace and quiet, so if you don't mind."

She tipped her head in the direction of the booth where Marcus sat watching.

"I was hoping to have a little AB negative, but since you got the last bag, I guess I'll have to go without. That is unless you'd like to share some of yours."

"Not gonna happen, buddy." The woman pinched the bridge of her nose in exasperation and let out a deep sigh. "Look, no offense. I'm sure you are a great guy, but I'm not looking for company tonight, so if you don't mind."

"Perhaps I could buy you another drink. Surely one isn't enough. We could get to know each other."

The woman rolled her eyes, which glowed with anger. "Okay, now I'm getting pissed. Please leave. I don't want to get to know you. I don't want any company. I just want to sit here and enjoy my drink in peace, and you are making that impossible."

When the waitress placed their drinks on their table, Marcus heard Demetri say, "Fine. I'll take my leave. My drink has arrived at our table anyway. Excuse me for trying to get to know you. Goodbye, female."

Demetri turned on his heels and walked back to the booth with a disgruntled look.

Marcus couldn't contain the smirk on his face. "Struck out, huh? She didn't want the pleasure of your company?"

Marcus inadvertently gave his friend the opening he needed, and Demetri wasted no time seizing the opportunity to change the subject. "Speaking of company, how's your heartmate situation? It's been several weeks now."

Marcus took a long draw of his drink before answering. "Not that it's any of your business, but by the end of the week I expect my heartmate will be with me. I'm going to ask her to move into the plantation on our next date."

"I'm very glad to hear that. It must have been hell for you with her in the same city, but not with you in your home. I don't know how you have stood it this long. A lesser vampire might have lost it by now."

Marcus took another swig of his Bloody Mary and replaced the glass with a clink on the table. "The only way I have been able to do it was by seeing her every night since we met. But it hasn't been easy to leave her every morning, unprotected."

"I bet. I don't know how you do it." Demetri took a sip from his glass, and Marcus mirrored the act. "If she were my heartmate, I would have thrown her over my shoulder and taken her to my lair long ago."

Marcus snorted at the notion just as he spied Michael enter the bar. He waved him over.

Michael approached the booth with what looked like a forced smile plastered on his face, and Marcus scooted over on the faux leather-covered bench to make room. Their fellow Alpha grabbed the waitress by the arm as she walked by and whispered his order in her ear. His eyes tracked her hips when she strolled to the bar to retrieve his drink.

Michael slid into the booth, clasping his hands together on the table. "Sorry I'm late. I just got your message, Demetri. Did I miss much?"

Marcus' grin stretched across his face. "You missed Demetri crash and bu—"

Demetri spoke over Marcus, and Michael shot Marcus an inquisitive look. "Where have you been, Michael?"

The younger Alpha donned an insouciant expression on his face, shifting under the ancient's discerning glare. "I was out...around the city."

Demetri's brows furrowed with trepidation. "Did you happen to see anything strange? I'm getting concerned. There seems to be an increase in criminal activity lately. Every time I turn on the TV, there is a news report about a death or a missing person."

Marcus nodded his head in agreement, his hair falling over his eye. "I noticed that too. I wonder if they are related." His voice hushed as the waitress placed a glass of blood in front of Michael.

Michael gave a nonchalant shrug. "Probably not." He took a large gulp from his glass, swallowing it quickly.

Michael crinkled his face. "I prefer my blood at 98.6."

"They have live donors," Marcus offered.

"I do not want to pay an exorbitant amount of money to take it fresh from the vein at the bar."

"Suit yourself," Marcus mumbled and brushed his hair from his eyes. "I thought I might call Stephan and discuss the missing women with him."

"I don't see why you would want to bother him," Michael commented casually.

Marcus faced him. "I was thinking we might need the Alpha Council to look into this."

Michael finished his drink in one more swallow, the empty glass landing on the table with an audible clink. "I don't see what the Council could do. I'd wait. It's too soon to call Stephan."

Demetri finished his drink and rejoined the conversation. "I agree. Let's wait. If there are any more murders, then we'll call Stephan and start an investigation, if need be."

The waitress came over, gathered the empties and asked the males if they needed a refill. Demetri and Marcus indicated they would like another round, but Michael declined.

"Not drinking tonight, Michael?" Demetri motioned to the empty glass cradled between Michael's hands.

"I already had some earlier." He placed the palm of his right hand over the glass. "I don't need any more right now."

Michael tapped the lip of the glass with his finger as if irritated. He obviously didn't want to be here.

"What's going on with you, Michael?" Marcus narrowed his eyes and tried to push into the Alpha's mind. He butted up against a mental wall, gleaning nothing.

"Nothing is going on. Demetri invited me, and I'm here. It's not like I'd turn down a summons from an ancient and risk insulting the guy."

Demetri scoffed and pinned the younger Alpha with his steely stare. "Insult me? You do not have to grace us with your presence, Michael. If there is someplace you'd rather be, by all means go."

"Okay. I've got things to do. I'll see you later, then." Michael stood before either of his fellow Alphas could protest and headed for the door. Demetri and Marcus stared at his back as he left.

Marcus swore he heard him mumble, "I'm so outta here," as he pushed through the glass doors.

He watched Michael disappear from sight. "You know, Demetri, he's a bit strange."

"I've met stranger, believe me." Seemingly mesmerized by the sway of her hips, Demetri watched Miss AB Negative glide out of the dining room,

"The one that got away," he murmured into his glass before slugging down the last of his drink. "Marcus, you make sure that you claim that heartmate of yours. There is no reason for you to keep suffering like the rest of us."

Marcus nodded and smiled as he thought of his Christina with her beautiful face and auburn hair. He raised his glass and tipped it toward his friend in salute. "I intend to do just that."

Chapter 13

Marcus opened the front door of his home and greeted Christina with an azure-blue silk scarf and a peck on the lips. "I have a surprise for you, Red. Put this on."

Marcus tied the blue scarf around Christina's eyes as a blindfold, the silk cool on her face. He took her arm and led her a short distance. Her heart pounded in her throat with the thrill of anticipation. When they stopped, Marcus carefully removed the blindfold.

As Christina's vision adjusted, a wooden door adorned with a large red ribbon came into focus.

"This is your game room," she observed, smiling at Marcus, who had a mischievous gleam in his eye and a grin to match. "Is the surprise a new arcade game?"

Marcus gave a noncommittal shrug of his shoulders. "Why don't you open the door and find out?"

Christina turned the knob and pushed open the door. The room had been transformed. The billiard table was absent, as were the arcade machines and the foosball table. Along one wall full-length mirrors now hung, the kind found in a ballet studio. Around the periphery of the room sat a variety of matching padded chairs and loveseats. In the center of the space stood the *pièce de résistance*—a magnificent grand piano. Its shiny black surface reflected in the mirrors, making it appear as if there were multiple pianos in the room.

"Oh my gosh, Marcus. What did you do? Where is your game room?"

Marcus turned to face Christina, taking her hands in his. "Christina, I have something I want to ask you.

"My people have a concept called heartmates. A heartmate is kind of like a spouse, only stronger. Heartmates never tire of one another. There is no such thing as divorce. As the years go on, their love always grows stronger, never weaker."

He gazed deeply into her eyes while she absorbed the information. "The first night we met, I knew you were my heartmate. I love you, *cara*. I want you to live with me here from now on. I want this to be your home, our home. And I thought if this house was going to be your home, you should have a special room, so I turned my game room into a music room for you."

Marcus paused and studied Christina's face. His brows furrowed, and the corners of his mouth dropped.

"You are very quiet, *cara*. What are you thinking?" His voice sounded low, slightly above a whisper as if he waited on bated breath for her answer.

Christina stared at him in disbelief for a few seconds while she processed what he'd told her. He had said he loved her, wanted her to move in. She'd not been expecting this. They had only been dating a few weeks. A job awaited her in Atlanta. It was too fast.

Wasn't it?

"I am shocked," she finally replied, when she found her voice. "So, are you saying you want me to move in with you?"

"It's more than that." He left her hands in his as he

lowered himself down onto one knee. "I want you to not only move in with me but be my heartmate, my wife to use the human term."

His heartmate! He wanted her to stay with him in this amazing home. Her dream man asked her to live with him in this fantastic setting. If what he'd told her was true, he'd love her in a way that went beyond what any husband could. To stay, she would have to give up her job in Atlanta, but look what she would get in return. It seemed like the plot from one of her romance novels, her innermost fantasy come true. But did she dare to say yes?

Chapter 14

"What do you say, will you marry me?" Marcus knew a moment of trepidation, unsure what her answer would be.

"I-I don't know what to say."

The smile on her face reached her eyes, and Marcus hoped that was a good sign.

"How about saying yes? Say you'll be my heartmate."

Christina threw herself into his arms. Luckily, he was stronger than a human or he would have fallen flat on his ass.

"Yes! Yes I'll be your heartmate or wife or whatever you want to call me!"

Marcus embraced Christina in his arms and spun the two of them around the room before lowering her back onto her feet. His chest swelled with happiness. This amazing woman just agreed to be his, and it made his heart sing.

Her beautiful smile lit up the room as her eyes fell on his gift.

"May I touch it?" She nodded toward the piano.

Her emotions poured over him, felt overwhelming, inspirational. And he knew she needed to play them out.

"You can do more than touch it. Please play for

me."

Christina approached the piano and ran her fingers along the glossy black satin lines of the instrument. As she rounded the edge, she looked taken aback. "It's a Bösendorfer."

Marcus smiled with satisfaction. "An acquaintance in Vegas helped me to get it. I hope you like it."

"Like it?" She clasped her hands together in glee. "I love it! I've always wanted a Bösendorfer."

Christina pulled out the bench and sat. She carefully lifted the wooden cover, removed and folded the rectangle of velvet found underneath, and then gently caressed the keys. After her fingers found their resting spot and her feet located the petals, she played a dark, romantic melody.

Marcus stood spellbound by the concerto for a moment before he glided toward the piano as if drawn by magic. A hauntingly beautiful song, he'd never heard such a piece. Its romantic melody and fast trills that crescendoed into majestic chords were utterly magnificent. He watched Christina while she played, knowing she played only for him. When she completed the sonata, their eyes met over the shiny black surface.

"That sounded absolutely beautiful. It stirred my soul." Marcus walked around the piano and sat beside his mate on the bench. "What is it?"

"It's a piece I composed the night we met about a woman who falls in love with a vampire and gives herself to him body and soul, loving him like no other. I'm going to call it *Heartmates*."

Marcus rose from the bench, taking Christina by her shoulders. Lifting her to her feet, he drew her to him, crushing her to his chest. He leaned in to capture her lips with his. Her lips parted in offering, and he accepted, thrusting his tongue deep inside. The kiss deepened as she melded against him.

Marcus broke the kiss. "I want you, Christina."

He hoped his love for her showed on his face, and her answering smile seemed to say it did. Her hand cupped his cheek. "Then make love to me."

She didn't need to make the request a second time. Their lips locked in a searing caress. Without breaking the kiss, Marcus scooped her into his arms. Using his preternatural speed, he took her to his bedroom and closed the bedroom door with a mental command. With his next thought, he willed the candles in the room to life, bathing them in a golden light.

Marcus laid her gently on the black satin sheets. "You are so beautiful, Christina." He gazed deeply into her emerald eyes, drinking her in.

His hands moved under her sweater so he could span her ribcage with his fingers. Christina arched as he removed the sweater. He cupped one breast, taking the weight of it in his hand. With his other hand, he popped open the clasp on the front of her bra, and her breasts spilled free.

"Umm," he purred. "Stunning."

His head bent and captured her nipple in his mouth. She groaned as she ran her fingers through his hair. She cupped his head in her hands, holding him to her. The scent of her arousal perfumed the air with each draw of his mouth.

He felt her need grow into a palpable force that surrounded him. His inner beast roared with relief to finally be able to claim its mate.

Marcus moved his hands along her ribcage and

slowly lowered them, spanning her flat stomach until they came to rest on the waistband of her pants. His fingers deftly undid the fastenings. As he slid them over her hips, his fingers hooked the edges of her white lace panties and took them along for the ride—down her supple thighs, over her muscular calves, and finally past her toes to the floor.

Marcus rose above her on his knees and stared at the buffet before him. Her sex blossomed in front of his eyes like beautiful petals of a delicate flower, glistening with the morning dew.

"Why did you stop?" Christina bit her lower lip, making Marcus' hard shaft jump in response.

"You overwhelm me, *cara*. The way the candlelight dances on your skin takes my breath away. I had to stop and enjoy the view for a minute while I remember how to breathe."

Christina's concerned expression turned to one of wanton anticipation. She sat up reaching for the buttons on his shirt, her fingers trembling.

He gripped her fingers, stilling them as he looked down into her sweet face. "You don't have to do this, if you aren't ready."

"No, no, I want to."

He didn't know how he would manage it, but if she wanted to stop he would somehow find a way. However, it would have to be before she got him naked, because once there was no cloth barrier between them; he didn't think he would be able to stop. "Are you sure, *cara*? I don't want to pressure you."

Christina smiled and looked at him from under the fan of her lashes. "I'm sure."

Thank the heavens above! The Alpha released her

hands so they could complete the path down his shirt until it opened, giving her a view of his muscular chest.

She ran her hands over his abdominals. A finger traced each of the distinct lines between his six-pack. They rose, glided over his pectorals to catch the edges of his shirt and push it from his shoulder. Marcus shrugged out of his shirt with Christina's help, then shimmied out of his slacks, very grateful he had decided to go commando.

He lay beside his heartmate, turned her face to his, and took her lips in a gentle kiss. When she parted her lips in welcome, his tongue danced in her mouth, and she responded in kind. As their tongues glided between their lips, Marcus lowered his hand to the junction of red curls between her legs. His fingers found the tiny spot he longed to touch. As he began to rub Christina's sensitive nub with tiny circles, she relaxed her legs, allowing them to fall open. The sinuous sensation pushed her body higher and higher. Marcus felt her tighten in anticipation.

The rhythm of her heart increased, her face grew flushed. His mate ground her hips into his hand in encouragement, abandoning all inhibitions. He pushed one finger into her as he drove her skillfully over the precipice. Her velvet folds gripped his digit tightly, milking it with a silky heat.

"So tight," he whispered as he slowly withdrew his finger and added two more in its place. He worked her sex by scissoring his fingers within her softness, readying her for his thick shaft.

"You are so wet. I can't wait to be inside of you." He withdrew his fingers and licked them while Christina watched. The erotic sight made a new pool of moist heat spread down her thighs. Marcus rolled over, putting his knees between her legs. He fisted himself in one hand and then positioned his shaft at her creamy entrance as he braced his weight on his other hand.

Marcus gently pushed the tip of his penis against her opening. Sweat broke out on his forehead from the effort to go slow, to allow her body to stretch and accommodate him so he would not hurt her.

When he reached her barrier, Christina tensed beneath him. She closed her legs, locking Marcus between her thighs.

"Look at me, Christina," Marcus whispered. Holding still, he remained poised over her, their bodies barely joined. He captured his lover's eyes, holding her to him. "Stay with me, *cara*. Relax for me, sweetheart. I promise I've got you."

Marcus reached down between their bodies. Easily finding her most sensitive nub, he began rubbing the spot. As his thumb made slow circles, Christina began to relax, giving in to the sensation he created.

Marcus moved his hips slightly in time with his circles, careful not to breach her barrier. When Christina's legs fell open and her eyes closed, he pushed into her mind and found her drifting on the sensuous wave. Marcus drove her body higher toward the heavens; a feeling of warmth consumed her as hot as if she neared the sun itself until she thought she would burn from the flames licking over her skin.

She gripped the sheets in tight fists, tossing her head from side to side, capturing her lower lip between her teeth. As she floated to heaven for the second time, Marcus thrust forward.

With one quick surge, he broke through her barrier

and buried himself to the hilt. Christina gasped. Her eyes wide, she gripped his shoulders, looking for a way to anchor herself to earth.

He didn't move, simply filled her feminine channel, allowing her fiery inferno time to adjust to the size of him. "That's it, baby. One moment of pain. From now on only pleasure. I promise, only pleasure."

Marcus captured her lips in a scorching kiss that drove all thought from her mind. The pleasure of having him over her, in her, consumed her. Marcus moved slowly in and out, building the heat between them. As his timing increased, Christina met each of his thrusts with a rise of her hips. She clung to the warrior's broad shoulders as if they were her lifeline when her next climax raced through her body.

Marcus felt her nails score his back, reveling in the pleasurable pain. A soft keening sound escaped her pouty lips, drawing his gaze to her face. Her lashes lay on her flushed cheeks in dark crescents. A fine sheen of perspiration glistened on her forehead. The light of the candles danced over her skin, creating a swirl of patterns. She looked like a goddess with her hair fanned out over his pillow.

The Alpha knew true happiness for the first time in his long life. This felt right—felt like coming home. This amazing woman lying beneath him, giving him pleasure like he had never known before, was his. His love.

His heartmate.

A growl escaped his throat as his inner beast voiced its approval. His balls drew up tight, and an orgasm boiled up from below, gathering in his loins, in his brain. His vision tunneled to only her.

His hips pistoned faster, in a rapid tattoo, against her flesh. Marcus brought her over the edge once more, this time going with her. Her tight folds gripped him like a fist, milking him with her hot sheath until he exploded into her. Her spasms rolled over his shaft, causing it to jump inside of her.

Breathing hard, gasping for air, Marcus slowly separated himself from Christina and rolled to her side. Gathering her in his arms, he nuzzled her hair with his chin.

She sighed, snuggling into his hold. "That was amazing, Marcus. I had no idea sex would be like that. I hope it was okay for you."

"It wasn't okay, it was incredible. You were so brave." His hand rubbed tiny circles on her back. "I love the way you feel. I love the way you trusted me. You are perfect, *cara*! As long as I live I will never forget this moment with you."

Marcus willed the shower on and lifted Christina into his arms. "Come on, let's get cleaned up."

When the water washed over her, the look of contentment on her face made Marcus push once again into her mind. The water warmed her as it poured down her skin. She felt a little sore, yet deeply satisfied.

She found him very loving, making her first time special and very pleasurable. His mate thought he had been wonderful in bed, and she considered his body a thing of beauty. She loved the way his muscles played under his skin, the way they felt under her fingers.

Christina's heated gaze raked his body, and his cock stood at attention in a passionate salute, ready for round two. He needed something to focus on or he would take her again here in the shower. But that would be uncomfortable for his mate. And making her uncomfortable in any way, physically or emotionally, was unconscionable. He reached around her and grabbed the soap and a washcloth.

After he lathered the cloth, he brought it to Christina's shoulders, gently making tiny massaging circles over her sensitive skin. He carefully made his way down her body, washing away the evidence of her innocence mixed with his seed from her thighs. Once she was clean, he took the bottle of shampoo and squeezed a circle into the palm of his hand.

"Turn around," he commanded, his voice husky even to his own ears.

When Christina did as he asked, he washed her hair, taking care not to pull it. A low moan pushed from her throat, and she closed her eyes.

"That feels *sooooo* good." Her body swayed as if her legs were boneless.

Marcus' mate leaned back against his hard frame, allowing his sturdy body to support her. Her exhaustion pulled at him. His protective instincts demanded he let her rest, make sure she got what her body needed.

He quickly rinsed the suds from her hair, watching the soapy bubbles dance down her body. He intended to get her into bed so she could rest, but before he turned off the water, Christina grabbed the soap and began to lather her hands.

The Alpha clasped her hands between his much larger ones.

"What do you think you are going to do with that soap?" he inquired, one eyebrow raised.

"I was going to return the favor and wash your back."

"Lover, you do that and I'm not sure we'll ever be able to get any sleep tonight. You touch me with those soapy hands, and you will awaken the sleeping giant," Marcus quipped with a wink before looking pointedly down at his long member that jerked under her gaze.

"Oh." Color flushed up Christina's neck into her cheeks.

He took the soap from her and quickly washed himself before turning off the water, giving her no chance to protest. After stepping from the shower, he wrapped a towel around his waist and grabbed another to towel her off. Reverently, he wiped away the beads of water from her body, then led her back to the bed. While they lay naked together on the satin sheets, he wrapped his body around hers, her warmth enveloping him. His heartmate snuggled into him and closed her eyes. When sleep took her, Marcus looked down and wondered what in his long life he had ever done to deserve such a gift as her.

Chapter 15

Keeping her lids closed, Christina awoke thinking about the wonderful dream she had about she and Marcus making love. *Marcus.* Memories from the previous day flooded her mind. He had asked her to marry him, be his...*heartmate.* It was like a dream. Opening her eyes, she looked at her beloved and realized the dream had been real.

She stretched, scissoring her legs to discover she didn't feel as sore as she expected. When she stirred, Marcus rolled and captured her lips with his. Her lover claiming her lips pushed the sleepy haze from Christina's mind. His kiss, soft and welcoming, created a blaze of desire within her. When he pulled back from their kiss, the look on his face humbled her.

His love and reverence for her showed. His expression said the words he did not. The heat in his eyes said he adored her, found her desirable. He slipped a hand under the covers, finding the juncture of her thighs wet and ready for him.

"You're incorrigible." Christina smiled, parting her legs in wanton invitation.

He gladly accepted her summons, moving over her.

"You mean insatiable, not incorrigible." Marcus smiled down at her and gently kissed her cheek as he slipped inside her body.

****

That evening, Christina glanced over the paper as she and Marcus enjoyed the meal Payton had prepared. When she read the headline, she gasped.

"This is awful. Listen to this, Marcus. According to the paper, they found one of the two missing girls."

Marcus' dark brows furrowed deeply over his eyes in confusion.

"Remember the two sisters, tourists visiting from Virginia who were missing and believed to have met with foul play?" she clarified. "One of the girls is still missing, but the other was found dead in an alley. It says her neck was broken.

"What is happening to this town, Marcus? It used to be so safe. Now every day it seems like someone is going missing."

"You've got a point." Marcus wiped his hand down his face and pulled the skin taut. "I need to make a phone call. I'll be right back."

His heartmate was correct. Someone disappeared every day...or rather every night. Marcus suspected a vampire might be behind the disappearances. His thoughts traveled back in time to an eerily similar situation.

It had only been a short time ago that he had noticed people disappearing from Las Vegas. He and his fellow Alphas investigated and discovered a hunt club run by a vampire named Gage Lucio. Though they destroyed Gage and freed the humans who had been kidnapped for the hunt, it did not escape Marcus' notice that all the humans taken for the hunt had been seized at night, and so far all of the women kidnapped from Savannah had also been taken at night. Perhaps that was no coincidence. He wondered if there might be a hunt club springing up here in Savannah.

Walking away from the table, Marcus pulled his cell phone out of his jeans pocket and scrolled through his contacts, choosing Stephan. As he hit dial and waited, he glanced back over his shoulder to be sure he would not be overheard.

"Hey, Marcus, what's going on? We haven't heard from you since you moved out of our place. How ya been?"

"I'm good, man."

"What's up?"

"I think we might need to convene the Council again. We got something going on here in Savannah." Marcus ran his fingers through his hair.

"You moved back into the plantation house?" Stephan asked.

"Yeah, I'm crashing in Savannah for a while. In fact, Demetri and Michael are in town, too." He took a deep breath before continuing. "Look, we've got women going missing here. Every night one or two disappear. I think we might have a problem that the Alphas need to deal with."

"What makes you think this is a Council matter? It's possible a human is doing this."

"Everything in my gut tells me it's one of our kind. Some of the news reports the past few nights have shown the crime scenes. Something's off. I can't put my finger on it, but I just don't think a human is taking all these girls."

"What do Michael and Demetri think about all the disappearances?" his sire asked, obviously questioning Marcus' ability to correctly read the situation.

Marcus sighed in frustration. He always had to prove himself to Stephan, who acted like an older brother more often than a friend. It didn't matter how long they'd fought together, or the fact that Marcus happened to be over two hundred and fifty years old. He was younger than Stephan, who always questioned his opinions.

"They have mixed feelings on the issue. Demetri thinks it might be something vampiric happening, but Michael thinks it's too soon to bring in the team."

Stephan sighed across the line. "I'll come to Savannah. Since Michael and Demetri are already there, the four of us will meet. I want to investigate the disappearances before we convene the whole Council."

Well at least Stephan agreed to look into the matter, and Marcus appreciated the effort. He paced the room. "When can you get here?"

"I'll materialize there in three hours. You contact Michael and Demetri and let them know we will meet tonight."

Marcus hung up the phone, his thoughts instantly returning to the woman waiting for him in the kitchen as he made his way there. They had much to discuss now that they were fully mated.

She was his to protect and care for. His to love and cherish. And the burden made his heart heavy. He didn't want this ugliness to touch her. The Alpha silently vowed to do everything in his power to keep her safe, and to that end there were a few things he must do before too much longer.

They must exchange a small amount of blood, so they could create a mindlink. She also needed to become a vampire, because he could not live without her or watch her grow old. But all that would have to wait. For now, he just wanted to be with her and drink in the happiness they shared.

Marcus rejoined Christina in the kitchen. When their eyes met, she gave him a wide smile.

"Everything okay?" Christina asked, popping a strawberry into her mouth.

He slid into the seat beside her at the kitchen table. "Yep. I have some people coming over tonight for a meeting."

"Anyone I know?"

Marcus took a bite of fruit and chewed it before he answered. "No."

"How many people are coming?"

"Three. The people who are coming are my fellow Alphas."

Christina looked at him questioningly. "What are Alphas?"

She listened intently while Marcus explained about the Alpha Council. After several minutes of answering her questions, Marcus took a strawberry off the plate and fed it to his heartmate. His gaze followed a small amount of juice dripping down her chin. He wiped it off with his thumb and licked it clean. It tasted sweet, with a hint of Christina in the aftertaste. Utter perfection.

Christina looked pensive. "Should I make some *hors d'oeuvres* for the meeting?"

He was amazed at how easily she accepted the fantastic things he told her. It was almost an inhuman response to not question such tales in disbelief, but his heartmate took what he said in stride, believed his stories.

"I don't think that will be necessary, but thanks for

the offer, my love." Marcus rested his hand on the side of her face, rubbing the pad of his thumb along her jawline. "You really are something, always thinking of others. I'll never know what I've done to deserve you."

Marcus wrapped his hand around her neck in a loose grip and pulled her toward him.

Their foreheads touched as she whispered, "You are the sweetest man I have ever met. I love you so much."

"I love you too, *cara*. You make my heart sing."

Payton interrupted the moment by clearing his throat to announce his presence as he walked into the kitchen, and Marcus released her to inform him about the guests he expected for the evening.

Time ticked by, and the trio prepared for the meeting in their own way. Payton straightened the mansion and stocked the wet bar. Christina decided to stay out of the way by working out then going for a swim in the indoor pool. Marcus put a fresh supply of blood, especially some O negative for Stephan, in the fridge. He replayed the crime scene in his head, searching for the details that might help Stephan understand why he was convinced a vampire was behind the deaths. Before he knew it, his home filled with guests.

Marcus sensed Stephan materialize on the front porch and made it to the foyer before the doorbell rang. As the bell sounded, Marcus opened the door and grasped his sire's forearms in greeting.

"Welcome." Marcus stepped aside so Stephan could enter before he continued. "Michael and Demetri are already here. They are waiting for us in the library."

Stephan followed Marcus down the hallway and

into the library. Marcus watched his sire's eyes scan the room. When they came to rest on Michael, he nodded his head in acknowledgement from where he stood against a wall with his arms crossed.

Demetri raised his glass of brandy, drawing everyone's attention with the gesture. "It's good to see you again, comrade."

Marcus motioned toward one of the wingback chairs. "Can I get you anything to drink?"

Stephan sat down and placed his ankle on his opposite knee. "No thanks, maybe later. Right now I want to get down to business. What do you know about what is happening to the women?"

Demetri spoke first. "We don't have a lot of firsthand information. All we know is what has been in the paper and on the news. I personally agree with Marcus. I think there may be a vampire behind all of these disappearances. It reminds me of what happened with Lucio."

A muscle ticked along Stephan's jaw, the only indication of his anger at the reminder of what had happened in Vegas. One of the women Gage had kidnapped had been Stephan's heartmate, Katrina. Stephan assembled the Alpha Council to deal with him and save Kat but not before she suffered at Gage's hands. They barely arrived in time to save her.

"But we killed Gage," Stephan growled through clenched teeth.

Demetri nodded his head in acknowledgement. "I didn't say it's Gage, but it's *déjà vous* all over again."

Demetri was as old as Stephan. They had both been converted by the virus in the thirteen hundreds when the plague devastated their countries. They had fought together for hundreds of years. In that time, trust formed into friendship. Marcus knew Stephan trusted Demetri's judgment like no other.

Stephan nodded in agreement. "We need to figure out what we're dealing with. We need some reconnaissance. Marcus, you, Michael, and I will divide up the city tomorrow night and begin patrols. Maybe we'll luck out and find something interesting. Demetri, can you contact the Vampire Enforcement Squad for this area? Maybe the VES agents will know something."

"Will do, comrade. I have someone I can contact. I will let you know what VES has to say."

"Very good." Stephan gave his old friend a tilt of his chin in a show of confidence before turning his steely gaze on the vampire who stood stoically against the wall. "Michael you've been very quiet. What do you think is going on?"

Straightening to his full height as he steeled his features, the supercilious Alpha responded, "I think we are wasting our time. It's probably a human. A very sick human, but a human, nonetheless. However, I'll do the patrols as you suggested, Stephan."

"Good, so we have a plan. Tomorrow night we will patrol the city and see what information VES has."

Marcus leaned forward, resting his forearms on his thighs. "Stephan, where is Kat? I thought she might come with you."

Marcus missed his friend. They had a special relationship that in the past went beyond friendship. The saying "friends with benefits" fit them nicely. At least until Stephan came into their lives. Now Kat belonged to him, and even if Marcus wasn't completely in love with Christina, she would be off limits.

"She can't dematerialize yet or she would be here. I don't like leaving her alone, so I'm going back to Vegas tonight. She and I will fly here tomorrow on my jet."

"I'll send Payton to pick you up from the airport. Just let me know what time. Of course, I offer my home to you both. Please stay with us."

"Thank you. I accept your hospitality." Stephan's head snapped around, doing a double take. "Wait, who is 'us'?"

****

As Marcus blathered on to Stephan about his heartmate, Michael slipped out of the library. His nostrils flared to life when they caught a compelling scent. He used his predatory senses to track the aroma down the hallway and into the sitting room. When he stepped through the doors of the room, the sight of a beautiful redhead standing in front of the window, bathed in the light of the moon, greeted him.

Marcus didn't mention he'd arranged a snack.

The human turned from the window and faced him. She smiled. "Oh, hello. I thought you might be Marcus. I'm Christina."

"Well hello, Christina. My name is Michael." He gave her a sanguine smile, the sharp ends of his teeth glistening.

"Can I get you a drink?" Christina offered, indicating the wet bar beside her.

Michael swaggered across the room and stopped in front of the attractive woman. Leaning in to her, he braced his hands on the windowsill to wall her in. She backed against the sill, her legs pushing against the marble.

Michael licked his lips. "I'd love a drink!" His head moved toward Christina's neck.

Christina brought her hands up on his chest in an attempt to push him away. Terror crept into her eyes. Her futile struggles barely registered to him as he wrapped his arms around her and pulled her to him until they were so close not even air could come between them. His taut muscles and sinew flexed while he gripped her to him. He breathed in her scent—a delicate aroma of jasmine and honey with a hint of chlorine.

"Yummm," he purred, feeling his fangs extend from his gums. "You smell good enough to eat."

Chapter 16

"Let her go. Now!" bellowed Marcus. He sprang from the entry of the room, landing on top of Michael just as the son of a bitch released Christina. The two hit the floor in a ball of limbs. They rolled around the hard wood, appendages flailing. Marcus came to rest on top of Michael, straddling his chest.

"Christina is my heartmate. You will not touch her, ever."

Marcus turned his angry stare on the rest of the group gathered by the French doors. "Did you hear me? No one is to touch her."

Demetri put his hands up in front of his chest in a gesture of surrender. "We got it, Marcus. We got it. No one is going to hurt your mate." His voice sounded like smooth silk, and Marcus detected the enchantment in his voice trying to push through the rage.

Lowering his hands, Demetri continued, "Marcus, get off Michael. It was a misunderstanding. Wasn't it, Michael?"

"Yeah," Michael replied in a breathy voice. The weight of Marcus on his chest obviously made it difficult for him to breathe. "I'm sorry. I thought she was a snack."

Marcus' head snapped back to Michael. He bared his fangs, and a hiss pushed through his lips before he yelled, "A SNACK!"

The Alpha pulled back his arm, his fingers curled into a tight fist. It made a satisfying crunch when it contacted with Michael's nose. Before the sound ceased, Marcus brought his other fist down upon his cheek, assuring it was broken.

He felt Christina grab his fist when he lifted it for round three.

"Marcus," Christina's voice came out a whisper. "Please stop this. I am all right. No harm done. He didn't bite me. Look at me, I'm fine. Please let him up."

Marcus' stare raked her trembling body from toe to head, spending extra time to thoroughly examine her neck. He eased open his fist, then slowly rose off Michael and stepped back.

"I was just kidding, Marcus." Michael rose and wiped the blood from his mouth and nose.

When Michael got to his feet, Marcus lunged forward, pinning Michael against the wall by his throat. "This is your only warning," he growled, fangs bared. "If you ever touch her again, I'll finish what was started here tonight. *Capiche*?"

"I *capiche*," said Michael, holding himself stone still. His eyebrows furrowed over his eyes.

Stephan cleared his throat and drew the attention of everyone in the room. "So, Marcus, now that you've proven what a deadly Alpha you are, are you going to growl at Michael all night or are you going to be polite and formally present your heartmate to us? Which, I might as well point out, had you done earlier we might have avoided this misunderstanding."

Marcus removed his hand from Michael's throat and raked it down his own face.

After a deep, cleansing breath through his clenched teeth, Marcus turned and reached a hand toward Christina. When she placed her hand in his, he said, "This is Christina Prescott. Christina, this is Demetri Romanoff and Stephan von Haas." He threw a disdainful look at the bloodied Alpha. "And you've met Michael."

Christina's smile appeared strained as she nodded toward the two large males in the doorway. She wrapped an arm around Marcus' waist and leaned into him. Her scent enveloped him, calming his nerves in a way nothing else could in that moment.

"It is a pleasure to meet you, Christina." Stephan bowed at his waist. "My heartmate, Katrina, will be here tomorrow. I hope you don't mind, but Marcus invited us to stay here. We will be flying in tomorrow evening from Vegas. Katrina will be excited to meet the woman who stole Marcus' heart."

"I can't wait to meet her. It will be nice to have another woman in the house. There is too much testosterone in here." She threw a chastising look toward first Marcus then Michael, making Stephan chuckle.

Crossing his brawny arms across his thick chest, Demetri tipped back his head and laughed, the sonorous sound coming from deep in his chest cavity. "I like this human female. I think she might actually be able to keep Marcus in line—which is no small miracle. Tell me Christina, do you have a sister that I could introduce to some of our comrades?"

"Sorry, I don't have any sisters." Christina looked up into the eyes of her love and smiled, appearing more relaxed now that some of the tension had eased from the room. "I'm hungry. If I go get something to eat, do you think you can behave yourself?"

"I'll try," Marcus promised and wrapped his arm around her shoulder. He gave her a reassuring smile and pulled her to him, tucking her head against his shoulder.

After a quick squeeze, Christina pushed away and turned to address the group. "Would anyone like something to eat? I'd be happy to make something."

All the vampires shook their heads in unison, refusing the offer.

Stephan stepped closer to the door and said, "We need to be leaving anyway."

Good. Marcus couldn't deny that a little time alone with his mate would calm him. Maybe calm wasn't the correct word. Perhaps excite would be a better descriptor. For the thought of having her to himself made his blood boil and wicked thoughts come to mind.

Marcus gave Christina a little pat on her rump and flashed his sexiest smile. "We're fine. You go make something to satisfy your hunger. I'll meet you in the kitchen after I see these guys out."

Michael seized the moment to make a hasty exit. "I know when I'm not wanted," he murmured, then dematerialized without saying farewell.

"Good riddance," Marcus muttered, his deep baritone voice rumbling in his chest.

The remaining vampires walked together to the front doors with Demetri in the lead. "Well, comrade, thanks for the interesting evening. We have to do this again some time." The Russian Alpha slapped Marcus on his shoulder.

"Yes," chimed in Stephan. "Just try not to lose it when Kitten is here tomorrow. Okay?"

"I'll try to control myself with Katrina in the house." Marcus flashed a toothy grin at his sire. "But I have to say it was fun kicking Michael's ass. You've got to admit he had it coming."

Stephan grinned and clasped each of Demetri's forearms in the grasp of the warrior. "Bye, my friend. Safe travels."

"And to you, Stephan." Demetri returned the valediction before dematerializing.

"Safe travels to you and Kat," Marcus said, turning to his sire. "Call me tomorrow and let me know what time to expect your plane. I'll have Payton at the airport to pick you up."

"Thanks again, Marcus. I'll be in touch." Stephan's form wavered then disappeared, leaving only a black wisp of smoke in the air.

After Stephan dematerialized, Marcus punched the code into the alarm keypad and headed for his mate.

He joined Christina in the kitchen, coming up behind her as she sat on a bar stool by the granite island. He wrapped his arms around her waist and leaned down next to her ear. "What did you find to eat, my dear?"

"Ice Cream. Want some? I'll make you a sundae. I've got the chocolate syrup, cherries, and whipped cream right here."

"Not right now, but those cherries look good." Releasing her, he sat on the stool beside her and popped a cherry into his mouth.

"How did the meeting go?" She scooped a spoonful of the sundae, then presented the spoon to Marcus and raised both eyebrows giving a want-some look. He wrapped his lips around the spoon and took the offering.

"It went well. Stephan and his heartmate will be flying into Savannah tomorrow evening. I hope you don't mind that I invited them to stay here."

Christina fed him another spoonful. "I think it will be fun. Tell me about Katrina. What is she like? How long have Stephan and she been together?"

"First of all, her friends call her Kat not Katrina, so she'll want you to call her Kat. Stephan calls her Kitten, but he is the only one who can get away with that."

"Why does he call her Kitten?" Christina popped a spoonful of sundae in her mouth.

"When I introduced them, I called her Kat, of course. Because she is so much younger than Stephan, he referred to her as a kitten to make fun of her age. The name stuck." Marcus lifted the spoon from its resting spot in the bowl and sucked down another chocolaty spoonful.

"You introduced them?"

"Yep. Kat and I were roommates."

Before he could clarify, Christina shot him a look that told him he needed to explain and quick.

"We were friends back in Vegas. When we met, she was down on her luck. I offered to let her stay with me for a little while because she didn't have anywhere else to go. Once she was there, she just stayed." He gave a casual shrug of his shoulders. "Most nights she was out dancing, so we barely crossed paths."

Christina raised an inquiring brow. "Dancing. What is she, a showgirl?"

The Alpha nodded, popping another cherry in his mouth. "She *used to be* a showgirl. She danced in a club I own on the strip, but once she married Stephan, she gave that up. He helped her open a dance studio. She manages the place and teaches some of the dance classes. And boy, are those kids lucky. That woman really knows how to move."

Christina pinned him with a jealous glare. "So just how close were you and this Kat?"

Marcus noted the wary look on his heartmate's face, but she worried for nothing. Christina was the perfect woman for him, and he would never look at another woman again.

"She is Stephan's heartmate, you have nothing to worry about. Our relationship is strictly platonic. There is only one woman for me and that's you, my dear. Plus," he added with a shit-eating grin, "Stephan would kill anyone who got near Kat, and I don't have a death wish."

Marcus ducked as Christina threw a cherry at him.

"You giving me your cherry again, babe?" he quipped when she grabbed a handful of the red fruit.

"I'll…give…you…my…cherry…" Christina pitched a series of cherries toward Marcus to emphasize each word of her sentence. He used his preternatural reflexes to catch each in his mouth. As he chewed the fruit, he dipped his finger into the whipped cream mound atop the ice cream and deposited the dollop on the tip of Christina's nose.

"I can't believe you just did that." Christina smiled as she wiped the whipped cream from her face and grabbed the canister. She pointed the can toward Marcus.

"You're in trouble now, mister." She pushed the button and drew a creamy line up his face.

Marcus licked the whipped cream from his lips and

wiped it out of his left eye. "Oh, you are asking for it now."

"Am I?" Christina pulled his shirt away from his body and launched the cold cream down his chest with a laugh.

"Think that's funny? I'll show you funny." Marcus grabbed the chocolate syrup and gave it a squeeze, sending a little onto Christina's chest. She let out a yelp when the cold liquid slid down her body.

"Oh, too cold for you, baby? Here, I'll get that off."

Marcus leaned in and used his tongue to lap the chocolate off her bosom. A rush of heat coursed through his body. Once he had gotten every last bit off, he noticed Christina had stilled in response to his attention, and he slowly raised his chin and saw lust in her eyes. Marcus pushed into her mind to glean her sinful thoughts. Delicious images of the two of them in his bed with the sweet cream played in her mind for him to see.

Half of her mouth crept up before she wagged her eyebrows in insinuation. Christina glanced at the can of whipped cream she still held in her hand and took off at a full run toward Marcus' suite with him in tow holding the bottle of chocolate syrup.

"I'm going to get you, my sweet," Marcus called as he followed his love. "I have some delicious ideas about what we can do with these toppings."

And did he ever.

Chapter 17

The next evening Christina sat in the kitchen, busily making *hors d'œuvres*, when Marcus reached over and plucked one off the tray. He tossed it into the air, easily catching it in his mouth.

"Yum, babe, those are delicious. You shouldn't have gone to all that trouble for little old me."

Christina smacked the back of her heartmate's hand playfully when he reached for a second treat. "Little old you needs to keep your big old hands off of these. They are for Stephan and Kat."

"But I thought you liked my big old hands. I didn't hear any complaints when they were all over your body last night." A sly grin took Marcus' face, matching his wagging brows.

Christina took a tray from the oven. "Ha, ha. Very funny. Listen, I thought I'd go to my apartment. There is an outfit there that I want to wear tonight."

"Okay, I'll get my keys, and we'll go over there now."

"Excuse me, sir." Payton stood in the doorway looking concerned. "The contractor would like to see you before he leaves for the night. He has a question about the panic room."

"He'll have to wait. I was just about to take Christina to her apartment." Marcus leaned against the counter as she placed the *pâté en terrine* on the perfectly polished silver tray.

"You go deal with the contractor, my love. I'll run over to the apartment real quick. I'll probably be back before you even finish with him."

"I don't like you going out alone." Marcus glanced over at his valet. "Payton will go with you."

"Of course, sir." Payton gave a quick nod. "I'd be happy to escort Miss Christina."

Payton crossed the kitchen and pulled the plastic wrap from the cabinet before making his way to Christina.

"I don't need anyone to accompany me, Marcus. I can go by myself."

"I'd prefer Payton to go with—"

"Excuse me, but may I speak with you a moment, Mr. B?" The burly contractor interrupted Marcus' protests as he walked into the kitchen. "I need you to show me where you want the security cameras installed, so we can run the wires before we leave for the night."

Obviously noting his employer's reluctance, the contractor hastily added, "It should only take a couple of minutes."

"All right," Marcus agreed reluctantly. "I guess I can give you a few minutes."

The Alpha leaned over the island and placed a quick kiss on Christina's lips before leaving to confer with the contractor. After the men left the kitchen, she turned to her companion.

"Payton, I don't need a sitter. Besides I'm sure you have lots to do before you go to the airport to pick up Kat and Stephan. I'll just go to the apartment on my own. It won't take but a minute, and then I'll be right back."

"But Mr. Marcus said I should accompany you."

"I heard what he said, but there is no reason for you to take me over there. I know you have things you need to do. Please, don't argue. I will go by myself."

Wrapping the *hors d'œuvres* in plastic wrap, Payton placed them in the refrigerator. "Madame, I really think—"

Ignoring the valet's protest, Christina effectively ended the discussion by declaring, "Marcus is just being over protective."

She washed and dried her hands on the tea towel which hung by the sink, then turned to look at Payton over her shoulder with a smile. "I'll be fine. Please stop arguing with me."

An exasperated breath puffed out the butler's cheeks. As if knowing it was never wise to argue with a woman, he simply responded, "As you wish, madam."

****

A short time later, as Christina ascended the stairs to her apartment, her spidey senses began to tingle. Her instincts screamed to her something was wrong, but she quelled them and continued up the stairs, silently chastising herself for being paranoid. When she reached the top, she glanced left then right, looking for anything out of the ordinary. Finding everything in place, she admonished herself once more for letting her imagination run wild and turned left down the hallway to her apartment.

She withdrew her keys from her purse and reached for the door knob. Suddenly the hairs on the back of her neck stood on end. She realized the door stood slightly ajar. Peeking through the opening, Christina realized the inside doorframe was splintered, as if it had been broken when someone bullied open the door. Christina eased open the door slowly, looking around her beautiful apartment that now lay in shambles.

The couch cushions lay strewn about. Her pictures, knocked from the walls, sat on the floor with the glass and frames broken. Her television and electronics rested in a heap of plastic and metal off to one side of the room.

She made her way into the kitchen. All her cabinets hung open like gaping mouths. Broken pieces of dishes and drinking glasses covered the linoleum. She spied some pink and blue flowers on a white porcelain background and realized her grandmother's china rested among the wreckage. Christina's stomach heaved at the sight of her things broken and damaged. A horrible sensation overtook her; tingly and warm like a rash. Christina rummaged through her purse for her cell phone. She snapped it open and scrolled through her contact list to speed dial Marcus.

"Hello, babe. Whassup?"

In a shaky voice Christina whispered, "S-someone broke into my apartment. It's a mess. S-stuff everywhere. They b-broke my grandmother's china." Her voice hitched on a sob. "Wh-Why would anyone do this?"

"I want you to get out of there right now. Run, as fast as you can, find a neighbor, the doorman, anyone."

The concern in his voice sent fear racing up her spine.

"I'm on my way. Stay on the phone with me. Don't hang up!"

Gripping the phone to her ear, Christina turned to run, but something hard and strong came around her waist locking her free arm to her side like a vise. When she looked down, she discovered a thick arm trapped her. She opened her mouth to scream, but a hand clamped down on her mouth, causing her muffled scream to come out as a little whimper.

Who the hell grabbed her? Did this person want to hurt her? Her mind raced through the possibilities, finding none that made any sense. Her adrenaline spiked, she thrashed against the steely hold in vain.

Losing her grip on the phone in the struggle, it dropped from her hand, and shut off when it contacted the floor. Her newly freed hand attempted to pry the hand holding her mouth loose, in a desperate effort to get away. She kicked her legs, fought to pivot around to get a look at the person who attacked her, but the person's grip held her fast.

Hot, sticky breath oozed over her ear. From behind a deep voice said, "Don't bother to struggle, you can't win. You're no match for me. However, it you want to keep rubbing your body against mine, go right ahead. It's a turn on."

She struggled with all her might, and it seemed of no consequence to him. When he spoke, he wasn't even winded by his effort to contain her. Well, if she couldn't fight him, she could at least keep from stimulating him.

Christina drew all her will power and silenced her fight-or-flight instinct, which screamed at her to struggle. Her body stilled. The evidence of his arousal rested against her bottom. The realization made bile rise in her throat, and tears clouded her eyes. She refused to give the bastard the satisfaction.

"What, stopped so soon? I would have thought you were the type to put up a good fight." The evil voice sent a shiver through her. "I've been waiting for you. I'd hoped you'd be here when I first got here, but you weren't."

The attacker took in a deep breath and let it out slowly.

"I can smell him on you...Marcusssss." The attacker hissed her love's name into her ear.

Christina trembled uncontrollably as fear snaked up her spine and wrapped around her brain in a strangling grip.

"His scent is all over you. You stink." The attacker rubbed the front of his body against Christina's backside, pressing his erection against her, his intentions perfectly clear. "Perhaps I should take you into your shower and wash him off you. My scent is the only one I want you to wear."

Her mind raced. He knew Marcus. Given his strength and his obvious heightened sense of smell, he must be a vampire. She realized she was at his mercy. The way he spoke to her said there was no mercy to be given. Tears fell down Christina's face, dripping to the floor to mix with the broken shards of china.

"Now, now, tears will get you nowhere, my dear."

The attacker used the hand holding her mouth to pull her head toward her left shoulder, exposing her neck. A sharp stinging sensation burned into her flesh. As the pain of his bite eased, her attacker pulled at her neck with insistent draws that hurt her sensitive skin. Awareness hit her square when her vision started to fade. She was going to die!

****

Marcus materialized into the hallway of Christina's apartment building and burst through the door to her apartment, his heartmate his only thought. When the phone went dead, panic flooded his body, giving him a boost of adrenaline that focused his concentration like never before. For the first time, he'd been totally focused on only one thing, getting to his mate. Sensing her in the kitchen, he used his preternatural speed to take him there.

In a puff of black wispy smoke, the coward dematerialized just as Marcus entered the tiny space. *Dammit!* One second sooner and he might have at least gotten a look at the bastard. Obviously, the attacker had been one of his kind. The Alpha sent a silent prayer up to the heavens thanking the powers for his ability to dematerialize. If he'd driven over here, he would have arrived too late. The realization sent a wave of sickening fear through his body, cooling his blood.

Christina's legs refused to hold her weight. Marcus ran to her, catching her as her knees gave out, and she fell toward the floor.

"I have you, *cara*." He lowered her into one of the chairs by her dinette set and came to rest on his knees in front of her.

Christina trembled, wringing her hands in her lap. "H-he…" she stammered in a faint voice. "A…v-vampire."

Marcus took her hands in his, and cocooned her in a wave of soothing comfort. "I know, sweetheart. I didn't get a look at him. He dematerialized as I entered the room, but I knew as soon as I got here what he was."

Marcus noticed the trails of blood rolling down Christina's neck and followed the eddying to the brutal wound torn open at the base of her throat. "Christina, he bit you."

"I know," she whispered, and pulled one of her hands from his to place it over the throbbing wound on her neck.

His eyes softened as he captured her gaze. "I need to close the wounds he left. I don't want to scare you, but I need to lick the wound. It will help it to heal. Do you understand, Christina?"

He watched her carefully, waiting for an answer. Her eyes widened slightly, the only indication she heard him. She looked at him with fearful determination, as if she had to force herself to allow someone to touch her neck.

Marcus rose on his knees and slowly leaned toward Christina, while he pulled her hand away. His mate flinched when his tongue licked the wound to quell the bleeding. Once the wound started to heal, the Alpha pulled away and immediately recognized that his touch had caused his mate anxiety. Anger flared white-hot in his gut.

How could anyone hurt someone as wonderful as Christina? It didn't make sense. She wasn't a threat. Why would one of his kind come after her?

Marcus stood and wet a paper towel, making sure the water felt tepid. "I'm going to use this to get the blood off your neck, if that's okay."

Christina nodded approval then stared ahead, like a deer caught in headlights, not acknowledging the act while he wiped at her flesh.

Marcus gently pushed into her mind to discover the

thoughts she wasn't capable of stating. She found the water warm, but it could have been like ice for all she cared. Her body didn't seem like her own. She sat, allowing his ministrations with impartial detachment, as if all of this was happening to someone else. No emotion registered while he carefully washed away the evidence of her attack.

Wash. Get a new paper towel. Wash. Get another paper towel. His eyes scrutinized her intently as he went about the task. She sat stone still, observing Marcus with sightless eyes, not reacting to his aid.

When he'd finished, Marcus crumpled the paper towels in his large hand, then stood and whispered, "All done, sweetheart. You're clean now. The blood is all gone."

Christina blinked once, twice, then looked at Marcus. Tears welled in her eyes when her brain allowed her to finally process all that had happened. The events played like a horror movie in her mind, there for Marcus to witness. The memories crashed in and brought with them helplessness and despair. "Oh, Marcus. I was so scared. I felt helpless, so afraid."

She finally spoke. He never thought the sound of someone's voice could bring such relief. A little of the tension left his shoulders. He struggled with what to do. He wanted to take her into his arms, hold her to him to reassure himself as much as her that she was now safe, but she didn't seem ready to be touched. He barely stifled the roar of frustration that rumbled in his throat.

"I know. That's actually how I was able to get here so fast. I felt your fear. It called me, like a beacon signaling where I would find you. My every thought became about getting to you fast. I dematerialized for the first time. My love and concern for you finally let me do it. I willed myself to your apartment, because I knew you needed me."

Christina stood and wrapped her arms around Marcus' waist. "Hold me. Please hold me. I need to feel safe."

Marcus folded his strong arms around her back and pressed her to him, tucking her head against his chest. As her tears wet his shirt, his heart felt like it was being torn from his chest.

"Let's get out of here and go home," he said, stroking her hair. "I'll send someone to pack up your things and move them to the plantation, so you won't ever have to come back here."

"That's a good idea," Christina muttered and released her grip. She wiped the tears from her eyes then squared her shoulders as if willing herself to start to put this attack behind her. "There is nothing left for me here but terrible memories. I don't want to see this place ever again."

They left the tiny apartment hand in hand. Her hand seemed so cold compared to his. Christina hesitated in the doorway and turned around, taking one last look at the place.

Once on the street, Marcus opened the passenger side door for Christina and helped her into the car she had driven to the apartment. He got in the driver's seat and brought the engine to life. Only the rumbling of the engine screaming through the gears broke the silence of the drive back to the plantation.

Marcus glanced at Christina as they drove. She seemed so forlorn, sitting with her hands folded in her lap, staring unseeing out the windshield. While thankful the tears had stopped, he worried she still appeared very troubled. He reached over and took her icy hands in his.

"Everything will be okay. You're safe now. I've got you, *cara*."

"I know," she quietly replied, though her eyes never shifted in his direction.

He knew she must be deep in thought, thinking over all that happened to her tonight. He wanted to push into her mind, take the traumatic event from her memories, but she went through a brutal attack and did not need him forcing anything on her, even if it killed him a little inside not to be able to help her.

They rode the rest of the way in silence, with Christina staring ahead and Marcus trying to decide how best to help.

When they arrived at the house, Marcus handed her from the car. Before she took a step, he draped his arms around her and rested his chin atop her head.

He rubbed her back, lightly running one hand up and down. "I know what you need, *cara*. How about a nice hot bath?" Marcus pulled away slightly to look down on her with caring eyes.

Meeting his gaze, Christina sighed. "That sounds great. I can wash away the past hour."

They walked in silence to Marcus' suite. He reluctantly allowed Christina to pull from his side to go lie down. She looked so tiny, vulnerable, curled into the fetal position on his large bed.

His heart seemed to drop to his stomach. It ripped him in two, seeing her like that. There must be something he could do to make her feel better. Marcus went into the bathroom to fill the tub. As the water rose, he paced the room. He leaned on the vanity looking at his reflection in the mirror.

What are you going to do? You can't let something like this happen again. You have to protect her. She's your heartmate, and her safety comes before all else, your desires or even hers. You have to have a mindlink with her but that will involve drinking her blood. She probably isn't ready for that after what happened tonight. Dammit!

The Alpha banged a fist on the vanity, sending the items there shaking. He wanted to tear something, rip something to shreds. He needed violence—itched for a fight. What he wouldn't give to get his hands on the bastard who had attacked his mate.

Noticing the tub was about to overflow, Marcus shut off the faucet and returned to Christina. She hadn't moved. Tears of concern pushed at the backs of his eyes.

"Christina," he whispered softly. "The bath is ready."

Chapter 18

She didn't remember walking through the house. When Christina became aware of her surroundings, she discovered she lay on Marcus' bed with him saying something about a bath. She couldn't care less about a bath, not now.

But it would be nice to be warm. She'd been so cold. So utterly, unbearably cold. It bore into her, freezing her mind and heart until she felt numb.

"Sweetheart, the water is getting cold."

Christina uncoiled bit by bit and pushed into a seated position on the bed. In a haze, she allowed Marcus to help her to her feet. His arms wrapped around her in a bracing hug. Taking a deep, steadying breath, she allowed the heat of Marcus' body to soak down into her bones. It warmed her slightly, but not enough to take away all the cold. Maybe that bath was a good idea after all.

Reluctantly, she pulled from his embrace and tried to undress, but her quivering fingers made the task impossible. Marcus assisted her with the fastenings, slowly helping her disrobe. He carried her to the bath and placed her gently into the balmy water.

Surrounded in the soothing warmth, she became pliant. The heat soaked into her skin as she drew her knees to her chest and wrapped them in her arms. She rocked, making little ripples form around her.

"Oh, sweetheart." When Marcus spoke, her eyes discovered the warrior blinking back the sheen of unshed tears as he picked up a bar of soap.

He lathered the wash cloth then gently washed away the horrors of the night and vowed to the heavens to get retribution on the vampire who had done this to her. He ran the cloth over her body, careful of the raw wound on her neck. His gentle touch surprised her, given his mood.

"I want to be out there hunting down the bastard who hurt you," he confessed. "I cannot begin to tell you what seeing you like this is doing to me."

The pain in his voice cleared some of her mental haze. She needed to pull it together. He needed her to be strong. He'd saved her. It could have been so much worse. A shiver went through her body.

"Go," she croaked, her voice rough from the injury as much as from her tears.

The look Marcus gave her made tears push from her eyes.

"I would never leave you tonight, *cara*. My place is here with you, seeing to your needs. *You* are my priority. Vengeance can wait. But I swear to you it will happen. I will find the male that attacked you."

He dipped the wash cloth into the warm water before wringing the material so the water flowed over her shoulders and down her back. She thought she heard the sound of the material ripping in his hands but couldn't be sure, for it ended too quickly to focus on.

The aroma of pine and spice from the soap filled Christina's senses. The combination of the woodsy smell and the gentle rubbing soothed her. Marcus gingerly straightened her arms and legs as he attended to her, uncurling her like a butterfly from a cocoon. Her stare remained straight ahead the entire time, never wavered, never made contact with his gaze.

The attack made her feel weak and vulnerable. She'd always thought of herself as a strong woman, able to face whatever life threw at her, but tonight that hadn't been the case. She'd felt utterly helpless. When Marcus moved behind the head of the tub to wash her back, a thought occurred to her.

"I want you to convert me."

"What?" asked Marcus, his voice high with incredulity, his body still as a statue.

Christina slowly turned her head and looked over her shoulder into Marcus' eyes. Lucidity cleared her vision for the first time since the attack. "I don't want to be weak or scared anymore. Convert me. I want to be a vampire."

Marcus gazed down on her with pity in his eyes. His hands gripped the tub, knuckles white. Warm breath ghosted over her face when he took a deep breath in through his nose and let it slip through his lips.

"Christina, if I convert you, I want it to be for the right reasons. I don't want you to do it because you are scared. I want you to do it because you love me and want to spend centuries with me."

"But I do want to spend centuries with you." She turned around and sat on her knees, sending water spilling over the edge of the tub.

The soft timbre of his voice brought tears to her eyes, which threatened to spill over as she contemplated what he said. She needed him to convert her. She never wanted to feel vulnerable ever again. She needed to feel safe and secure, and how better to do that than to have superhuman strength and speed.

She loved him, wanted an eternity with him. Weeks ago she decided to convert. Why not do it now?

"You know I love you, Marcus. I want you to convert me, tonight."

"No, I won't." The Alpha shook his head from side to side.

"Not ever?" The dam broke, and tears streamed down her cheeks.

Marcus wiped the tears with the pads of his thumbs. "Just not tonight, sweetheart. I want you to think about what you're asking. It will be permanent. You can't ever go back to being human.

"It will also be very painful, and my heart can't take seeing you in any more pain tonight."

He wiped another tear from her cheek. "Please don't cry. The look on your face is tearing my heart from my chest."

In a blur of movement, he grabbed a tissue from the vanity and handed it to her.

"There is something else, something that might make you feel safer." Marcus slid a hand to Christina's jaw and feathered his thumb back and forth under her chin while she patted her tears.

"What?" Christina looked at him from under lashes that were spiked together from her tears. Hope blossomed in her chest.

Marcus hesitantly replied, "We could create the mindlink. That way we could communicate with each other using our minds. It would allow me to know how you are at all times and communicate with you instantly."

"Yes, do it. Do it now." Christina enthusiastically nodded her head up and down.

It wasn't superhuman strength, but it was a way to be closer to Marcus, a way to be safer. The thought of being able to communicate with him using her mind comforted her. If she needed him, he would know instantly.

"I would need to drink from you. It will require that we exchange blood, sweetheart. You will have to drink from me as well. Can you handle that after what you have been through tonight?"

Marcus drinking from her neck, taking her blood like the monster had. Could she handle that?

She could, she decided.

This was Marcus. He would never hurt her, not the way the beast did. Christina hesitated for only a moment before she placed her hand on top of the one Marcus held to her face. With complete resolve, she said simply, "Yes."

"Are you positive? Once the link is made we will be forever in each other's minds."

Forever linked to Marcus...wasn't that what she planned on anyway? She knew she wanted to be with him for eternity. Hell, she was willing to give up her humanity and live the life of a vampire to have her happily ever after. What was a small mindlink?

Decision made, Christina found the strength to stand. She could do this—allow him to drink from her—if it meant keeping her safe in his world.

As she exited the tub, her stomach tightened, and she wondered what drinking Marcus' blood would be like. It would be coppery and thick, she imagined.

Hopefully, it would stay down. Her determination to create the mindlink was strong, but if she was honest, admittedly some reservations about the process existed. Her heartbeat quickened at the thought of anyone at her neck. She wondered if she would be able to allow him to do it, but Christina pushed all doubts aside, knowing that if Marcus wouldn't do the conversion, at least the mindlink would help her feel safer.

Marcus dried every inch of her body slowly. Too slowly. She needed to get this done before she chickened out.

"Are you stalling?"

He gave her a sly smile which almost brought an answering grin to her own lips. He looked like a little boy caught with his hands in the candy jar.

"Maybe," he replied, working the towel over her arms. "I'm attempting to give you time to change your mind."

"Why? Don't you want to make the mindlink?"

His gaze snapped to her, letting her see the wealth of emotion held within. "I desperately want to create the mindlink. It is a natural part of the mating process for vampires, but I'm hesitant about the way the process is done. I'm concerned about how you will feel when I bite you."

She wondered that as well. But with every inch of her skin now dry, she knew he could not stall any longer. Her heartmate wrapped her in a towel then led her to the couch at the foot of his bed.

"Are you sure about this?" Marcus asked when he sat down.

"Positive." She sat next to him and gave him a sad smile that did not quite reach her eyes. "Let's do this."

Chapter 19

Marcus heard Christina's heartbeat increase as he cupped the back of her neck with his large palm. *She wants this,* he reassured himself, leaning down slowly. His eyes blazed a trail along her face, over her petite nose and emerald eyes, down her rounded chin, to the marred skin on her neck.

His saliva had closed the wound, but only time and his blood could heal it. Creating the mindlink would give her enough blood to heal the ragged injury. Rage at the sight tried to push into his mind, but he refused to give in to the anger. He'd be damned if he'd allow anything to ruin this special moment.

Like most men, his anger demanded action, and he would have it, just not this night. Determined to make this experience special for her, he pushed his ire down ruthlessly and decided to let it fester until he found the male who'd hurt her—then all bets were off. He'd unleash the beast within.

Marcus watched Christina pull her hair around to one side, baring the side of her neck opposite her wound. His muscles tightened in anticipation. He had longed for this moment for so long.

His fangs lengthened, aching, as he lowered his lips to her neck. When his lips brushed the soft flesh she flinched, and he pulled back immediately.

"We don't have to do this tonight, *cara*."

"I'm sorry. I want to do this, really. Maybe if you bit something other than my neck. It reminds me of…"

The quiver in her voice told him she didn't feel as brave as she tried to sound.

She trembled under his hand as he slid it from her neck to rest on her shoulder. "If you really want to do this tonight, there are other places. Your wrist, leg, breast. You pick."

Marcus waited patiently, allowing her time to think about her choice. When she looked at him, the trust in her eyes humbled him, making him take her into his arms.

"You've decided." His heart pounded while he waited for her response.

"Yes, here. I want you to bite me here." She placed her hand over her breast.

Surprise widened his eyes. "Are you absolutely sure?"

Her breast…as if this act wasn't intimate enough, she wanted him to put his lips to her bosom. Fates give him strength.

"I'm sure." The resolve in her eyes bored into him. They possessed no fear—not anymore. The Alpha pushed into her mind to discover her decision firm, but he remained with her to make sure her resolve didn't falter.

Finding the assurance he needed, he eased her back in his arms and feathered a trail of kisses along her jaw and across her collar bone, coming to rest over her heart. Marcus ran his tongue over the creamy skin, making tiny circles. A small moan tumbled from her lips as she arched against his mouth.

He sank his fangs into her breast, puncturing the vein. She tasted like pure ambrosia, a delicious nectar that hardened his manhood. They sighed in unison when he first drew at her vein. The bite of a vampire could be a sensual experience for both the vampire as well as the donor, and as he'd hoped, the bite from her heartmate seemed to excite Christina.

She laced her fingers in his hair, holding his head to her chest. Her body became instantly alive. She found this completely different from the earlier attack. She felt excited by the sensation of Marcus' mouth on her breast, suckling her bosom. Her heart rate increased, and her breath quickened. Deep in her mind, he experienced her body's reaction. It throbbed and ached at the junction of her thighs. The sensation increased his own pleasure from the exchange.

Marcus tasted her arousal; it sweetened the blood. With each draw, he drove her higher and higher, pushed her body toward the precipice of release. When he'd taken enough to create a mindlink, he reluctantly flicked his tongue over the small puncture wounds to close them, tasting himself on her creamy flesh.

He raised his head and saw longing in Christina's eyes. She wanted this, wanted him. He read it on her face.

"It's your turn." His voice sounded husky as he brought his wrist to his mouth.

"Wait." Christina placed her hand over his wrist. "Why do I have to drink from your wrist? Can't I take from your neck?"

Marcus' smile showed his fangs. "You can drink from anywhere you want, heartmate." He strolled next to the bed and retrieved a dagger from his bedside table.

"Just happened to have a knife handy, huh?" Christina teased as Marcus returned to the couch. Her flushed face held a genuine smile that warmed the Alpha's heart.

It was so good to hear her more like herself. He knew she rode the euphoria his bite caused in her body, but he'd take it. At least she was talking.

Marcus graced her with a wide grin. "Always ready for any occasion. I'm always prepared, just like a good little boy scout."

Marcus leaned back, cradled in the arm of the couch. He wanted Christina to come to him rather than seem like he forced himself on her, so after leaning back, he bent one leg, resting his foot on the couch, and left the other on the floor, hoping the posture would appear open and inviting. He then sliced a small line across his neck. As his blood began to flow, Christina crawled up his chest toward the liquid she wanted. He knew she would feel his arousal, but he didn't care. In fact, he wanted her aware of what she did to him. The look on her face sent desire coursing through his body. He let it smolder until he knew it consumed her as well.

She tentatively lowered her body, allowing Marcus to take her weight, then placed her lips over the wound and took a tiny sip.

"Tastes good, spicy, like you," she murmured before returning for a second draw. By the third swallow, she appeared lost in the moment.

She gave herself freely to the process, enjoyed herself. With each swallow, he sensed she felt stronger, more alive. Grateful his blood provided for her, he wrapped an arm around her back in order to have more physical contact while she drank.

Christina moaned against his neck. The sensuous sound elicited a whole body spasm which caused him to drop the dagger. Fire licked over his sensitive skin, driving his passion higher.

He could have stayed like that forever, with her taking his essence into her. It took all of his carefully honed self-control to realize when she'd taken enough to create the mindlink.

The feel of the link connecting made him grab her by the shoulders and try to hold her from him. "That's enough, *cara*. You don't have to take any more."

Much to his surprise, Christina did not stop. She continued to draw from him and ground her pelvis back and forth against his hard shaft. Marcus gripped the couch, watching her hips move against him. The suction of her lips timed to the movement of her hips created a dual sensory experience that pushed him toward the edge.

He smelled the sweet scent of the moisture between her legs. He might be a strong male, but the erotic scent took the remainder of his self-control. He growled and brought Christina away from his neck. Lifting her by the shoulders, he brought her lips closer to his.

He kissed her hard, tasting his blood on her lips. As his body healed the wound on his neck, he lowered her back onto the couch, stripping away her towel. She lay with one arm stretched above her head as the other reached for him.

With one finger she wiped the small trickle of blood that had escaped from the wound before it closed. She brought her finger to her mouth and sucked it in, her cheeks going concave. Marcus groaned at the seductive sight. His cock jumped in response behind the zipper of his pants.

Christina pulled her finger from her mouth with a popping noise then grabbed the hem of his shirt, sliding the offensive material over his head. It dropped to the floor as she lifted her hands to his chest. She traced the contour of his pectorals, moving her hands down to trace the hard lines created by his abdominals. His mate followed the trail to his belly button, circling the outie with one finger before opening the hook clasp on his waistband. His shaft sprang free as she unzipped the pants with a quick pull.

Christina wrapped her hand around his manhood, stroking it slowly, fanning the flames of ardor that consumed him. Christina licked her lips and purred, "Come closer."

Marcus happily complied; nothing would have kept him from obeying at that moment. Christina gazed at him, holding his eyes as she took him into her mouth. She closed her lips around his thick shaft, surrounding him with the warm heat of her mouth. When she moved up and down the length of him, he thought the top of his head might blow off. Up and down, her hand traveled in the opposite direction of her lips, driving him mad.

Just when he thought he would lose himself in her mouth like a virginal schoolboy, she pulled away. Surprised, he glanced down and watched her tongue swirl around the tip once, twice before she again took him into the welcoming heat of her mouth. She pulled him out, licking the tip like a cat does cream, before she made his flesh disappear back into her mouth. She took him deep, so freaking deep, until he felt her throat work around him. His balls drew up tight in response.

Damn, his mate possessed a talented little mouth. A grateful moan pushed through his lips as he threaded his fingers in her hair.

She built the momentum, increasing her speed until he had no choice but to bite out, "If you don't stop, babe, I'm going to explode."

Christina pulled back slowly, releasing him from her mouth with one last tug around the tip. She continued to stroke him with her hand as he settled between her legs. He allowed her to guide him into her feminine core. Her silky opening gripped him when he thrust into her. He built the friction between their bodies with each slap of their skin. She matched the rhythm of his hips with her own. Their bodies moved as one, in perfect synchronicity.

Her nails scored his back until her hands rested on his buttocks. Her fingers bit into his flesh, encouraging him deeper.

Marcus lowered his mouth to her breast and punctured the delicate flesh with his fangs. Over their mindlink, he sensed the slight sting give way to a wave of ecstasy that coursed through her body, washing her in desire.

She rode the surge, while he drew her life-force into his mouth. Her body wound higher, her muscles tightened. She arched her back, fisting her hand in his hair to anchor her to this plane.

His mate screamed his name when her climax hit. Christina's inner muscles rippled around him, milking him, driving him higher with the incredible sensation. His body tightened, throbbed for its own release. It built from his toes, coursed through his body and demanded he follow his heartmate over the precipice. Giving in to temptation, his release pushed through him so they tumbled together in a fall of ecstasy.

When they came back to earth, Marcus leaned his head forward. Christina watched him lick the puncture wound closed then laid her head back on the couch. Through their mindlink, Marcus sensed she reveled in the sated, tranquil sensations that coursed through her body. Her body no longer ached. Both her neck and her breast had already healed.

She knew he had bitten her, but no pain throbbed in her body. With her finger she traced the place where the wound had been, astonished to find nothing there.

"What did you do? I can't feel it anymore."

Marcus nuzzled her other breast, his lips brushing over her sensitive skin as he spoke. "My saliva contains healing properties. When I licked your breast, it took the pain away."

Christina rubbed her hand over her delicate breast, looking for his mark. She found nothing. Her hand moved up her body to her neck. She shifted her hand to the other side, as if she might have inadvertently touched the wrong side.

"My neck is fine. How did you do that?"

Marcus smiled against her breast. "That was my blood. It healed you."

"That's amazing," she murmured and held him to her by placing her hand on his head.

"*You're* amazing, *cara*. The taste of you drives me wild." He raised his head and captured her gaze, allowing her to see the love and reverence in his eyes. "Now do you understand why I didn't drink from you that night in the library?"

Christina smiled a sated grin. Breathlessly she answered, "I most certainly do."

Chapter 20

"I was so fucking close!"

The vampire licked his lips, savoring the remaining taste of blood. *Her* blood. Until they had been interrupted by that meddlesome Alpha, he enjoyed the mouthwatering taste of fear in her blood. He would have to wait to take the woman—live to fight another day or in his case make a strategic retreat to attack another night. He hoped he'd dematerialized out of the apartment before the other vampire had seen his face.

He stormed down the street, sending a series of vile curses into the air until someone accidently bumped into him. When he growled his frustration, a look of surprise and fear crossed the man's face, but he didn't care what the human thought. Edgy and pissed, he needed a way to work off his frustration. And up ahead he spied what he needed.

The vampire ducked into the seedy, dark bar. It smelled of stale beer and perspiration. Dressed in jeans, a black T-shirt and leather jacket, he looked like he belonged. While he waited for the bartender to pour his whiskey and cola, he saw her in a corner table. A petite woman with mahogany hair sat surrounded by a group of four burly men. The vampire squinted, his vision blurring until the woman looked a lot like the one that got away.

"She'll do," he muttered, slamming down his drink in one quick gulp. It burned like the sun down his throat.

He tapped his empty glass with an index finger. "Another," he said to the bartender and dropped a C-note on the bar. "Keep them coming."

The bartender nodded before the vampire turned his attention back to the woman and waited for opportunity to strike. After thirty minutes, she headed down the hallway toward the bathrooms. *Ahhhhh.* An opening rewarded his patience.

The motto "Good things come to those who wait," came to mind. If patience was a virtue, he must be a saint. Most his life, he'd reaped the rewards of his persistence and patience. And it seemed tonight would be no different.

The vampire crossed the distance and caught up to the woman in the hall. He grabbed her arm, forcing her to turn toward him. His eyes roamed her face. Though not as beautiful as Christina, this one wasn't bad. Looking into her eyes, the vampire captured her gaze.

"You are tired of this place." He gave her a mental push to punctuate his command. "You are too good for your companions. You want to leave with me. Now."

The woman went with him willingly, unable to do otherwise. His ire, more than necessity, kept his grip on her arm tight as they walked through the bar.

One of her companions noticed the two heading for the door and called after them. "Hey, you…Barbie. Stop!"

The table emptied, and all four men followed the couple out of the bar.

The vampire turned on the quartet. "Let's get this

over with. I'm in a hurry."

He moved his second-place prize behind the establishment, with the men following in tow.

"Sit," he commanded, and the woman promptly complied with his directive.

He rounded on the brawny men, tucking into a fighter's stance. One of them let out a warrior's yell and lunged for the vampire. The monster pivoted to the side then grabbed the back of the man's leather vest with both hands. He spun the human head first into the brick wall of the bar, leaving an indentation from the man's head in the bricks. He dropped the guy unceremoniously onto the ground atop the debris from the wall.

The vampire rounded on the remainder of the group. He leapt in the air, coming down between two of the men. Grabbing each by the head, he brought their heads together with a loud crunch. Blood poured from their crushed faces. He listened to their hearts stutter in an interesting rhythm before they ceased to pump and silenced.

The last man pulled a switchblade from the pocket of his jeans and opened it with a flick of his wrist. "I'm gonna slice you up."

The vampire smiled in response to the threat. He held his arms straight out in a submissive stance. "Come and get me."

The man shot forward with his knife extended in front of him. The vampire grabbed his arm and throat at the same time. He brought the man's arm down over his knee, causing an open fracture. He squeezed the man's throat, cutting off his scream of pain. Held tightly in his grasp, the man's body jerked with its effort to take air into his lungs. But the exertion was for naught as the vampire simply tightened his grip in response. When he heard the man's heart stop, the vampire let the body fall to the ground in a heap.

The male looked around at the carnage and smiled, pleased with his handiwork. He came looking for some action, and he'd found it, albeit human action. Too easy really, not nearly satisfying enough. Luckily, he still had more to look forward to this evening, a different type of action, a way to work off what remained of his frustration.

His prize still sat where he'd left her. The monster bent, grabbed a wrist and pulled her to her feet. He might not have who he wanted, but she was a good substitute, and he couldn't wait to get her to his playroom with the others.

****

Marcus and Christina lay side by side on his bed while the news played on the plasma TV. Her fingers trailed lazily along his black silk shirt.

Stephan and Kat are here, Marcus projected the thought.

"How do you know?" Christina looked up into his handsome face.

I can always feel when my sire is near.

Christina pushed off the bed, her eyes wide. "How can I hear you? You're lips aren't moving."

I'm using the mindlink. You can communicate with me using your mind too. Just close your eyes and concentrate. I'm using a mental channel to communicate with you. Follow the channel back to my mind.

Christina closed her eyes. *This is never going to*

work.

It just did, babe. You're good. Marcus squeezed her in a tender hug to his chest. *It usually takes a couple of tries to use a mindlink. You did it on the first try.*

"I can't believe you can hear my thoughts." Her excitement brought a boyish grin to her lover's face.

"The more we use the link the easier it will become until you will be using it as naturally as you speak aloud. Let's go up and greet Kat and Stephan." Marcus led Christina up the stairs toward the front door.

Christina wrung her hands and thought, *I hope Kat likes me.*

"Of course, she will like you. What's not to like?"

"You heard that?" She shook her head in disbelief. "It's going to take me a while to get used to this mindlink thing. Having someone hear your every thought is strange."

Marcus gave her a side glance and smiled. "I can't hear every thought yet. As I said, the more we use the link the stronger it will become."

Marcus opened the door wide. "Hello, Stephan."

His sire stepped to the side and ushered his heartmate through the door before him with a sweep of his arm. Marcus caught Kat up in a bear hug, lifting the leggy blonde off her feet. "Hey, Kitty Kat, it's great to see you."

"It's good to see you again too, Marcus. So are you going to put me down and introduce me to your heartmate or what?"

Marcus set Kat on her feet and placed his palm on the nape of Christina's neck, giving it a gentle, reassuring massage. "Yeah, of course. Katrina von Haas, this is my heartmate, Christina. Christina, Kat."

Christina expected the woman to be pretty, but she'd been unprepared for the graceful woman who stood before her. Katrina could only be described as drop-dead gorgeous, with her lithe dancer body, long blonde hair that flowed over her shoulders, and blue-gray eyes. At least a head taller than Christina, Kat had shapely legs, on display thanks to the miniskirt she wore, appeared to go on forever.

Christina swallowed her jealousy and pasted a welcoming smile on her face. "It's nice to meet you, Kat. I've heard so much about you."

"Not too much, I hope." Kat shot Marcus a mock glare. "Marcus has a big mouth and tends to go on and on and on—"

Marcus crossed his thick arms over his chest and cocked his head to one side. "Hey now, I resemble that remark."

"Yes, you do," Christina teased and gave his bicep a playful punch.

Kat looked up at Stephan and smiled. "You weren't kidding. She really can keep Marcus in line." Her eyes landed on Christina. "I can tell we will be fast friends."

Marcus *tsked* and wagged his finger. "Now, now ladies, no ganging up on this poor defenseless male."

Kat laughed. "Defenseless my butt. Christina, did he ever tell you about the time he single handedly took out four vampire body guards to save me?"

Stephan cleared his throat and hugged Kat to his side. "Who exactly saved you, Kitten?"

The blonde rolled her eyes. "Of course, you helped, too. Whatever! Don't get your dander up, heartmate. Anyway, it's history."

"History that doesn't need to be shared. Christina's

human, after all. I'm sure she doesn't want to hear all about our scary adventures." Stephan gave his mate a pointed look that spoke volumes.

What's that all about, Marcus?

He's telling her he does not approve of a human knowing about their conflicts with other vampires.

Meaning me?

Meaning, any human. He's got a thing about protecting our existence. It's a long story.

Christina leaned toward Kat and put her hand to the side of her mouth. In a stage whisper she said, "Come with me, Kat. You can tell me all about it while I get the *hors d'œuvres* from the kitchen."

"Lead the way. We have so much to talk about." Kat threw Stephan a smug smile over her shoulder before she followed Christina down the hall.

****

Stephan shook his head wearily from side to side and grinned. "The women seem to be hitting it off."

"Yeah, they are. I see Kat hasn't changed a bit since marrying you, old man. She's still as feisty as ever," Marcus quipped.

"And I wouldn't have it any other way."

The younger vampire chuckled. "I know what you mean."

The two males made their way into the living room. As they waited for their mates to join them, Marcus filled Stephan in on what happened in Christina's apartment.

A look of concern filled Stephan's face, furrowing his dark brows over his sapphire eyes. "This is very troubling."

Marcus nodded. "That's not all. There was a story

on the news tonight about a woman who is missing. She was at a bar with four men. The men were found behind the bar—all dead. The woman cannot be located. The news showed a picture of her, and she looks a little like Christina."

Stephan leaned forward, resting his forearms on his knees. "So let me get this straight. You interrupted a vampire attacking Christina. Now a woman who looks like Christina has been reported missing."

Marcus rested his elbows on the arms of his chair and steepled his fingers. "Yeah, and don't forget the four men found dead outside the bar. I don't see how a human could have taken on all four of them and won. The TV report showed their mug shots. They were big guys. I think we can be sure a vampire killed them and took the woman."

Stephan's long black hair flowed around his shoulders when he nodded. "You're probably right, Marcus, most likely the same vampire who attacked Christina earlier. I think it's time to convene the Council. We'll need all the help we can get to find this rogue." Stephan leaned back in his seat and rested one ankle on the opposite knee. "Demetri and Michael were here the other night. Have the other Alphas been here before, so they can materialize here?"

Marcus shook his head. "I don't think so."

Hearing the women approach, Stephan lowered his voice to a whisper. "Well, when you summon them, find out for sure who has been here. I'll send my plane to retrieve the ones who can't materialize here."

Christina joined them in the living room, carrying a silver tray with colorful *hors d'œuvres,* which she placed on the coffee table then sat on the couch, and

Kat followed, sandwiching Stephan between them. The tight squeeze caused the Alpha leader to scrunch his shoulders and sit with his thighs held together.

I love watching you cater to the females, Marcus sent using their personal mindlink. *You look like a school boy serving detention.*

Watch your mouth, Marcus, or I'll have to cross this room to teach you the meaning of discipline.

I don't think Kat would appreciate that.

Oh, I don't think she'd mind. She'd probably join in. I seem to remember a time or two when she kicked your ass.

Marcus grabbed an *hors d'œuvre* and popped it in his mouth. The memory of sparring with Kat played in his mind. Marcus relived the time Kat bloodied his nose, and he'd taken a good ribbing about it from Nicholai. *Yeah, she probably would like to do it again.*

He had no desire to relive that situation in front of his heartmate. Talk about embarrassing.

"How was your flight?" Christina asked, drawing Marcus from his thoughts. "Not too cramped, I hope."

Christina glanced between the couple sitting next to her.

"Just fine. We took my personal plane, so we had plenty of room." Stephan gave Kat a conspiratorial wink.

Stephan was an ancient, one of the original humans to be changed. With age came money—lots and lots of money if one knew how to make it. Everything bought was guaranteed to be worth more at some point, you just had to know when to sell things for a profit. Marcus envied Stephan's knack for making money. He seemed to instinctively know whether to keep a possession for five years or four hundred.

"Would you like an *hors d'œuvre*?" offered Christina.

"We ate a little something on the plane," Stephan explained, the deep timbre of his voice dropped when Kat placed her hand on his knee and squeezed.

I bet you did, sent Marcus over their mindlink, causing Stephan to throw him a disgruntled look.

Marcus knew all about Stephan's plane. It was equipped with a fully stocked bar and an oversized bed that accommodated him and Katrina very well.

"You have to try this," Kat said as she fed a creamy treat to Stephan. He took her fingers along with the goodie into his mouth.

"Ummm." He moaned around her fingers while she slid them slowly from his mouth.

The heat between them sizzled within the room with such fervor that Marcus guessed even Christina might feel the palpable force. It wrapped the couple in a cocoon of wanton lust.

Payton appeared in the doorway, breaking the mood. "Excuse me, sir. I have placed your guests' luggage in their room and turned down their bed. Is there anything else you require of me tonight?"

Marcus cleared his throat. "No. Thank you, Payton. You have been very helpful as always. Thanks for working late tonight."

"Of course, sir." Payton turned to take his leave.

Kat popped a fifth *hors d'oeuvre* in her mouth and stood. She made quick work of the delicacy, swallowing it as she crossed the room, her graceful gait taking her to Payton before he had completed his turn. She grabbed him by the shoulders and kissed his cheek.

"Thank you, Payton."

The valet rubbed his face, a deep blush flushed his leathery skin. "I'm happy to be of service," was all he managed to squeak out before he left in a rush.

Kat rounded to Stephan and winked. "It sounds like our room is ready. I don't mean to be rude, but I think I'll go to bed. Christina, you and I will spend more time together tomorrow. Okay?" She disappeared in a blink of Marcus' eyes, not waiting for a reply.

The Alpha leader stood and stretched, in an obvious feign of exhaustion. "Bed sounds like an awfully good idea. I think I'll join her."

He turned to Christina. "Thank you for the *hors d'œuvres*. They were quite good."

"Going so soon? We barely got to say two words to each other." Christina's lower lip jutted out in a pout.

Stephan put his hand over his heart, in an old-time gesture that bespoke of his age. "It was a long flight from Vegas, and Kat is ready for bed. Please accept my apologies. We'll visit longer tomorrow evening," he promised then turned on his heels and left.

"You'll have to forgive them, my sweet," said Marcus. "I'm afraid the draw between heartmates is very strong and grows the longer they are together. Stephan and Kat did not mean any disrespect. They just need time alone."

"But they just spent six hours alone on their plane. I would think they could have visited a little longer."

Marcus grinned. "I for one am glad they kept the visit brief. I have to agree with them; bed sounds like a wonderful idea."

Marcus threw Christina over one shoulder in a fireman's carry and headed for their suite.

Chapter 21

Three nights later...

Michael strolled into Marcus' library, taking his usual spot. Leaning his shoulder against the wall, he crossed his muscular arms over his chest. Stephan pinned him with a hard stare. "Nice of you to finally join us, Michael."

Michael inclined his head in response. He knew he arrived late tonight, had been late to every meeting. But he had things happening in his life that needed to be dealt with, things more important than the Alpha Council business.

Besides, these meetings frustrated him. Night after night, the Alphas discussed the missing girls in Savannah and went out to patrol the city, but they were no closer to finding the missing women or the person responsible. He seriously doubted tonight would be different.

Stephan had assembled the entire council this evening. Nicholai, Alexander, and Vladimir were finally here. The Alpha leader stood in front of the fireplace with his arm resting on the mantel. His commanding presence filled the room.

"So, as I was saying before Michael decided to grace us with his presence, this situation in Savannah has gotten out of control. The number of missing or dead girls has increased. Several of the girls abducted bear a striking resemblance to Christina. Given that a vampire attacked her earlier this week, I'm inclined to think a vampire is behind the abductions and killings. It's time for the Council to get involved. We need to find this male and take him out before he can get his hands on any more innocents.

"I want all of you here in Savannah, so we can do some team surveillance and find this sicko."

Stephan strutted across the room as he spoke. "Marcus has graciously offered his house for our use."

Stephan smacked Marcus on the back, in a friendly gesture. The younger Alpha straightened and nodded approvingly at the group. "I have plenty of room. Each of you can have your own guest room upstairs. I have a full gym, sauna, and indoor pool downstairs that you can use to train. I also have a range for target practice and a sparring building out back available. I know Michael and Demetri have their own places in town, but you guys are welcome to stay here too."

Stephan interjected, "That's not a bad idea. It's been over a century since we all lived and trained under the same roof. Demetri, will you stay here with the rest of the Council?"

"If you think that is best, I guess I can suffer my comrades' company for a while," Demetri retorted with a smile.

Stephan turned his steely gaze on Michael. "What about you?"

Michael shifted uncomfortably under the hard gaze. "I'll think about it."

"Better than an outright no," Stephan muttered,

nodding curtly. "After the meeting Marcus will show you to your rooms and give you the grand tour of the mansion so you can find the training rooms when needed."

Their leader shifted his weight onto his other foot as his gaze found the largest male of the group. "On to the next order of business. Demetri, what have you learned from the VES?"

"The Vampire Enforcement Squad is almost as stumped as we are." Demetri's attention focused on the newly arrived Alphas as he explained, "I've been emailing the Savannah VES agent my Russian contact recommended. He put me in contact with one of the agency's best trackers, Agent Bolovich. He seems like a decent enough gent from his e-mails. He's willing to work with us to take this murderer down. The VES wants this monster as bad as we do. I invited Bolovich here tonight so we can get an update and meet him."

"Excellent. I'm interested in what the agent has to say. Hopefully, he will be able to…" A knock on the library door interrupted Stephan.

"Come in," called Marcus.

Payton opened the oak door wide and announced, "Agent Bolovich to see you, sir." He remained in the doorway to await his instructions.

"Send him in," ordered Stephan, motioning inward with his hand.

Payton stepped aside to reveal a woman dressed in black. She wore the dark leather like a second skin. It started on her toes with laced stiletto boots that crept up to her knees. It continued upward to caress her shapely thighs and the slight curve of her hips in a pair of black pants. A leather bustier, which lifted her breasts, exposing the soft flawless skin as the twin globes swelled over the seam, topped her obsidian ensemble. The female's yellow, cat-like eyes seemed to glow against the shoulder length black hair that framed her beautiful face. The heel-length leather duster she wore flared slightly behind her with each step as she crossed the room and made for the fireplace.

Fates above, this *femme fatale* made the blood rush to his groin. Michael licked his lips at the sight his mind created of this female naked and writhing beneath him. The lust in the air hung heavily between the unmated males in the room. He'd have competition for her affections, but that suited him. He could handle anything the others wanted to throw at him. He'd be happy to take them on just to have a go at that.

****

Tatiana Bolovich had been a VES agent for over one hundred and fifty years. An incident early in her life had driven her to the agency. Because she gave the agency her all, she was the kind of agent VES prized.

She didn't have a family, outside of the agency. Tough, intelligent, and committed were words used by her colleagues to describe her. In fact, her partner and she were referred to as T-N-T, as much for their explosive attitudes as for the fact both their names started with the letter "T."

Once she took on a case, she saw it through to completion, refusing to do no less than win against the bad guys. VES always assigned her to the most difficult cases, and this latest vampire murderer was no exception.

With little to go on and no real leads, finding the Savannah murderer proved to be a challenge for her.

But she was more than up to the challenge. In fact, when one of the infamous Alphas approached her about helping them solve the murders, she'd jumped at the chance to work with the super-secretive group.

Tatiana stopped in front of the male with sapphire blue eyes, her duster settling around her body. "I'm Agent Bolovich. Which one of you is Romanoff?"

A male behind her stood. She turned and watched his beefy body glide toward her. The vampire possessed a fluid grace that most males his size would not. He appeared calm but in control, like a predator ready to pounce at the slightest provocation. Tatiana appreciated the way his muscles rippled under his clothes as he moved, though she would not give him or any male the satisfaction of showing any reaction. She steeled her features, refusing to allow any appreciation to show on her face.

In a deep baritone voice the burly male replied, "I am Demetri Romanoff. It is nice to meet you." He offered his hand, turning it as if he intended to kiss the back of hers. Tatiana grabbed the proffered hand and shook it vigorously.

"You're Romanoff?" she asked

"I am. I must admit I am surprised to see you."

The VES agent cocked her head in disbelief, a confused look crossing her face. "You should have been expecting me. In our last e-mail, I said I would attend the meeting tonight."

"I thought you were a male." Demetri raked her body with his gaze. "But obviously you are not."

"Obviously," she echoed and surveyed the buffet of beefcakes in the room.

Her gaze carefully scrutinized each male as she

sized them up. She had grown up hearing stories about the Alpha Council. Studying their history had been part of her VES training. She knew their reputation for being specially trained warriors who took out the worst of their breed with efficient ease. Their features were steady, showing no hint of what they were thinking as she glanced over them. Well-built, big males, each carried an air of confidence that came from years of proving their skills on the battlefield. Copious amounts of power filled the room, pushing down on Tatiana like an avalanche.

She turned to the male with the blue eyes and squared her shoulders, her mouth in a hard line. "I think introductions are in order. You all know who I am, and I now know Demetri. What are the rest of your names?"

"I am Stephan von Haas." Mr. Blue Eyes began the introductions. "I am the leader of the Council."

He took Tatiana's hand, dwarfing it in his own, and kissed it before she could start a handshake. Her eyes widened when he brought the hand away from his supple lips. She tried to pull her hand away, not wanting the intimate contact.

Seeming to detect her reluctance, Stephan raised a questioning eyebrow but did not say anything, instead released her hand. One by one the rest of the Alphas were introduced.

Marcus waved in greeting after his introduction. "Hey. Welcome to my home."

Tatiana appreciated the relaxed way he spoke to her. Being in the room with these males might have been rather intimidating. Their reputation certainly preceded them. She was prepared for…well, she wasn't entirely sure what she'd been prepared for.

VES possessed little information about the members of the group. She knew of their history and some of their greater escapades, but as to specific information about the group's members, that was a tightly guarded secret. It was one of the reasons the Vampire Enforcement Squad had agreed to work with them. The agency wanted a better relationship with the group. They had the same mission—to stop unruly misfits of the vampire population—so her superiors at VES instructed her to ingratiate herself with the Alphas. The commanders wanted her to develop a positive working relationship with the group, win their trust, so the two groups might foster a more cooperative relationship.

Nicholai rose from his chair and bowed when he was introduced. The tailored suit he wore fit perfectly on his large frame and made him look like a mafia don. His handsome face sported a smile that added a sexy element to his youthful appearance.

"It is an honor to meet you, agent," he greeted in a thick Russian accent.

Across from Nicholai sat Alexander, who wore blue jeans and a dark T-shirt that molded to his defined muscles. His short, blond hair barely showed from under his baseball cap. He remained in his chair and greeted Tatiana by tipping his hat saying, "Nice to meet ya, ma'am."

His southern drawl intrigued her with its singsong quality. His accent and rugged good looks reminded Tatiana of a farm boy.

On the settee, next to where Demetri had been, sat Vladimir. The black jeans and snug black sweater he wore accented his rippling muscles. Tatiana watched his muscles flex when he stood and bowed to her in greeting. "It is an honor to meet you, Agent Bolovich."

Stephan cleared his throat, bringing her attention back to him before he spoke. "Lastly, back there is Michael Garsoe." Michael pushed away from the wall, straightening to his full height. He greeted her by a tip of his chin in her general direction. His lustful eyes grazed her body, blazing a trail hotly over her. His desire stood heavily behind his pants.

She knew she wasn't an unattractive woman, but being in the presence of these powerful, sexy males, made her feel very feminine. The weight of their combined stares pushed in on her, made her a little self-conscious.

They appeared reserved as if they were withholding their judgment of her, but she knew she *would* be judged. Males like these not only held themselves to a higher standard but others around them as well. She played with the big boys now, and she would have to man-up if she wanted to hang with them.

Go ahead boys, test me. She trusted her abilities and knew she'd pass. Not to mention they needed *her* or they wouldn't have contacted VES.

Tatiana stood a little straighter before she spoke. "It is nice to meet all of you. Before I share the intel from the agency, I need your word an agent can be included within your group. The agency wants to be with you every step of the way, especially when you take the murderer down."

Stephan furrowed his brows, eyeing her suspiciously. "Who would the agency assign to us?"

"Me." Tatiana placed her hand over her heart.

Demetri shifted his stance and crossed his large

arms across his massive chest. "Absolutely not! Females don't belong in the field."

Tatiana rounded on him, putting a fisted hand on each hip. "That's old-fashioned and chauvinistic. It's the twenty-first century, vampire. Get with the times. Females can take care of themselves now."

"Who made you?" Demetri demanded, raising a questioning brow before continuing, "Or are you a natural born?"

"That's a bit of a personal question, isn't it?" She coyly tried to deflect his questions.

She knew natural born females were protected at all costs, because they were considered special due to their ability to bear children. Unlike converted females, who took decades to conceive because of the damage to their uteruses during the conversion process, females who were born vampire were able to conceive as soon as they matured sexually. Naturally born females had no such physical damage to overcome and could produce an heir as soon as they mated, making them valuable to their kind.

Before Tatiana threw up any mental blocks, she felt a presence fluttering in her mind. Her gut twisted when she realized one of the males searched for the information she tried to guard.

"She is a natural born female!" Demetri accused in amazement. "She's a treasure, a rare gift. The female must not be allowed to be placed in danger. She must not be allowed to be put in harm's way, Stephan."

"I'll have you know I've taken down bigger bruisers than you, Romanoff," Tatiana countered, glaring at the beefy male.

"You have, have you?" Demetri chuckled. "Tell

you what, come at me. If you can land even one blow, you're in."

He beckoned her with a mocking wave of his hand.

Chapter 22

Irritation zipped through Tatiana at the arrogant gesture from the male, giving her a shot of adrenaline. He'd thrown down the gauntlet, and she was all too happy to pick it up. Demetri thought she couldn't touch him. Ha! He couldn't be more wrong.

She flew at him, taking a quick jab at his face. Demetri easily blocked her fist then flashed a supercilious grin that infuriated Tatiana. She growled and came at him with a series of upper cuts and left hooks. Each time, he either blocked her or ducked the blow in a blur of motion. She tried to catch him off guard with a sweeping kick to his ankles, but he simply jumped to avoid the swipe.

Tatiana paused, slightly out of breath from her effort. She narrowed her eyes in an assessing glare, seeking his weakness. He cocked an eyebrow, waiting. He toyed with her! Anger flooded her body in a rush of heat. How dare he! She went after him with renewed vigor, her punches and kicks thrown as fast as her preternatural speed would allow.

The broad-shouldered vampire blocked all blows but never came after her.

The realization made her pause once more, a scowl on her face. "Fight back," she snarled, lunging at him.

He zigged and circled her. "I wouldn't want to hurt

177

you." His eyes gleamed down at her with laughter.

"I can take what you can dish out," she hissed. "Come on. You're not afraid of a female, are you?"

Tatiana charged forward again. The Alpha stepped to the side, his fingers clamped around her wrist like a band of steel. Before she knew what happened, he twisted her arm behind her back, turning her away from him. Propelling her forward, he secured her against the wall, pinning her with his heavy body. Her cheek ground into the plaster.

"It's not fear I feel for you, female," he whispered in her ear.

He pressed his body against her back, every hard line of him sinking against her softness. His grip on her arm loosened, allowing her to bring it around and splay her hand on the wall. Tatiana forced her body to relax, soften. She subtly brushed herself against him, feeling his most manly part push against her backside.

His breath caught behind her, the sound causing the tiny hairs on her nape to rise. She smiled as he pushed himself against her. Tatiana rolled her body around so her back rested against the wall. He remained close, a wall of solid muscle and heat. His body flush against hers, he looked deeply into her eyes.

"Perhaps it is I who did the underestimating," she said, running her fingers up his bicep to rest onto his shoulder. She slid her fingers back down his arm as she brought her leg up against his side, until her knee rested against his waist. Leaning forward so their lips were mere centimeters apart, Tatiana's lips brushed his as she spoke in a husky voice. "Perhaps there are some things I could learn from you. Would you teach me your moves, Romanoff?"

"There is much I could teach you, woman." His breath came out in hard puffs, his voice raspy.

Her eyes held his intense gaze. "Then teach me, professor."

Tatiana closed the distance between their lips, thrusting her tongue aggressively into his mouth. His taste took her by surprise. She expected it to be repulsive but instead found it enticing, delicious—addictive. Her body betrayed her, tightening her muscles. Her nipples pushed painfully against her leather bustier as heat coiled in her belly.

Demetri didn't allow her to be in control for long. His tongue thrust back, pushed into her mouth with an aggression that snapped her back to her task. As they kissed, her hand went to the boot on the leg now wrapped around his waist and silently unsheathed the knife hidden there. She brought the knife to his throat and broke the kiss as the tip of the blade bit into his neck, leaving a drop of red.

"Gotcha." Tatiana gave him a smug grin then pulled the blade away so the male could see his blood on its tip.

Demetri put his hand to his neck. His brows flew up in anger and his nostrils flared, either from the smell of his blood or from wrath. It was difficult for Tatiana to tell which.

"Is that what you do when you are losing? Tease and use your feminine wiles to distract?" the wounded warrior roared. The centers of his steel-gray eyes glowed with fury.

"If needed." Her eyes widened, and indignation dripped from her voice.

"You cheated!" he accused, turning his back on the

vampire who bested him moments before.

"Actually, I won." Tatiana followed behind him as he stalked across the room. "You are bigger, stronger, faster. Those were your advantages during our fight. I did the same thing you did. I used my advantage, and I landed my blow. Now I expect you to let me in...Oh, and no more comments about how females can't handle themselves. I handled you just fine."

"Yeah, Demetri," agreed Alex in his southern drawl. "You gotta admit she got ya."

"She cheated," the large vampire growled, making his way to Stephan. "And it doesn't matter because no female, especially a natural born, should be put in danger. Right, Stephan?"

Tatiana slid around Demetri and sat down on the settee beside Vlad. The leader of the Alphas eyed her for a moment, silently weighing his options.

After a moment of careful consideration, he reluctantly responded, "Chivalry dictates that I not allow you to fight." He raised a quelling hand, stilling Tatiana's protest. "But we need the intelligence from VES, and I have to admit you did handle Demetri beautifully. All right. You're in, Tatiana."

Demetri huffed in protest, but Stephan stayed his frustration with a slight shake of his head. "Now if you'll please inform us about the intel the VES has on the murderer."

Tatiana crossed her legs and, after wiping the blade of the knife on the sleeve of her duster, sheathed it back in her boot. "I have your word that I'm in. I'll be included in everything. You'll share information with me, and I'll be there if you try to take down the murderer?"

Stephan nodded. "You have my word as a warrior and an Alpha."

The female vampire tipped her chin in acknowledgement. "Very well. We have a profiler who came up with an outline of the killer. The vampire we are looking for probably lives in Savannah. He is a loner with a superiority complex.

"He wants to be in charge—thinks he *should* be in charge but isn't. He would be someone who is working under others. He has a warped sense of humor but can appear normal in social situations for a short time. We think he is an old vampire because of the power it takes to control multiple humans at one time. We believe he probably turned rogue slowly over the past century, so those close to him haven't noticed."

Still seething with anger from her besting him, Demetri walked over to Tatiana. "Nice profile, but how exactly does that help us?"

"We can put the description out to the vampires in Savannah to see if any of them know someone who fits the profile. We also have narrowed down where he might be living. All the killings have occurred within a fifteen-mile radius. We believe the killer lives within those fifteen miles."

Stephan ran his hand through his dark hair. "Now that *is* helpful. We will patrol the area, search for anything out of the ordinary. Maybe we'll get lucky."

Tatiana drew a map out of her duster pocket and opened it on the coffee table. The Alphas gathered round. Marcus sectioned the area into fourths.

"We'll divide into groups of two, and each group will take an assigned section of the city to patrol. Check for any signs of the monster."

Marcus clapped his hands once in approval. "We have a plan."

Chapter 23

For the last six evenings, Christina watched the vampires train together and meet nightly to coordinate their patrols. According to the reports from Marcus, the teams scouted the city carefully, looking for signs of the murderer, looking for places a rogue vampire might be hiding, but all had appeared quiet. As Alex put it one evening, it seemed as if the murderer somehow knew they searched for him and went into hiding, as undetectable as a B-2 stealth bomber.

The house had been a whirlwind of activity, with all the large bodies moving throughout the plantation like bees in a hive. Meals were served in the formal dining room with everyone gathered around the large table eating together. Christina always felt very tiny sitting between the vampires. Even Kat's five-foot-ten-inch frame dwarfed her.

She'd discovered the vampires seemed to have an endless supply of energy. When they weren't working out or on patrol, they were swimming, playing games, or talking strategy. They especially enjoyed sparring in Marcus' gym. Even Katrina joined in the melee occasionally, appreciating the opportunity to spar with Marcus or Stephan.

Tonight the house seemed unusually quiet while Christina made her way through the halls. She discovered why when she opened the doors to the gym, and a spectacular sight greeted her. Her eyes scanned the room, taking in the massive bodies within. As if she'd gone to California and stepped onto Muscle Beach, everywhere she looked a perfect male specimen flexed, each over six feet and none under two hundred pounds. The caged lights from overhead illuminated the tiny beads of sweat that dotted their bodies, creating a glistening effect. The gym smelled of spice and musk, tickling Christina's nose.

Alexander lay on a black padded bench, wearing only a pair of blue gym shorts, while he pressed five hundred pounds. His muscles rippled beneath his skin, flexing with each lift of the bar. Darkened by perspiration, his blond hair lay tucked tight against his head. The grunting sound that escaped his lips with each rep indicated he strained from his effort.

Stephan, slightly more covered in a white muscle shirt and black shorts, stood behind him to spot. The Alpha leader removed the towel from his shoulder and wiped his own face and chest, while Alexander continued his presses.

Nicholai drew Christina's attention as he stepped toward the sauna, wrapping a white terry cloth towel around his waist. As if he'd just stepped from a pool, he too glistened under the harsh lights. He looked in her direction and smiled, tipping his chin up in greeting before he tucked the corner of the towel at his waist. Like all of the Alphas, his Adonis-like physique contained not an ounce of extra fat. His six-foot-five body filled the frame of the sauna door when he opened it and stepped in.

Demetri stood in one corner of the gym, going a

few rounds with a punching bag. Giving the bag hell, he punched it with a right hook, then a left uppercut, followed by a roundhouse kick. Like a martial arts fighter, he executed the moves perfectly.

Christina's eyes found Marcus. He sat on the thigh press, pushing eight hundred and fifty pounds up and down with ease. The metallic clunking of the machine kept steady time with each pump of his legs. She watched in admiration as her lover flexed and extended his legs, his muscles rippling with each pass. Marcus stopped with his knees bent and turned his head toward Christina. "Hey, babe. Like what you see?"

"Very much," Christina replied with a sly smile. "I thought I'd do a little treadmill time, if you guys don't mind." She waited for a response.

"Of course, go ahead. Help yourself." Marcus gestured to the series of treadmills located on the opposite side of the gym.

Vlad ran hard, working up a sweat on one of the machines, wearing only a pair of green shorts, shoes, and socks. The steady pounding of his feet created an echo in the room that accompanied the clanking of the weights. Christina tried to track his movements, but his legs were a blur of motion. Only his face remained still enough for her human eyes to register clearly. His sturdy features sported a dark goatee around a mouth set in a taut line. His black eyes held an intensity that made Christina inwardly cringe. He reminded her of a deadly assassin, ready to execute his assignment with cold detachment.

Christina chose one of the available treadmills, as far from Vladimir as possible, and brought it to life with the push of a button. She ran hard, striving for a runner's high. Christina loved the feeling she got when the adrenaline hit. Feeling she could run forever, she pushed herself, and ran longer then she usually did. Her steady rhythm, while much slower than Vlad's, added to the noise echoing in the gym.

She let her mind roam, allowed the thoughts to breeze in and out. She replayed the night she met Marcus, remembering how her first thought of her future lover had been that he was the devil. It brought a smile to her face. Her devil. He *was* a bit devilish, with sinfully delicious ideas of ways to please her, tempt her. Her mind raced through their time together, her focus on their time in bed. She couldn't help it. Her mind recalled the way he smelled, the feel of his fingers on her body. She lost herself to the sensation of the adrenaline, let her mind continue to wander.

She rode the high until eventually her body tired and her lungs burned from their struggle to consume enough air. A painful stitch stabbed her side, forcing Christina to slow her pace and finally stop altogether. She wiped the perspiration from her brow and arms before toweling off her legs.

Leaving the machine, she made her way to the middle of the gym to stretch her body as she cooled down. First, she bent at the waist and touched the floor in a hamstring stretch. She moved into a downward facing dog pose to stretch her calves. Next, she knelt down, and arched backwards touching her head and shoulders to the floor to lengthen her quads. Christina released the stretch and shifted onto her hands and knees for cat-cow pose—arching then rounding her back. A small moan escaped her parted lips as the tension in her muscles eased in much needed relief after the fierce workout. Finally, she sat on her bottom, spread her legs into a wide split, and laid her forehead and chest flat against each calf to stretch the backs of her legs one last time.

Realizing the gym had become very quiet, with only the hum of Vlad's treadmill and the sound of her own breathing perceptible to her ears, she looked into the mirrors that covered the walls of the gym from floor to ceiling, and found five sets of intense eyes watching her. She jumped to her feet, suddenly aware that she stood in the room with five very large, very male vampires, all of whom focused on her with hungry eyes.

An audible growl emanated from across the room.

Vlad moved first. He shut down his machine and silently dismounted as he flung his towel around his neck and wiped his face before he made a hasty retreat toward the indoor pool area. Alexander and Stephan were the next to go, heading for the showers while one of them muttered, "Good God." Demetri stilled the punching bag when it swung silently from his last punch. He almost tripped over the dumb bell rack in his haste to exit the gym doors.

Marcus rose from his machine and headed for Christina with the swagger of a male tiger prowling after its mate. His eyes darkened in hunger, strides quickened and ate up the space between them.

"Did I do something wrong?" asked Christina.

Her reply came in the way of a rush of cool air when Marcus used his preternatural speed to cross the gym and scoop her up in his arms before pressing his lips to hers in a crushing kiss.

"That stretching was the sexiest thing I've ever

seen," he managed to bite out before he kissed her again.

Marcus pinned her against the wall next to the sauna door, his body pressed into hers. Christina wrapped her arms around his neck and returned his kiss with equal urgency. His hunger fueled her desire. He built the lust between them, letting their passion mix in their mindlink until, like a tornado, their desire circulated between them, building until it became an unstoppable whirlwind.

Nicholai opened the door to the sauna and made a hasty exit. "Get a room, you two." Nicholai glanced at them quickly, a smile on his handsome face.

Marcus grabbed the open sauna door, catching it before it closed as he broke their kiss. "Sounds like a plan. I think this room will do."

Chapter 24

Marcus ushered Christina into the sauna. The heat and steam made it difficult for him to breathe. Or perhaps it was the power of his heartmate's desire, coupled with the feelings building between them. Lust rode him hard, and his heated blood rushed to his loins.

Marcus made quick work of her clothes, stripping her naked in record time to get to her luscious body. His gym shorts were the next to go. Christina took advantage of his momentary distraction to lay a towel on the teak wood bench that lined one wall. She lay on the towel, with one leg bent while the other hung off the bench, legs open wide in invitation.

Marcus stood for a moment just taking in the vision. His heartmate lay before him like a five-star buffet. Her soft pink nipples stood erect, begging for attention. Her flat stomach bobbed up and down like a gentle sea with each breath. She reached her arms out, beckoning him.

A demure smile lit the corners of Christina's eyes. "When you look at me like that, I think you want to eat me up."

"I do, my love, I do!" Marcus' voice sounded raspy, even to him.

"Well, what are you waiting for?"

Marcus fell to his knees before his mate. Taking

her hips in his large hands, he pulled her creamy core toward his mouth. She moaned when he pressed his lips against her, and his tongue swirled circles on her most sensitive spot. He sucked her delicate nub into his mouth, causing her to arch back in a sensuous way that lifted her breasts in offering. In response, his hand trailed up her body to her breast.

He palmed the soft globe, kneading it gently. Marcus rolled the nipple between his thumb and finger, making it tighten while he continued his oral ministration. He teased her nipples, first one then the other, until two hard and firm buds pebbled from his attention.

Christina tossed her head back and forth with delight. She fisted her hands in his thick hair, holding him to her as she thrust against him in wanton abandonment. Marcus fed on her, suckling, driving her body higher until it tightened with need. He moaned against her when she rewarded his efforts by climaxing a heady rush of creamy heat.

The Alpha crawled up her body, wrapping his arms around her back. He rolled their bodies and brought her to rest on top of him. With one thrust he surrounded his shaft with her amazing heat. It bathed him in its warmth. A fresh rush of passion pulsed through his veins, and flames licked over his skin.

Christina sat up, bracing her palms on his chest, taking charge of their pace. She moved slowly, hips rocking against him. Marcus watched her breasts sway to the rhythm. Noticing where his attention lay, she took his hands, encouraging him to caress her breasts, and he readily complied.

He loved watching her like this, licentious and

unrestrained. Her body undulated in sinuous gyrations. Christina bit her lower lip as a look of pure ecstasy took her face while she rode him.

The Alpha slid his hands around her back and pulled her down against him. Her hair surrounded his head, veiling them from the world. The pads of his fingers brushed down her back before they gripped her hips. He quickened their pace, pounding their flesh together. The slap of flesh aroused him further. He lost himself in the intoxicating sound, to the moment, the rhythm. His power moved within her, the friction nearly intolerable, the pleasure so intense he gave himself to her, losing himself completely.

He tucked her hair around to one side and exposed her neck. His fangs lengthened in anticipation. Marcus bit into her vein, taking her blood down his throat, sending her over the edge, when the ecstasy of his bite coursed through her. Her orgasm tore a scream from her throat. She gripped him tightly with her sheath, milking him as he moved. His thrusts deepened, burying himself to the hilt in her moist heat. His own orgasm boiled up, and he quickly licked the small wounds closed, before he succumbed to the sensation and followed her lead, growling against her neck as he spilled his seed into her.

They lay joined together, trying to catch their breath.

"I feel lightheaded," Christina muttered, as she trailed one finger over his shoulder and down his arm.

"Probably the combination of heat and steam." Marcus gave her a tight squeeze.

"And passion." Christina raised her head from his chest and placed her hand on her neck over the bite wound.

Marcus gently pulled her hand away from her neck. No mark remained. His eyes softened at the look on his mate's face. "I hope it's okay that I drank from you. I couldn't help myself."

Marcus feathered his thumb back and forth across the spot where he'd bitten her.

Christina smiled down at him. "I thought my orgasm would have been answer enough." She chuckled. "You can do that anytime."

He returned her smile, his chest swelling with male satisfaction, then sighed when reality pushed in on him. "I hate to say this, but I need to go. We are doing patrols again tonight."

"That's why you were all hitting the gym. You were getting warmed up in case you have to fight tonight." A look of apprehension crossed her face.

"Yes." He wouldn't lie to her.

"I don't want you to go."

The beseeching look on her face nearly undid him. Her concern for his safety radiated through their link. Marcus tucked a strand of her auburn hair behind one ear.

"I have to. It's what I do. It's what *we* do." He kissed the tip of her nose. "I'll be fine. I've spent centuries training with these guys. We're tight, a good team. And we're good at what we do. You have nothing to worry about, *cara*."

Famous last words, thought Christina as she dismounted his body and headed for the sauna door.

"I heard that, babe." *Remember our mindlink. I can hear your thoughts*. Marcus followed her out of the room.

"I keep forgetting about that," she muttered, holding the door for him.

They exited the sauna together, and each grabbed a towel located just outside the door. After wrapping themselves in their towels, Marcus tucked Christina under his arm, drawing her to his chest. He leaned down and planted a kiss on the top of her head.

"You really don't have to worry, you know. I'll be back before you know it."

"You'd better be."

They left the gym side by side through the double doors and headed for their suite so they could shower and change before Marcus went out on patrol.

****

A short time later, Marcus joined the Alphas in the foyer of his mansion. Dressed in black from head to toe, he matched his fellow warriors. His leathers were tight and tucked into his boots. He'd donned a dark turtleneck covered by a black leather jacket.

Nicholai shrugged into his leather coat and grinned at Marcus. "So, you get all your kinks worked out in the sauna there, my man?"

"More like he got kinky in the sauna," bantered Demetri.

The Alphas all laughed with the exception of Marcus, who feigned a disgusted look. "What did or didn't happen in the sauna is none of your damned business. Got it?" Marcus hauled off and punched Demetri in his bicep.

"Got it. Point made," Demetri growled, grabbing his shoulder and circling his arm to work out the sore muscle.

"Where's Michael?" Stephan smoothly changed

the subject, before the jovial mood could become violent.

"He told me he had something to do this evening. That's why he didn't join us to workout. He said he would be able to patrol his section of the grid tonight, though," Alex informed the group.

"He'd better," said Stephan, putting on his coat. "He's starting to get on my nerves, that one. He is increasingly unavailable. He acts like the Council is too much of an effort for him. Perhaps Michael and I need to have a little sit-down soon. He needs to get his priorities straight."

"Is it just me, or does he seem to be more of a recluse as of late?" Demetri asked.

"I noticed that in Vegas," Alex chimed in. "He seems to have a way of vanishing just when something needs to be done."

Nicholai zipped his jacket. "The male is in need of a serious altitude adjustment."

"You mean an attitude adjustment?" Marcus corrected, with a smile.

"We could give him an attitude adjustment by sending him to a higher altitude with a few hard punches," offered Demetri.

The Alpha leader raked a hand through his hair, securing it in a thong before continuing. "We'll deal with Michael later. Right now we have more important matters at hand, like finding the person responsible for those missing women. Marcus, you and Alexander will take quadrant one tonight. Demetri, you will go with your cousin, Nicholai, and patrol quadrant two. Vlad and I will take the third quadrant, leaving Michael to do the fourth with Tatiana, assuming Michael shows up."

"Speaking of, where is Tatiana?" Alex asked as he handed Stephan a knife.

Stephan tucked the switchblade into his boot. "She said she had something to do and would hook up with Michael in Forsyth Park at ten.

"If you find anything unusual, call in and we will rendezvous. This is strictly a recon mission. Do not engage, unless it is absolutely necessary."

The group of males turned to exit the house.

"Whoa there, big fella," Kat called, as she and Christina emerged from the living room. Kat stopped her mate in his tracks by grabbing the back of his jacket. "Where do you think you're going without a good luck kiss?"

Stephan turned toward her, and she jumped into his arms. "I don't need luck, heartmate, but I'll take the kiss anyway." Kat's toes dangled while they kissed. He lowered her to her feet, parting their lips. "I'll see you soon. Be waiting for me in that little blue number I saw you pack."

Her eyes widened. "You saw that? I wanted it to be a surprise."

"Be waiting for me in that, and I'll show you a surprise when I get back." Stephan winked at Kat.

"What about my kiss?" Marcus grabbed Christina around her waist and drew her to him.

"I don't think Stephan would appreciate me laying one on you, Marcus," Kat teased, and Stephan growled a warning.

Marcus shot her a look from the corner of his eye before turning his attention back on his love. "I wasn't talking to you, Kitty Kat. I was talking to the gorgeous woman in my arms."

Christina rose on her tiptoes and kissed Marcus—a deep kiss that made him push into her mind to glean her thoughts.

She had a bad feeling about tonight and didn't want him to leave. His mate wanted him to stay with her where he would be out of harm's way. That was sweet. She was concerned for his safety. It warmed his heart to know she felt that way.

When he released her to leave, her bereavement came across their link.

"You come back to me safe and sound," she called after him as he turned from her to leave.

"Will do," said Marcus before he set the alarm code and closed the door behind him.

Once outside and out of earshot of the women, Stephan motioned for his team to wait. "Hold up for a minute." He waited for their full attention, then continued. "We've been at this for six nights with nothing to show for it. We need to find this vampire. He's going to strike again if we can't find him."

Marcus shifted his stance. "I know. I'm surprised there haven't been any abductions this week. Maybe our patrols are keeping him away. Or maybe he moved on to a new city."

"According to Demetri, VES thinks he is still here in Savannah." Demetri nodded before Stephan continued. "They think he is laying low, probably because he knows we are looking for him."

"Well, one thing's for sure," said Alexander. "We won't find him standing around here."

Vladimir nodded once in agreement. A male of few words, he simply said, "I concur."

They headed for the three identical black SUV's

parked in the driveway. The teams loaded into the cars and brought the vehicles to life. Engines rumbling, the cars caravanned down the drive, spitting gravel behind them as they went.

****

The vampire watched the procession drive away. He knew the routine, had it down. The patrols would be gone for six and a half hours. Once they returned, there would be a briefing, after which the Alphas would disperse. While the single males did whatever, the ones with heartmates would go to their females to mate. Fates above, how he wanted that.

He wanted a female to call his own. Since meeting Christina, he'd tried to sate his appetite with other women, but they didn't smell or taste like her.

He wanted to possess Christina, and tonight he would finally have her. With the Alphas gone, the females would be unprotected. Of course, it would have been nice if Christina happened to be alone, but he'd take care of the other female easily enough. He had waited for the perfect time, and tonight was it.

His scheme was perfect. No one could stop him. He had planned carefully. He'd thought of everything. He knew it wouldn't be easy, but his plan would work. It must.

He licked his lips in anticipation and smiled.

Chapter 25

Christina and Kat settled into their usual evening plan. Every night for the past six evenings, the women kissed their heartmates goodbye before going to the media room to pass the hours. As they watched TV, they talked, getting to know one another. The two were becoming good friends.

Christina found she enjoyed Kat's company. When she first met Kat, she had been jealous, mostly because Kat had a longer history with Marcus than she did. With Katrina looking so beautiful and perfect, Christina expected Marcus' friend to be stuck up and snooty, but she couldn't have been more wrong.

Christina now genuinely liked the woman, found her to be caring and sweet. Kat turned out to be a wealth of information. Most conversations between the two consisted of Christina asking questions about either Marcus or life as a vampire, and tonight was no exception.

Christina watched Kat pop a handful of popcorn into her mouth. "What was it like?" she inquired grabbing some of the kernels.

"What was what like?"

"The conversion. What was it like when you were turned into a vampire?"

Kat stilled. She turned her gaze fully on Christina

and asked, "What did Marcus tell you about it?"

"He said it hurt like hell." Christina ate another handful of the corn.

Kat put her arm on the back of the couch and rested her head on her hand. "To say it hurts is an understatement. The pain is so great you start begging to die. And in a way, you kind of do."

Christina's brows narrowed in concern over her emerald eyes. "Is it always that bad?"

"Yeah, I think it is. Your human body does die in a way. Your muscles become longer, your bones denser. Your cells become depleted as your body literally eats itself for energy to complete the change. Your heart enlarges so your new body can have enough blood flowing through it. So yeah, it's always bad."

"But you got through it."

"I did, but it wasn't easy."

"Is it worth it?" Christina whispered in a soft voice. "Is it worth the pain to become a vampire?"

Kat ran her fingers through her long blonde hair as she carefully considered her answer. "What choice did I have? I am the heartmate of a vampire. If I stayed human, I would age and die while he remained young and agile. There really is no other choice, when you think about it. For me, I'd endure anything to be with Stephan. The few moments of pain were definitely worth centuries with the love of my life."

Kat turned her attention back to the show as Christina sat silently, contemplating what her new friend had said.

Centuries with Marcus.

She couldn't imagine it but definitely wanted to find out what that might be like.

The doorbell rang, startling Christina from her musings.

"I'll get that." Katrina offered. "I know Payton isn't here tonight."

Christina stood and brushed the popcorn crumbs from her slacks. When she looked around, Kat was already gone.

Making her way through the home, she reached the hall in time to see Kat disarm the system and open the door.

"Hi." Katrina moved aside to let the man enter. "I thought you were patrolling tonight. Is everything all right?"

The vampire stepped inside, closing the door behind him. "Where's Christina?" he asked, looking around.

"She's in the TV room."

Unease crept up Christina's spine, freezing her steps. Did he come to be the bearer of bad news? Had something happened to Stephan? To Marcus? Christina's stomach churned with apprehension.

"Why are you here?" Kat's tone of voice sounded shaky. "What's wrong, Michael? Why aren't you out patrolling with the other Alphas?"

Christina's eyes widened as Michael's fingers wrapped around Katrina's throat. His other hand gripped her shoulder. A quick jerk snapped her neck with a sickening crack.

A bloodcurdling scream pushed from Christina's lips.

Michael's hungry eyes met hers. A thick lump formed in her throat.

"There you are." Malice dripped from his voice.

He took a step in her direction, and Christina's fight-or-flight response kicked into gear. Knowing there was nothing she could do for Kat, Christina ran toward the safe room.

As she turned and ran, she heard Michael call out behind her, "Nothing I like better than a good chase, Christina. I'm coming to get you, my pretty."

****

Michael leaned over Stephan's mate, a look of abhorrence on his face. A broken spine would not kill her, but it would certainly keep her incapacitated while her body healed. Michael put two fingers to the female vampire's throat, feeling a thready pulse.

With Kat out of the way, there was no reason to rush. No reason at all. In fact, it was much more fun to stalk his prey. However, he'd need to make sure the prey couldn't call for help.

He sent his awareness through the home until he found Christina. Michael pushed into her mind, built a mental block between her and Marcus, then flooded her with the sensations of fear and dread before pulling back to himself.

Michael strolled in the direction Christina had gone. He sniffed the air, inhaled the smell he craved so desperately. Fear. Delicious fear mixed with the sensual aroma of Christina. His nostrils flared as he caught the arousing scent. It took him down the hallway, through a door, and down some stairs. At the bottom of the stairs, a steady pulsing beat came to his ears. *Her* heartbeat. It called to him like a beacon on a dark ocean, guiding him.

Michael increased his speed, rounded the corner, and discovered Christina.

Her little feet pounded at a rather fast pace for a human. A predatory growl escaped his throat.

Chapter 26

The hairs on Christina's neck rose. She sensed him behind her, a fierce predator seeking his prey. She was so close, just inches from the panic room. She put her hand on the door knob to the room as his hand closed around her ankle. Her momentum halted. Christina fell face first onto the carpet.

She rolled over onto her back and kicked as hard as possible with her free leg. Her high-heeled shoe intuitively found Michael's eye. The contact snapped his head back, and he screamed in pain when the heel punctured the orb. A clear liquid mixed with blood rolled down his face, and revulsion at the sight twisted her stomach. Michael covered his eye with both hands and rolled from side to side with pain. Her ankle freed, Christina scrambled backwards into the room and slammed the door shut.

"LOCK!" she screamed.

The door's special locking mechanism clicked into place, leaving Michael to scream his frustration on the other side of the door. Christina collapsed on the floor. Adrenaline and fear shook her body. Heavy breaths tore in and out of her lungs while the adrenaline slowly left her body. Pushing to her feet, she took a moment to gather her wits.

Christina took in her surroundings. On three walls

sat shelves with food and drinks, enough for two people to stay there a week if needed. Exploring the room, she discovered a bathroom with a toilet and sink. As she turned from the doorway to the bath, she noticed a long rectangular table. The metal table supported a wall of small TV monitors. One, two, three…ten in all sat on the table.

Why would anyone need ten TV's in a safe room, she wondered. Then she took time to focus on what played across the screens.

She noticed each monitor had an area of the house on it: the kitchen, the front gate, the stairway, and other various areas of the house all covered. Movement on one of the screens grabbed her attention, and she leaned on the table in front of the monitor, taking in the scene playing out.

Michael paced the hallway just outside the panic room, wiping the blood from his face, and cursed. She watched his form coalesce in on itself until only a wisp of black smoke remained in the hall.

Suddenly, he reappeared outside the door to the panic room. The vampire looked around the hall in disgust. Noticing the camera perched high on the wall, he turned his menacing scowl toward the lens and leered. With his injured eye mostly healed, his gaze met hers through the monitor.

"Marcus is smarter than I gave him credit for. Apparently, he lined your room with titanium so I can't materialize within. I hope you can hear me, woman. You will come to me, Christina. You will come out to me or Stephan's heartmate will die."

Wait! Kat was alive? Realization smacked into Christina. Of course, a broken neck wouldn't kill a vampire. She had to find a way to help her.

Michael turned and stalked away from the camera. Her eyes searched the monitors, trying to catch sight of him. She found him going up the stairs.

"No. Leave her alone, you bastard!" she yelled at the monitors, not knowing if Michael could hear her.

Her gaze flew to the next monitor, where she saw Michael stalk toward Kat in the foyer. He picked up her lifeless body. She hung limply over one of his arms like a rag doll. Michael looked up at the camera, finding it with intimidating ease.

"Christina, I'm going to drain her. If you come to me, I'll stop. If you come out quickly, she might even live. It's up to you. Her life is in your hands. Tonight you will decide if Katrina lives or dies."

He wrapped his hand around Kat's neck and brought her to his mouth. Looking up at the camera, he stared at the machine as he bit through the delicate skin of her neck and drank. He took long draws, gulping her blood down his throat. After several minutes, when Christina did not come out, he sealed the wounds and let Kat drape again over his arm.

He moved to the next camera, one closer to the panic room and said, "I'm going to keep doing this, Christina, until you come to me. I'm slowly draining her dry. You can stop this. You can save her. Come to me, and I'll stop." Michael again brought Kat to his mouth and began to drink.

Christina watched in horror as the vampire drank from her friend. Bile pushed into her throat. He *was* killing her. She had to do something. Her friend was about to die. It wasn't fair. Michael wanted her. Why should Katrina suffer for her?

After several more minutes, he moved on to the next camera and repeated the morbid process. Ultimatum. Bite. Drink. By the time he made his way to the camera in front of the panic room, Kat looked ghostly pale, a color whiter than white, her lips blue. Michael glanced up at the camera.

"Christina, this is it. Your last chance. She is still alive…barely. Her heartbeat stutters. I can hear it. She doesn't have much blood left. If you want her to live, you must come out. Now."

He hesitated a moment, then brought Kat's neck to his mouth. The end had come! He intended to kill her. Christina couldn't take it another second. As he bared his fangs, she hit the button to release the locking mechanism of the panic room with a click.

Opening the door to the room, Christina ran out and yelled, "Stop, Stop. No more. Don't kill her. Please!"

Michael dropped Kat's body onto the floor. With a thud, she fell limp like a sack of cement. When Christina tried to reach her friend, Michael's fingers clamped around her wrist, preventing her from checking on Katrina.

Wearing an evil smile, he flung Christina over his shoulder. His long strides took them out of the house. She bounced on his shoulder with every step. His clavicle bone cut into her stomach with each footfall. The pain in her abdomen couldn't compare with the pain in her heart as she thought of Kat lying helpless on the floor.

"Did you kill her?" Christina whispered.

"She is still technically alive, but fading. If she dies, it will be your fault. You took too long to come out. You should have come to me sooner, Christina. You know there will have to be a punishment for your bad behavior."

She didn't want to dwell on what punishment he might have in mind. She'd never trusted Michael, but this behavior seemed extreme, even for him. What happened to make him take these measures?

"What are you going to do to me?" Tears streamed down her face, falling on the gravel drive as he strode to his vehicle.

"That is entirely up to you. You will reap what you sow. Behave, and I'll take that into consideration."

As they moved away from the mansion, Christina glanced up for one last look at the residence, in case she never saw the home again.

Michael tossed her into the back seat of a silver Mercedes and slammed the door then walked nonchalantly around the car, slipped behind the wheel and brought the engine to life. Michael glanced at Christina from the driver's seat as she slowly sat up. When their eyes met, she fell into their depths. The sinister smile on his face made Christina's flesh crawl, just before the world went black.

****

Stephan and Vlad walked down Fifth Street for the third time in a week. Stephan had been itchy all night. He felt the cold tingling of something amiss, but all was well on the streets, nothing out of place. The humans went about their usual business of getting a bite to eat and meeting friends in the bars that lined the street. Nothing seemed out of the ordinary, but still something felt off to Stephan.

Suddenly a physical pain, like none he'd felt

before, gripped his chest. He dropped to his knees, the sidewalk digging in. The biting pain took the breath from his lungs. He gripped his shirt in desperation, trying to catch his breath.

Katrina! Stephan desperately tried to establish their mental connection, but only silence met his call.

Vlad put a hand on Stephan's shoulder and knelt beside him. "What is it, Stephan? What's wrong?"

"It's Kat. Something is terribly wrong. I can feel it. I must get to her."

"Can you dematerialize?"

Stephan closed his eyes and tried to imagine himself at Marcus' home. As his form started to waver, another wave of pain hit, and he became solid. "No. I can't concentrate enough to dematerialize. You have to get me to the plantation now!"

Vlad ran with blurring speed to where the two left their SUV. Jumping behind the wheel, he gunned the engine and took off with a screech of tires to pick up Stephan. He leaned over and opened the passenger door as Stephan stood. The Alpha leader struggled into the vehicle on legs weakened by pain and fear for his mate.

"Go, go, go. NOW!" commanded Stephan as he closed the door.

His mind sought Kat through their mindlink. No response. He stilled, sensed nothing from her, no thoughts, no feelings, just a blankness that sent a wave of desperation through him. If he couldn't reach Katrina, perhaps Marcus could get to the plantation before they would. His mind searched for Marcus, finding him with perfunctory ease.

Marcus, something's wrong. I can't connect with Kat. Vlad is taking us to your place now. You need to get your ass home.

I know. Alex and I aren't too far from the plantation. Just pulled a U-turn. We're on our way.

Can you contact Christina? Find out what's going on?

I've tried. I haven't gotten through yet, but I'll keep trying.

As will I.

Twenty minutes later, the two SUV's pulled into the drive one behind the other. They ground to a halt, skidding on the gravel drive as they arrived at the front door. The door to the homestead yawned open, and light streamed from within, casting an eerie glow onto the front porch.

Stephan bolted inside. He closed his eyes and sent his senses flaring out through the home, searching for his beloved. When the other Alphas crowded into the foyer behind him, he hushed them so he could concentrate. A faint, erratic beat reached his ears, the sound familiar yet strange at the same time. The Alpha leader concentrated hard on the sound, attempting to place it.

Recognition hit him. Opening his eyes, Stephan took off toward the noise as fast as his preternatural speed allowed. He raced through the house, Vlad and Alexander hard on his heels.

Finding Kat lying on the floor in the hall outside the panic room, Stephan scooped her limp body in his arms and brushed the hair from her face. The warrior hugged his mate to him, rocking her as his gaze roamed her body, assessing her injuries. Her head listed to one side, exposing her neck. It was broken and ravaged with multiple bites.

His eyes clouded, and her features blurred. He closed his eyes to keep the tears from falling and pushed his emotions aside so he could send his consciousness into her body to continue his assessment. The muscles in her back were bruised in multiple places and her neck had yet to begin to fuse the ruptured spinal cord. The lack of blood made her heart struggle for each beat. It sputtered in her chest.

He leaned back his head and allowed the pained roar to escape his throat, the sound akin to the howl of a great animal losing its mate. The bellow shook the walls.

"Don't you leave me, Kitten," the Alpha pleaded, brushing Kat's hair from her face. "Don't you go. You stay with me. Dammit."

****

Marcus searched wildly for Christina, using his preternatural speed to physically check every room, but she was nowhere to be found. When Marcus approached the panic room, the scene with Stephan and Kat greeted him, as did the mighty roar of grief from his sire.

Shock slowed his steps, bringing him to a stop next to the couple. Anger shook his body as he looked down on his friends. Questions pinged around his brain. Who would do such a terrible thing? Why would anyone attack Katrina? And just as importantly, where was Christina? If Katrina was this badly injured, how was *his* heartmate? His concern spurred him into action.

"Vlad, Alexander, where are you?" he called, making his way down the hall, past the couple.

"In here," Vlad replied from the panic room.

Marcus' long strides took him into the safe room

where Vlad and Alexander watched the monitors. As his gaze flew to the screens, he stilled. Like a Saturday Night Horror Movie of the Week, the video of what transpired while the Alphas were on patrol played before his eyes. Marcus watched Michael drain Kat slowly until Christina sacrificed herself to save their friend.

Anger flooded his blood at the cruelty and betrayal of one of their own. He'd fought beside that bastard for decades. He'd called him brother, and even though he'd not been himself lately, Marcus never expected this type of duplicity from Michael.

The monster would pay. He'd make sure of that.

Marcus reached out again to his beloved. *Christina, can you hear me? Cara, I need you to respond. Speak to me!*

The silence that met his plea was deafening. Desperation pushed in on him. His stomach knotted until he couldn't breathe.

Alex took control. "I'll stay and help Stephan. Vlad, you and Marcus go to Michael's place. See if you can find Christina. On your way, call Demetri and get him to meet you there."

Marcus knew Stephan possessed a special ability to heal using his aura, and Kat would need his special talent to survive. Kat would also need a lot of blood to replace what Michael had taken, and he hoped Alex and Stephan had enough between them. If Vlad and he were lucky, they would reach Christina in time to save her.

They *had* to reach her in time. The Fates only knew what Michael intended for her. He sent a quick prayer to the heavens that they weren't too late.

****

Wake up, Christina. I don't want you to miss a minute of what I have planned for you.

Christina awoke with a jolt of fear and pushed up into a seated position just as the vehicle passed the large graveyard located on the outskirts of Savannah, far away from the inner city. The car turned down an obscured dirt road. Spanish moss hung from the live oaks and maples like spidery fingers swaying in the wind as they made their way down the bumpy lane until they came to a clearing. The moonless night cast the yard into darkness, making it difficult for Christina to discern her surroundings, but she could tell the tree-cluttered lawn concealed them from the highway.

Michael rolled to a stop in front of a compound. Christina knew if she went into that building she would never come out, so she pushed open the car door and ran for all she was worth.

By her fifth step, Michael stood in front of her, like an immovable wall of stone. He grabbed her arm in a bruising grip and spun her around, marching her into the compound. "Don't ever try to run away from me again. I have been more than patient with you, but my patience is wearing thin." He looked down at her with a chilling smile. "Come with me. I have something I want you to see."

Michael marched Christina around the back of the compound to the smaller of the two buildings. Opening the door with his mind, he escorted her inside. The smell of the room washed over her when they entered, death and decay. It smelled similar to the morgue at the hospital, without the scent of antiseptic.

A few candles scattered throughout dimly lit the room. Christina's human eyes had difficulty adjusting—which was a blessing because the things she could see brought bile into her throat.

She noticed a woman with red hair lying motionless on a rack. The woman's wrists and ankles were strapped down, her eyes closed. Unable to tell if her chest moved, Christina didn't know if the woman lay dead or unconscious.

Training as a nurse compelled her to try to help the woman. She shifted her weight, taking a step toward the table, but Michael tightened his grip on her arm, keeping her by his side. "Where do you think you are going?"

"I'm going to help her."

"She's dead. She didn't survive the fun I had planned. Humans break so easily, you know."

The similarities between the woman and herself struck Christina. The dead woman was about her size, same red hair, similar frame. Her voice sounded small as she squeaked, "She looks like me."

"Yes," her captor agreed. "When I didn't get you that evening in your apartment, I needed to find a substitute.

"At first, I became furious when Marcus interrupted us in your apartment. But it actually turned out to be a good thing. She taught me that in your human state, you will be too weak for the things I have planned, so I'm going to convert you."

Panic gripped her with its icy claws. A shiver raced down her spine. Christina rounded on Michael, a look of terror on her face. "You're going to convert me?"

Before Michael responded, she heard a cry from a pitch-black corner of the room.

"What was that?" Christina turned toward the

sound.

"That is your first meal. After I convert you, you will need to feed. I will bring you here to feed from her."

Her eyes, wide with a combination of fear and repulsion, returned to her captor. Michael took a deep inhale, his nostrils flaring.

"I do so love it when my special toys are scared." A twisted smile took his face, and another shudder went through Christina's body. He bent, lowering his voice as he whispered in her ear, "And after you feed, we will put this playroom to good use."

Chapter 27

Demetri and Nicholai exited the SUV. Having finished driving their section of the city, they planned on walking the streets, so they could look in the nooks and crannies of the buildings when Demetri's cell phone vibrated against his chest. He pulled the phone from the pocket of his shirt and accepted the call with the push of a button.

"Hello."

"Demetri, Vlad here. We are at the mansion. There has been an incident."

Demetri listened to Vlad explain what he and Alex saw on the security monitors at the plantation. The warrior stopped walking and gripped the phone harder, the cracking of the case evidence of his anger.

"Michael's place is near here. We can be there in five. You and Marcus meet us there."

He slid the phone back in his pocket and informed Nicholai about the emergency. The warriors jumped back into the SUV, and two minutes later the vehicle screeched to a halt in front of the brick building Michael called home.

Demetri bounded up the stairs, his cousin in tow. Tearing the door from its hinges, he burst through the entryway. A cloud of dust kicked up when Demetri's booted foot hit the floor. His eyes roamed the space, discovering a layer of dust an inch thick covering everything within. No prints marred the dusty floor. The house appeared abandoned.

Once inside, the cousins split. Demetri took the downstairs, while Nicholai headed up. As Demetri searched through the house, he wondered if Michael had *ever* lived there. Dust covered the furniture so thick it looked like a sheet. The kitchen sat empty except for a bottle of rum in the back of the pantry. The refrigerator stood bare, as vacant as a campsite during a hurricane. Demetri turned to head upstairs, but the sound of soft footsteps walking through the back door stilled his feet.

When he turned, he found Tatiana staring at him.

"What are you doing here, female?" he inquired, the look of derision twisting his features.

"Michael never showed up to do our patrol. I was on my way here to get him when Vladimir called and told me what happened at the mansion. Have you found anything?"

"No, the place is empty, and it looks like he hasn't been here in quite some time. He must have another place in the city we don't know about."

"I had more luck upstairs," Nicholai stated as he pushed through the archway and joined them in the kitchen. "I found Michael's bedroom. There are signs that he's been there recently."

"What have you got in your hands, cousin?"

Nicholai lifted up the tomes held in his grip. "Journals. I glanced through them. It's all here. You can read the decline of his mental faculties. They go back almost to the time he turned."

"You are kidding me," Tatiana scoffed in disbelief.

"There are only a few of them. I thought Michael was centuries old."

Demetri made an inelegant snort of disparity. "He's relatively young. The Alphas only brought him into the Council a few decades ago." He turned his attention to his cousin. "I don't see how we missed the signs."

Nicholai shrugged. "He has always been a loner. He was the first to volunteer when we had an assignment that would require long periods of seclusion. Remember the time he spent in the barren lands of Alaska pursuing that one vampire?"

Demetri nodded. "The one that got away? I remember. Michael spent years tracking him. And before that there was the time he went into hiding to monitor the New Yorkers we thought were preparing for a hunt club."

"And before that he was gone for years—overseas supposedly—gathering information about the Asian ring. However, that was not the case. According to these, he found the Asian ring and joined them for a time. It's all in here." Nicholai held up the journals. "It's obvious when you read these that he was never quite right. Since the night of his conversion, his mind slowly deteriorated, but something happened in Asia because that seems to be the turning point. I will not even share the horrible things he wrote about Christina. It is disgusting what he plans on doing with her."

Tatiana stepped forward. "Some people can't handle turning. Do the books suggest where we might look for them?"

Nicholai shook his head. "Unfortunately, no. But they do, however, mention he is responsible for Gage

Lucio finding Katrina. It's all in here." He tapped one of the journals.

His anger growing, Demetri sent a series of vile curses into the air. "How could we not have known?"

The VES agent put a friendly hand on his shoulder. "Sometimes those we think we know the best, we actually know the least. Rogues are like serial killers, they can turn on the charm when they want to. They can seem normal, even charismatic. It is how they lure their victims, but inside they are pure evil."

They heard a commotion in the foyer and rushed to find the cause. Vlad and Marcus burst through the doorway at the same time, ricocheting off each other like a couple of pinballs. They stumbled to a halt in front of the trio.

****

"Where is he?" demanded Marcus, the look of hatred on his face so intense it could be felt as a presence in the room.

"He's not here, comrade."

"We have to find him. He has my Christina! God only knows what he will do to her."

Tatiana stepped forward and laid her hand on Marcus' forearm. In a gentle voice she said, "Marcus, try using your mindlink. See if you can find out where she is."

"Don't you think I've been trying that?" Marcus barked.

Christina, answer me, now! He sent over their private channel of communication.

Silence.

Fuuuuuuuuck! Why couldn't he contact her? An answer came immediately to his mind. His concern, his

218

fear of losing her consumed him.

"I can't reach her! Something is blocking the connection." Marcus growled in frustration and slammed his fist into the wall, leaving a jagged circle in the plaster.

Tatiana stepped in front of him, cradling his face in her hands.

"You're too upset. Calm down and try to push through the barrier. Concentrate hard. You can do this. Slow, calm breaths." She captured his eyes in hers and took long, slow breaths until he could push down his emotions. He began to breathe with her. She slowed his breathing until they breathed as one.

"Now try again," the VES agent instructed, keeping her voice soft and soothing.

Marcus took one more calming breath and let it out slowly along with the tension from his shoulders. He closed his eyes and concentrated on his beloved.

He put his full strength behind his thoughts. *Christina, can you hear me?*

Chapter 28

The vampire took her to his sleeping chamber, his bruising grip on her arm never lessening. The pain didn't keep her from taking in her new surroundings. Christina found the room sparsely decorated. It consisted of a large bed—apparently Michael liked his comfort—and a dresser. The cinderblock walls weren't even painted. The drab color seemed fitting in this prison-like room.

He pushed Christina onto the bed. Her body bounced from the force. She scampered away from him until the metal headboard cut into her back.

Curling her arms around her bent knees, she rested her chin on her forearms, attempting to make herself as small as possible. Her eyes tracked Michael while he crossed the room to the dresser. Maybe she could change his mind. Maybe she could talk her way out of this.

Michael's form blurred when tears welled in her eyes. She blinked them back, refusing to allow him to see her cry again. He wouldn't care about tears. He didn't care about her feelings at all.

Nothing she could do would stop this from happening. Against a vampire, she'd be as helpless as a child. Her only recourse was to take the abuse and hope she might live through it.

Suddenly tenderness and love surrounded her, infusing her with its warmth as she heard Marcus calling to her through their mindlink.

I can hear you! Help me! Michael kidnapped me. He's holding me hostage.

Their mindlink! Why the hell hadn't she thought to use this to contact him earlier?

Probably because you were too scared to think of it. Even if you had tried, it wouldn't have worked. Something was blocking us. I need you to calm down, sweetheart. We know all about Michael. We're trying to find you. Can you tell me where you are?

Relief flooded her body. Marcus was on his way to save her…and he'd bring the Alphas. Hope infused her body for the first time since Marcus left her sight that night.

We are in the old marsh outside the city on Route Eleven. He has a compound. Look for the old cemetery. The dirt drive leading to the compound is just past the cemetery entrance.

We're coming. Hold on, cara. *I love you Chri…*

She felt Michael's evil presence in her mind. Like a coating of tar, it covered her brain with his black hatred. His presence replaced the warmth of her heartmate with the icy tendrils of malevolence.

****

Michael felt a subtle shift in the emotions in the room. Christina's fear was an aphrodisiac to him. He breathed in, taking the fragrance of her terror deep into his lungs, and noticed the sweet perfume subsiding. It was subtle but noticeable. He pushed into her mind, enraged to find Marcus there. What the hell? How had the Alpha managed to break through his barrier! No matter. He knew how to fix it.

Michael reinforced the barrier, making it thick and tough as steel. Just like that, Marcus disappeared from her mind. Christina's gaze met his.

"How dare you communicate with another male in my presence! You are mine, not his. Once I convert you, I'll have sire rights, and Marcus can't touch you."

Michael noticed the look of confusion on Christina's face before she turned her gaze to the floor. His self-righteous laugh sounded like a cackle as he crossed the room and sat on the bed. "Did Marcus not explain sire rights to you?"

Christina shook her head no. He caught her chin in a hard grip and forced her to look at him. "Well, let me give you a little education then. See, young one, when one vampire creates another vampire, he has the rights to that vampire. He can do anything he wishes with the one he sired. He owns it, and it is considered his responsibility and his to command."

Michael knew that sire rights were an antiquated concept, a throwback to the time in history when kings and lords were obeyed unquestioningly. The concept had been outlawed in the vampire community centuries ago, but he did not wish to share that with this woman. He believed in the rights, so as one he created, she would obey him in all things—as she should.

In a small, shaky voice Christina asked, "So if you convert me, I'll have to do whatever you say. I'll be your slave?"

Michael grinned, exposing his extended fangs. "That's precisely what it means. You learn fast, and that pleases me."

Michael brought his wrist to his mouth and used

his fangs to score a wound. "Now drink." He shoved his wrist to her mouth.

"Never!" She recoiled, pushing at his proffered arm.

Blood from his arm dripped onto her silk blouse. He could force her to drink, seize control of her body and force her to comply, but he wanted to play with her mind. He wanted her to come to him, take him willingly into her body so it would be her doing. He bet she would blame herself if she came to him of her own will—feel guilty that she had betrayed Marcus. And as an added benefit, Marcus would never forgive her the transgression, which would complete her misery.

No, he would not force her to drink but, instead, trick her into drinking.

Michael ruthlessly seized control of her mind and shoved through her memories until he found one he could use—the memory of the night Christina had first drunk from Marcus.

He let a sanguine smile bare his elongated fangs.

Michael lay down on the bed, creating an image in Christina's mind of Marcus, his features blurred. Her mind struggled to make sense of the situation, but Michael ruthlessly pushed farther, taking complete control. He forced her mind to believe it all seemed logical, and in the dream-like state, she didn't question the abnormalities.

He motioned for her to come to him with one finger. Christina snaked her way up Michael's body, believing him to be Marcus.

"Drink, Christina," he demanded, placing his wrist to her lips.

This time she complied without hesitation. The

sucking sounds she made as she gulped the blood caused Michael's muscles to tense, sending a rush of blood to thicken his shaft. A vicious smile pulled at the corners of his mouth as he thought of all the fun they would have in the playroom.

With his free arm, he circled her back and turned their bodies, bringing her to rest under him. Using his free hand, he tore her blouse, exposing the soft flesh of her breast above her bra. Her heart beat under the supple tissue. It called to him. He sank his teeth deep into her left breast and moaned as he drank, savoring her taste while her life flowed through his lips. She tasted as good as he remembered, like honey and jasmine.

Michael drank from Christina, until he gradually detected the change in her blood. What began as sweet became tainted with the dark, musky flavor of Michael. The conversion was happening.

****

Marcus' eyes snapped open in panic when something severed his connection to Christina. "Michael has a compound out on Route Eleven past the old cemetery. I think I might know where it is. You three follow Vlad and me in the SUV."

As Vlad drove away from Michael's house, Marcus reached out to Christina again with his mind. An image, blurry and out of focus, formed in Marcus' mind. He closed his eyes in concentration, attempting to clear the image.

His stomach knotted when he realized what he saw. His head snapped in Vlad's direction. "Michael's converting her. He's controlled her mind. She thinks he's me. We have to find them now!"

Vlad hit the gas, screeching around the corner with Demetri, Nicholai, and Tatiana following in hot pursuit.

****

"That's enough," someone commanded.

Christina struggled through a mental haze. Marcus licked her skin, sealing the small wounds as he pulled his wrist from her mouth.

The hold on her mind lifted, and like a cold breeze blowing away the cobwebs, Christina's mind cleared. Realization of what had transpired knocked into her consciousness. She wasn't with Marcus but *Michael*. She recoiled in disgust and pulled her shirt together. She put the back of her hand to her mouth. "What did you do?" Her voice sounded thick with repulsion.

Michael *tsked* and waved his hand in dismissal. "I gave you a gift. The gift of immortality, with me. My blood will start to change you, and, after you are converted, you will be mine…forever."

Christina's limbs felt heavy. She could barely move as the virus from Michael's blood started to take effect. Warmth crept throughout her body. It slowly increased in intensity, until within minutes she felt as if she roasted in an oven on the broil setting. Her skin burned, and her muscles felt like they were being torn apart. A fiery pain swept over her.

"Help me!" She lifted her hand toward Michael.

He looked down his nose at her and gave a dismissive shrug of his shoulders. "The conversion has begun. You'll live. I have to go get the playroom ready for us."

With apparently no thought for anything but his own pleasure, he left her to suffer through the conversion alone.

****

The small caravan of SUVs tore through the streets of Savannah, making its way to the outskirts. The warriors neared the cemetery and slowed their speed, not wanting to miss the dirt drive Christina mentioned. The inches turned into feet, feet into yards, and one mile became two as they snaked the vehicles down the mostly abandoned road.

Marcus hissed an exasperated sigh. "I think we've gone too far, Vlad. Let's turn around and go back."

Vlad made a U-turn, taking the SUV over the grassy median like a bucking bronco and headed back in the direction from which they had just come.

Marcus strained his eyes. He did not want to miss the turn-off again. As the cemetery came into view, Marcus noticed a small place along the tree line that looked about four and a half feet high by five feet wide. "There!" He pointed. "That might be it."

Vlad turned the SUV into the opening. Branches scraped the sides and top of the large vehicle while they drove down the overgrown dirt path. It reminded Marcus of going into a bear's cave, and he would be more than happy to tear a bear named Michael apart when they arrived.

The path seemed to go on forever as they made their way slowly along. It wound its way through the trees and brush, no end in sight. The SUV pitched as it hit rocks and divots in the dirt path. The two vehicles trekked through the dense woods, detritus spitting from their tires.

Marcus tried again to reach out to Christina using their mindlink. Burning, searing pain swamped him and forced him to grip the dashboard of the SUV for support. His fingers bit into the hard plastic, leaving indentations.

Vlad glanced over. "What's wrong?"

"It's Christina. She's going through the conversion." Marcus felt the blood drain from his face as bile rose from his stomach.

Vlad hit the brakes, coming to a stop in front of a compound just in time for Marcus to jump out of the car. He doubled over, rested his hands on his knees, and gagged. As the remnants from his last meal made a second showing, Demetri's SUV pulled up behind him.

Demetri and his two companions exited their vehicle quickly.

"What's wrong with Marcus?" he asked Vlad.

"It's Christina. She's going through the conversion."

Nicholai advanced toward Marcus with long purposeful steps, a look of concern on his face.

"*Chyort voz'mi!* He must be feeling it through their mindlink." Nikko placed a comforting hand on Marcus' shoulder. "That is something no one should have to go through twice."

He moved his hand in the middle of Marcus' back when the Alpha began to dry heave. "Breathe through it, my friend. You should close your mind to her while she goes through this. You will need a clear mind to take on Michael."

Marcus shook his head back and forth, straightened to his full height and wiped his mouth with the back of his hand. "I can't let her suffer alone. I have to be there to see her through this."

There might be one blessing in all this. Going through the conversion might have broken down the mental barrier keeping them from using their mindlink. He decided to test his theory.

Hold on, Christina. We're here. I'm coming to help you. Hold on, baby.

Marcus. Help me. Please! I need you!

I know, cara. *It will get better, I promise. Just a little while longer.*

I don't think I can stand it. Her exhaustion crossed their link; the brief moments of relief between the waves of pain were not nearly enough to allow for any recovery.

You are the strongest woman I know. The bravest woman I know. You can do this. I know you can.

Marcus felt a wave of pain start to overwhelm Christina as he walked to the back of Vlad's SUV. He managed to open the tailgate and remove a sheathed sword from the arsenal he and Vlad had placed there before leaving his mansion. The scabbard was beautifully carved from the toughest mahogany, wrapped in leather that formed X's, and finished with gold patina.

Marcus strapped the titanium-coated sword on his back as his friends loaded their own personal arsenals. Each had a preference for a particular type of weapon, and since Marcus had loaded most of his extensive collection into the back of Vlad's SUV, everyone found what they wanted. Demetri slipped his shoulders into a leather holster and sheathed a dagger on each side. Tatiana looked from the holster to his eyes and raised her eyebrows.

"Not carrying guns, Romanoff?"

"No, I don't need guns. I prefer daggers. They don't make any noise," he explained.

She grabbed two forty-fives, shoving one into the waistband of her leather pants and cocking the other before palming it.

Marcus' knees went weak when another wave of pain from Christina hit him hard. His hand snapped out and grabbed the side of the SUV to steady himself.

Breathe through it, Christina. It will be over soon.

Steeling himself against the pain, he turned to his fellow warriors, met their eyes with a determined stare and said, "Let's go get that bastard!"

Chapter 29

Christina lay curled in a fetal position. Every cell in her body felt like it was being drained of its moisture from the heat consuming her. When the virus caused her hormone levels to soar, her synapses all fired at once. Adrenaline and serotonin blanketed her body. Everything, right down to her kidneys and toes, hurt. Her muscles burned as if a blowtorch seared all of them at once with its white-hot flame. Her limbs contorted from the pain, sending her body spasming off the bed onto the concrete floor below. With a loud thud, the back of her head slammed into the hard floor when she arched from another spasm of pain.

She actually felt her bones grow denser to support her thickening muscles. It seemed like every bone in her body broke at the same time to accommodate the need for growth. She wept so hard, tears no longer fell, and her dry sobs added to the jerking of her body.

Her heart nearly beat out of her chest as it enlarged, pounding hard against her sternum. Her lungs grew at the same time, making it difficult to breathe as the two organs pushed against one another, fighting for room within her tiny rib cage. As if an elephant sat on her chest, Christina struggled to get the oxygen her growing muscles so desperately needed. She believed she'd die, gasping for air until, at last, her stomach shrank, allowing her heart and lungs room within her chest cavity. Finally able to take a breath, she gulped the sweet air that brought her a moment of comfort before the next spasm hit.

Her body curled in on itself, pulling her into a tight ball. Bile rose as her stomach pushed out its contents, no longer having room for the meal she'd eaten earlier. Wave after wave of pain continued to beat at her, twisting and contorting her body, the concrete floor rough against her overly sensitive skin. She could take no more and wished the pain away. She wished for respite.

For death.

****

Marcus led the group down the side of the compound, their line pressed firmly against the wall. The building contained no windows, so they walked upright, not worrying about being seen. They trod lightly with their backs to the rough cinderblock. A scent drifted to him on the wind, and Marcus' nostrils flared.

Michael!

The mated warrior held up a silent fist, indicating the group needed to stop and hold their positions. Marcus crouched down, easing forward like a mountain lion stalking its prey. He peered around the corner and watched Michael leave a small shack, locking the door behind him.

"I'd better go check on Christina's progress," he muttered just loud enough for Marcus' sensitive hearing to catch. The Alpha watched Michael wipe blood from his hands and make his way into the larger of the two buildings.

Marcus rejoined the others and in a hushed voice explained, "There is a small building in back. I just saw Michael leave and lock the door, wiping blood off his hands."

"Do you believe Christina is being held in there?" whispered Vlad.

"No, he said he was going to check on her and went into the main building. I think we need to split up."

Demetri nodded. "Vlad, Nicholai, you two go into the shack and see what you can find," the warrior said, taking charge. "Marcus, Tatiana, and I will take the main building."

The group nodded in agreement as a cool wind whipped over them, bringing the smells of the marsh with it. Death and decay surrounded them like a bad omen of things to come.

****

Vlad and Nicholai moved first. In perfect synchronicity that came from decades of fighting together, they made their way toward the shack. When they reached the front of the building, Nicholai felt it first, the ground made a subtle shift under his feet. Vladimir's eyes met those of his fellow Alpha when the realization registered on his face.

In the time it took for the two of them to look down, the ground gave way, sending them plunging down a metal tunnel. They clawed at the tunnel walls looking for purchase, but the smooth surface provided none. They slid quickly, Nicholai in the lead, until at last they went through a metal door that swung shut behind them.

The tingling under his skin told Nicholai exactly

what type of cage held them. Not much could hold a vampire, but titanium could. The metal, because of its special properties, would not allow atoms to pass through, could keep them from dematerializing. In fact, the vampires were so sensitive to the metal that it would burn their skin if they touched it. And of course, the cube they had dropped into was made from titanium, a perfect trap.

Nicholai glanced around for a way out and discovered they were sealed up tight. The hinged door through which they fell appeared to be the only opening.

"Where are we?" Nicholai examined the pitch-dark cage with his preternatural vision.

"It would appear we are in a titanium square." Vladimir turned, looking at their jail. With no seams, other than those around the trap door they fell through, it appeared to be one solid box.

"Nicholai, I think our only hope is getting out the way we came in."

"I agree, get on my shoulders. I'll lift you up."

Vlad balanced his feet on Nicholai's shoulders, and Nicholai's hands clasped his friend's calves. When the Siberian warrior pushed on the opening, Nicholai's nose instantly registered the smell of burnt flesh from the titanium touching his hands. It didn't move. Apparently this was a one way roaches-check-in-but-they-don't-check-out kind of door.

"It won't budge," Vladimir grunted. He shifted his weight, bearing down on Nicholai's left shoulder.

Nicholai adjusted his stance to keep them balanced. "How bad did you get burned?"

"It's nothing," said Vlad as he tore the sleeves

from his shirt and tried again, this time putting the cloth between his flesh and the titanium. He pushed several times, but even his thick muscles could not budge the door. His feet pushed from Nicholai's shoulders, and he landed on the balls of his feet.

Vlad examined his hands. "We're trapped."

Nicholai's gaze dropped to his friend's hands. "You're hurt."

"It will heal, but there is no doubt this place is made of titanium."

"Vlad?...Nicholai?" a deep baritone voice bellowed from above.

"We're down here, cousin."

"Are you okay?" Tatiana's voice called down. Nicholai could see the tiniest amount of light pushing through the cracks where the trap door met the rest of the enclosure, as if a flashlight shone down the shaft.

Like a caged tiger, Vladimir paced the metal container. "Yes, but this box is made of titanium. We can't dematerialize out of here."

"We'll need a rope," Tatiana called down. "If Demetri can lower me down, I'll open the door and then we can pull you and Vlad out."

"Not a bad idea," agreed Demetri. "There might be some rope in the SUV. I'll go check. Hold on. We'll be right back."

Nicholai thought he heard Tatiana mumble "Where's Marcus?" as her voice trailed off.

Chapter 30

Marcus watched Demetri and Tatiana go to examine the hole through which the Alphas had dropped. The sound of a heavy door sliding drew his attention. He quickly glanced around the corner of the building and saw a door closing. Using his preternatural speed, he caught the door with two fingers before it closed.

He carefully pulled the heavy door wide and sent a silent prayer up to the heavens that the hinges didn't squeak, though why they didn't for such a heavy door was anyone's guess. The Alpha prowled on silent feet, making his way down the long hall, his way lit by the harsh fluorescent lights that dangled from the ceiling. Marcus spied Michael walking away from him at the other end of the hall, oblivious to the danger stalking behind him.

Marcus saw red. Anger infused every cell, flooding his mind with rage. His teeth gnashed together, jaw clenched with his hatred for the male. Michael had not only kidnapped Christina, but treated her and Kat harshly, bringing both women great pain. He swore a silent vow of vengeance.

The sound of a soft click behind him signaled the door sliding closed. It pushed a waft of air down the hall and carried Marcus' scent to Michael. The Alpha flinched at the rookie mistake. He knew better. He couldn't count the number of times he'd purposely kept upwind of his prey to avoid detection. But he'd allowed his heartmate and his determination to make her captor pay, to distract him.

Her pain was his own. Her emotions flooded his mind, keeping him unfocused and edgy. Coupled with his unmitigated desire to excoriate Michael's flesh, they filled in his mind, pushing his training out. He'd made some stupid mistakes—mistakes that could get him killed.

Michael stiffened his shoulders slightly, but the vampire kept walking and ducked into a door on his left. Marcus unsheathed his sword, sure Michael had detected his presence. As Marcus approached the door through which Michael disappeared, the door flew open. Marcus leapt backwards to avoid being hit.

Michael emerged with a samurai sword clutched tightly in both hands. The lights from above reflected in the blade. Marcus barely had time to register the glint on the steel before Michael swung the first blow, sending Marcus crashing back against the wall.

****

Christina slowly straightened her arms as the latest pain receded. The bursts were shorter and less intense now. The waves of searing pain gave her enough respite between them to realize the conversion must be ending. A clash of steel, of two enemies locked in mortal combat, grabbed her attention, and she swung her head toward the noise.

Her eyes locked on Marcus. A mountain of rippling muscle, he battled Michael with a fierce grace. The warriors grunted with their efforts as the opponents moved back and forth in front of the chamber doorway. Christina heard a distinct whistling sound as one of the swords crashed into the doorframe, sending wood splintering to the floor.

This was a two-handed sword fight. No points for finesse. Brute strength. Males growling. Flexing muscles that wielded the weapons with the perfection achieved by centuries of training.

Marcus backed through the door, and Michael advanced with his sword by his head ready to deliver a finishing blow. Michael swung, putting his full strength behind the blow. Marcus blocked the swing, the shock vibrating down Michael's body.

The combat became a flurry of blurred movement and clash of metal meeting metal. Christina's pulse increased when anxiety mixed with fear. She no longer gave her pain a thought, her sole concentration on Marcus and his battle. He must win. Must survive.

Marcus rounded with a swipe of his sword that left a red line across Michael's stomach. The red stain spread across his shirt, but the wound was not fatal. Michael staggered back into the wall, one arm holding his stomach. Marcus attacked, blade raised above his head, but the warrior moved a moment too late.

The evil vampire sprang into a somersault and landed free from the path of his adversary's sword. He sprang up into a fighting stance.

Christina lay motionless on the floor while she watched the vampires fight their way across the room, exchanging blows. The conversion exhausted her body, making her limbs heavy as stone. Above Christina their blades clashed in a sweeping blow toward the floor. Survival instinct rolled her out of the way when the swords swung in a scything arc. Christina smacked into the corner of the bed, hitting the tender part of her elbow on the metal frame. She frantically crawled away, sheer will enabling her leaden body to move in search of safety.

Marcus wheeled around, bringing the whole weight of his motion into the stroke. Michael countered by arching back out of reach. The sword narrowly missed his neck. Michael turned and drove back in with a blow of his own. The tip of his blade sliced through the tendons of Marcus' right arm, causing it to hang limply from his body. As if renewed by the small victory, Michael thundered a rain of blows. Christina's stomach knotted with concern, and she suppressed a scream, for her love didn't need the distraction.

Marcus staggered back under the onslaught, deflecting as best he could with his one-handed grip until Michael brought his sword down on Marcus' good wrist. The pained look on Marcus' face suggested the agony of the blow arced to his brain, vibrating along every nerve.

The sword dropped to the floor as Marcus fell to his knees with a violent curse. Michael circled Marcus, taunting the Alpha. A smug smile of triumph lit his eyes.

Chapter 31

Michael twirled his sword spitefully, playing with his prey. Obviously believing victory was his to take, he seemed in no hurry to make the killing blow, apparently unaware of the warrior lying in wait at the door.

Demetri crouched down, dagger in hand, waiting for the moment to strike. "Stay back," Demetri hissed at Tatiana as she came running up. "I've got this."

Tatiana gave him a look of contempt when she approached the doorway, her stealthy movements cat-like.

"Where are Vlad and Nicholai?" he hissed to the female.

"There are women in the shack," the VES agent informed him. "Nicholai and Vlad stayed behind to help them."

"You should have stayed with the women. An Alpha should have come to back me up."

She rolled her eyes. "Shut up and watch for an opening."

Tatiana drew her gun from its holster, sliding the safety off before cradling it between her delicate hands.

Demetri growled a low rumble of disapproval. He did not need a female backing him up. She'd probably get him killed.

His eyes returned to the room to discover that the opportunity Demetri waited for presented itself at last. With Marcus on his knees, Demetri finally had a clear shot at Michael.

"Closer," the female beside him muttered.

Demetri didn't spare her a glance or a moment's thought, totally focused on his target. He reared his dagger back and let it fly, aimed at Michael's heart. A wisp of black smoke drew his gaze, and he turned to discover Tatiana gone. She'd dematerialized.

As Demetri's dagger flew silently toward its mark, Tatiana materialized in front of Michael, gun in hand.

The danger of the moment gave a still calm that seemed to slow time itself. Demetri watched in horror. Tatiana raised her weapon toward Michael, unaware of the dagger careening toward her back. Her breath failed when it struck the base of her neck. She arched forward and dropped face first to the floor, the knife buried to the hilt in her spine by the force of his throw.

Demetri rushed to her and pulled the dagger from her flesh. A fraction higher and it would have pierced her skull. Blood poured from the wound and welled around the fingers he used to attempt to stay the bleeding. She would recover, but the dagger had been made of titanium. Healing would be slow. He faced an impossible choice, get the female to safety or attempt to save his fallen comrade.

Demetri glanced up at Michael, who stood motionless, watching the scene before him in disbelief. The shocked look on the vampire's face indicated he'd not realized other warriors might be in the building. It wasn't much, but Michael's stunned surprise might be used to Marcus' advantage. Demetri tossed Tatiana's gun to the Alpha and hoped that with the pause in the action, Marcus might have healed just enough to use it.

With the life of a natural-born female at stake, Demetri knew duty to the vampire race dictated he must save Tatiana. The burly Alpha pulled the agent's body toward the door, putting space between them and the rogue vampire.

Demetri gathered her in his lap and scored his wrist with his fangs. "Drink, Tatiana, my blood is ancient. It will speed your healing."

****

Without hesitation, Tatiana gratefully took what he offered. Her nails dug into his arm as she held his wrist to her lips and gulped down the life-giving elixir. His blood fed her cells, and her wound began to knit close. It strengthened her, warmed her, sent a rush through her body that made her feel…wanton?

Mine! The thought brushed her mind as Michael bared his fangs and hissed.

He advanced on the couple with slow, purposeful strides, taking his time as if to savor his moment of victory. His sword poised to take Demetri's head. His eyes gleamed with hatred as he stalked toward the pair.

To seal the small wounds her fangs made, Tatiana flicked her tongue against Demetri's skin. Her hand flew to her thigh holster but found the damned thing empty. After quick search, her gaze located the gun near Marcus.

Demetri peered up. Obviously reading the intent in Michael's advance, he reached in his holster for the other dagger. As he pulled the blade from its sheath, Tatiana noticed something glistening in front of Michael's heart. It created a bull's-eye for the knife.

She blinked, and it disappeared as fast as it had appeared.

Michael dropped to his knees, then fell forward. His face hit the floor with a smack. A pool of red formed under his body. Tatiana's gaze rose from Michael's body to Christina. The newly converted vamp stood swaying, holding Marcus' sword in both hands as the red dripped from the blade.

Now there's an example of Woman Power. A smile came to Tatiana's lips.

****

Marcus watched the air huff from Christina's lungs from her effort. The sword she held crashed to the concrete floor with a loud clang. Apparently too weak from the conversion to support her any longer, her legs folded beneath her. She crawled through a stream of blood to Marcus, who sat on the floor, his back braced against the wall.

"Marcus," she cried, her eyes wide with panic as she examined his wounds.

"It will be okay. The cuts are deep, but they will heal. All I need is a little rest and some blood."

Christina swept her red mane to one side. "Drink."

"No!" Marcus bit out a little stronger than he would have liked, causing Christina to wince. "I can feel your hunger. It's almost as strong as your need for sleep. I can't take from you. You need to sleep, rest, and, when you awake, you'll need to feed."

"No, I'm fine," Christina lied, as she looked at him from beneath hooded eyes. "You need blood more than I do. You must drink from me."

A weak smile played on the corners of his mouth. His mate had just endured the conversion and then taken the life of Michael to save them, yet her concern for him outweighed her concern for herself. Her exhaustion beat at him. She desperately needed to rest and feed, yet she thought only of him and his injuries.

And he knew just how she felt. The pain from his injuries throbbed with each beat of his heart. He bled profusely, his strength draining with every drop of his blood. He, too, needed to rest and feed. Marcus relaxed his head against the wall and sighed deeply.

"I'm too weak to argue, Christina. You must rest now." Marcus gave his command a mental push, expending his much-needed energy to provide what his mate needed. Christina's health and safety came before all else, and Marcus would make sure she got what her body required.

She laid her head in his lap, exhaustion taking her as her heavy lids slowly closed. Her last thoughts went to the women, who like herself, had been tortured by Michael.

"The women...playroom..." was all she managed to say before she succumbed to the overwhelming need her body had for rest.

"Vlad and Nicholai are on it," Demetri quietly assured from the doorway.

Marcus' eyes never strayed from his mate. He longed to smooth her rumpled hair, but his arm and hand still hung uselessly to the floor. "We know, sweetheart," he reassured her, not sure if his words of comfort would reach her in the dream state. "Vladimir and Nikko have them."

Chapter 32

"Can you sit up?" Demetri asked Tatiana as she leaned against him.

"I think so."

Demetri helped her into a seated position. When she swayed slightly, she locked her elbow and rested her hand on the floor to brace herself. Demetri's powerful blood healed her wound quickly and renewed her strength. If only it hadn't also made her feel strange.

Her sexuality had been brought to life as she fed, in a way that had never happened before. Infused with warmth, her body craved the touch of the one who fed her—a most curious reaction. But knowing this was not the time to examine those feelings, the female warrior ruthlessly pushed them to the back of her mind, saving them until a future time.

Demetri crossed to Marcus and Christina. When he knelt next to the couple, his pants absorbed Marcus' blood from the floor. "How are you, comrade?"

"I'll be fine. It's Christina I'm worried about."

"She'll be fine, once she feeds." Demetri bowed his head in a formal, courtly gesture. "With your permission, I offer your heartmate my blood."

Marcus glanced down at the proffered arm.

"I thank you for your offer, but you can't let her feed from you, my friend." The younger Alpha had obviously noticed the fading bite mark on Demetri's wrist. "You have already given this night."

"I'll be fine."

Marcus brushed off the offer with a shake of his head. "No, I can't accept, but thank you. When we get back to the plantation, we'll see that she gets the blood she needs." Marcus winced in pain when he attempted to shift his arm. "Tell me about the women in the shack."

"Nicholai and Vlad stayed with them. They should have gotten the women to safety by now. Tatiana and I will go out and send the males back in here to get you and your female." He turned his attention to Tatiana. "Tatiana, can you walk?"

She rose slowly, carefully testing her body. "I can. I'm stiff and sore, but no worse for wear. Let's go."

Demetri held onto her arm as they left the compound, sending something akin to electric current coursing through her body.

Tatiana jerked her arm from his grasp. "I'm fine. I don't need any help."

Having this large male so close made her feel…uncomfortable. She considered herself a strong, independent female. She didn't need the help of any man, certainly didn't want *his* help, but something seemed to pull her to him. She needed some space, whether from the desire to be autonomous or the need to put some distance between her and the attraction she felt, she couldn't be sure. She couldn't wait to clean this mess up, so she could put the Alphas and Demetri in her rearview mirror.

****

As the couple made their way around the building,

approaching the vehicles, Vlad advanced toward them. "The women are in the car," he said and gestured toward one of the black SUVs.

Nicholai pinned Demetri with his stare. "They don't look good, cousin. I'm not sure they will make it."

"Show me," Demetri commanded, reaching for Nicholai's mind, using the mindlink they had established centuries ago.

The Alpha easily picked the images from his cousin's photographic memory. He clearly saw the women chained to the wall, the instruments used for torture sitting on the trays. The dead woman lying on the metal table. The scene played out before him as clearly as if he had been in the disgusting room himself.

Tatiana pushed past the males and climbed into the SUV, leaving the back door open. He tracked the way her leathers enveloped her heart-shaped ass when she bent at the waist to crawl inside. She was a sight to behold, that female. With her black hair and cat-like eyes, she looked as deadly as a panther.

Too bad she hadn't been deadly. Instead, she had been injured because she'd gotten in the way of his blade. It just confirmed what he had always believed; females did not belong in combat.

After a few minutes, she exited the vehicle with a grim look on her face. The female had paled considerably, her olive complexion now white. Was her ghostly parlor more a result of the physical expenditure or the emotional distress at what she found in the back of the car?

"They have been terribly abused." Tatiana answered his unspoken question. "They require medical and psychiatric care. We need to get them to a hospital."

Vlad crossed his thick arms across his chest. "They can't go to a hospital. The doctors will ask questions. And what will the women say? 'We were kidnapped and tortured by an evil vampire who drained us and kept us around for his sick pleasure'?"

The female rounded on Vlad with her seething temper and bit out between clenched teeth, "You're suggesting we let them die so we can keep our existence a secret. They haven't been through enough at the hands of one of our kind; they must die for us, too?"

Demetri stepped between the two, facing the incensed female. "There may be a way for them to be able to go to the hospital. I could wipe their memories."

Nicholai shook his head. "Cousin, you know if a memory is too traumatic, it can't be erased. Besides, don't you think the doctors would be suspicious if three women show up seriously injured, and none of them can remember what happened?"

"I'm not talking about a complete memory erase. I could *change* their memories, make it so they think a human kidnapped them. I can remove only the memories associated with vampires, like I did in Vegas."

"You can do that?" Tatiana asked incredulously. "I've never heard of a vampire being able to do that."

The thickly muscled Alpha nodded. "Yes, I can do that. It is just one of my many talents."

"I can only imagine your talents," Tatiana muttered.

Was that an attempt to flirt? No, Demetri quickly decided, looking at the angry expression on her face.

Definitely not flirting. He shook away the thought so he could concentrate on what his cousin said.

After more discussion between the members of the group, they decided Tatiana and Demetri would take the women to the hospital. Nicholai came up with a plausible story to tell the doctors about how he and Tatiana were out hiking and came across the women in a cabin in the woods.

With the cover story decided, Demetri climbed into the SUV. One by one, he touched each woman on her forehead and began the arduous task of easing their memories. He sent a wave of comfort and peace to surround each mind, then changed the memories of Michael so that all vampiric characteristics were gone.

The difficult task took a physical toll on Demetri, especially since Tatiana had fed from him just a short while ago. When it was done, he slumped into the driver's seat and laid his head on the steering wheel. Exhaustion weighed heavily upon him but, determined to see the situation through to the end, he refused to give in to his weariness.

Tatiana slid into the passenger seat beside him and placed her hand gently on his forearm. "Thank you. You have done much this evening, and I can see it has taken a lot out of you."

Demetri sat up and started the engine. "I'm fine. You should check on the females."

"They have names." Tatiana looked back over her shoulder.

"I know, I touched their minds. I know more than just their names."

Yeah, he knew a lot more. He'd lived their memories, the sound, the feel of every torturous act.

He'd known it would be like that, but he'd done it anyway, because it had to be done.

"I know." Tatiana's voice softened. "I don't know how you tolerated reliving their horrors."

Demetri shrugged and put the vehicle in gear. He eased the SUV down the dirt drive.

The female glanced over her shoulder again as they bumped along. "What is your name?" she asked the thin woman with short brown hair in the back seat.

"M-my name is Catherine." The weary woman took a deep breath and let it out slowly. "I think they said their names are Anne and Tammy."

Demetri nodded his head in agreement from the front seat, confirming to Tatiana he knew their names. He also knew Anne and Tammy would not reply. Once Demetri had eased their memories, exhaustion overtook them. They both rested, their heads leaning on the back of the bench seat. In contrast, Catherine sat very still, staring out the window while they drove.

Tatiana remained turned around in her seat, watching over the women, and Demetri mentally rehearsed the cover story he would tell the doctors. They made the trip in silence, all lost in their own thoughts. And really, what could they say?

****

After they dropped the women off at the hospital, Tatiana and Demetri drove to Marcus' mansion. Since leaving the hospital, Demetri had been stewing about injuring Tatiana. Guilt rode him hard about the incident, about how his blade injured the female now sitting next to him. He hadn't wanted her there in the first place, to prevent just such an accident. Only sheer luck made her injury easily repairable. It made his stomach turn to think he might have killed her.

The vibration of the cell in his pocket pulled him from his reflection. He took it out, looking down at the caller identification before punching the "talk" button.

"Hello, cousin. What's going on?"

An explosion sounded in the background.

Nicholai's voice sounded strained. "We got Marcus and Christina out and torched the place. It just went up in a blaze of gory, as they say."

"I believe the correct word is *glory*, cousin." Demetri chuckled. After all these centuries, some English vernaculars continued to give his cousin trouble.

His mood turned serious once more as his thought turned to the bastard that had caused all this trouble. "And Michael's body?"

"We burned it and left the bones outside for the sun. Once it rises, his ashes will scatter in the wind. How did everything go at the hospital?"

Demetri gave a heavy sigh. "It took a little mental persuasion with the doctor and nurses, but eventually they believed the story about us finding the women in the woods. Obviously, they called the police."

"You allowed them to do that?"

"Yes, in order to authenticate the validity of the kidnapping story. It is standard procedure for the police to be notified by hospital personnel."

"Oh. Of course. What happened after they arrived?"

"Catherine gave the police a detailed description of Michael. In fact, the police sketch artist did a fair representation. Obviously, Michael will never be found." Demetri palmed the steering wheel and turned the SUV. "How are Marcus and Christina?"

Nicholai hesitated. In a whisper he replied, "Marcus is in pain, but his wounds are not fatal. Christina does not look good. She needs to feed, soon."

Demetri heard the concern in his cousin's voice. "Get them to the plantation as quickly as possible. Tatiana and I are on our way there now."

Chapter 33

Stephan followed as Marcus and Christina were helped to their bedroom suite. With his arm draped around Nicholai's shoulders for support, Marcus watched Vlad carefully lay Christina on the bed. Supported by Nicholai's arm around his waist, Marcus limped around the bed and lay down beside her. Each movement sent a streak of pain through him, making perspiration dot his brow from the effort.

"What happened?" the Alpha leader demanded of Nicholai, nodding in the direction of the bandages on Marcus' arm and wrist.

Nicholai informed Stephan of the night's events. Stephan paled, then sat on the edge of the bed by Marcus.

Marcus had been drifting in and out of consciousness during the ride home, but his concern for his mate forced him to remain in the moment. "I must help Christina," he stated, trying to rise. Pain raced throughout his body and the room tilted on its axis.

Stephan splayed a staying hand on Marcus' chest. "She will be fine. You are home and safe. I will see to it that no harm comes to you or your heartmate."

"She killed Michael, you know," Nicholai shared.

Stephan's head snapped in Nikko's direction. "But Michael converted her."

Marcus winced. He hated thinking about his heartmate having blood ties to anyone other than him. A converted vampire experienced a special tie to one's sire. If Stephan were to die he'd know it immediately. It had been described to him like something akin to having a part of you ripped from your body, the pain both physical and psychological.

"Since she had just completed the conversion, is it possible that their bond wouldn't have been deeply established?" Marcus asked hopefully.

Stephan shrugged. "Our bond certainly grew over the years. I guess it might be possible that she might not have felt much discomfort since she killed him right after he converted her."

"Not to mention, when she killed him, she had just experienced the pain of the conversion. I'm sure the pain of her sire dying was nothing compared to that," Nicholai reassured Marcus.

"Good point." Marcus gave a small, satisfied smile.

After a glance at his mate to assure himself she still slept soundly, Marcus watched Stephan wearily scrub a hand over the grim expression on his face. It reminded him of how his sire looked with Katrina's limp body in his arms.

Marcus settled back onto the mattress. "How is Kat?"

"Alex and I both had to give her blood, she'd lost so much. Michael almost drained her. She lay near death. If Christina hadn't come out of the panic room when she did, I would have lost Katrina. I will forever be grateful to your heartmate for her sacrifice for Kat...and me." Stephan glanced over to Christina. "She needs to feed. With your permission, I offer my blood to your heartmate. It is the least I can do, since she saved both you and Kat. And you need to feed as well, Marcus."

Marcus laid his bandaged hand on his sire's forearm to forestall his attempt to rise. "No, I can't let you do that. You, Alex, and Demetri all gave blood tonight. I won't let any of you give to us."

"There is some bagged blood in the fridge, no?" Vlad said.

"Feeding directly from the vein would be better," Stephan responded. "You need the extra strength it would provide."

Nicholai walked to the bed, next to Stephan. "You and your heartmate both need blood. Vlad and I have not yet given tonight. I offer my blood to you."

"And with your permission, I will gladly give my blood to your heartmate," Vlad offered in his dark voice, his thick Siberian accent rolling his *r*'s.

Marcus thought for a moment about Nicholai's offer and found he had no choice but to accept. He needed blood to heal so he could take care of his mate. His eyes met Nicholai's dark gaze. After a slight nod, Nicholai slid the sleeve of his black shirt up his arm and extended his wrist.

Marcus brought the wrist to his mouth, looked up to meet his friend's eyes in thanks, then bit deeply into the flesh. The blood rushed past his lips, down his throat. The powerful liquid fed his cells, giving them new life. With each drink, his strength returned a little more. When he drank enough to sustain him through the night, he sealed the puncture wounds and released the proffered arm.

"Thank you, Nicholai. Your generosity will not be

forgotten."

Nicholai bowed his head. "I was happy to be of help to a warrior such as yourself. Now we must see to Christina."

A flare of jealousy spiked within Marcus at the thought of another taking care of his mate. A low growl of warning escaped his chest.

Chapter 34

Nicholai lowered his sleeve back down over his forearm, then moved from Marcus' bed. His eyes met Vladimir's, and the two warriors exchanged a knowing look.

"Marcus," Vlad said quietly, "you need to awaken Christina so she can drink."

Marcus breathed out a heavy sigh as his mind balked at the suggestion. Completely depleted by the conversion, her body needed time to recover. But it also required blood, so reluctantly he pushed into her mind and gave his heartmate the mental command to awaken, choosing to remain there to monitor her thoughts.

Christina's eyes fluttered. While she fought the sleepy fog, her mind churned through the tumultuous memories of Michael. The kidnapping. The pain. The conversion.

In her hazy, confused state, she didn't know where she lay and let out a blood-curdling scream. Her fingers curled around the sheet, pulling the satin up to her throat, not realizing she was now safe.

Marcus turned to face her, easily reading her fear. "Shhhh. It's okay, *cara*." He took Christina's hand gently in his and rubbed the pad of his thumb across the inside of her wrist. The intimate touch quieted her scream. "You're safe. Michael's gone."

Her eyes squinted in concentration at her surroundings, before she turned silently toward him. The fear disappeared from her eyes, and he exhaled a relieved sigh.

His mate truly amazed him. Her courage and complete trust in him humbled him.

"That's my girl," he soothed as he tucked her hair behind her ear. "You need to feed, sweetheart. You are weak from the conversion."

Christina nodded without hesitation. Her stomach burned like fire, and Marcus knew feeding would quench the terrible feeling. She allowed him to settle her back onto the pillows, so she lay on her back.

Christina watched Vlad step forward. He rolled his shirtsleeve up to his elbow, and her eyes widened with concern. "Who will feed me?" Her voice quivered.

Stephan stood and answered, "Vladimir has offered. His blood is strong and will give you the nourishment you need."

"No!" Christina's voice raised an octave. "I don't want to feed from anyone but Marcus!"

Nicholai moved around the bed, placing a restraining hand on Vladimir's bare forearm. He lowered his voice, putting a soft warmth behind it as he spoke to Marcus' heartmate. "Christina, please, you need to feed. I know you might prefer Marcus, but Vlad is the only one of us who has not yet given to another. The rest of us are unable to supply you. Allow Vladimir the honor of providing for you."

Christina shook her head adamantly from side to side. Drawing her lips into a tight line, she reminded Marcus of a child refusing to take her medicine. The sight tugged at his heart, made him take her in his bandaged arms to cocoon her in the soothing warmth of his body.

Stephan looked down at the couple as they cuddled together on the bed. *I owe Christina much after what she has done for Kat and you this night, and seeing she is well fed is the least I can do. Let me try talking to her, Marcus.*

Good luck, Marcus sent back over their mindlink. *I can sense she feels strongly about who she will feed from.*

And really, Marcus couldn't blame her. In fact, he wasn't entirely sure how he felt about another sharing blood with her.

"Christina, please be reasonable," Stephan pleaded. "Marcus has been injured; he himself needed blood. He can't feed you. Vlad's blood will make you strong. Please take what he offers."

"No, I won't. I'll only drink from Marcus. If Marcus can't feed me tonight, then I'll wait until he is better."

"That could be a night or two. New converts should not wait that long to feed for the first time, and bagged blood will not be strong enough. You need to feed from the vein." Stephan turned his attention to Marcus.

This is ridiculous; if she won't feed willingly, let me put a compulsion behind the command. I could erase her memory afterward. It is for her own good.

Marcus sat up, taking Christina with him. *No, Stephan! She has been forced through enough tonight. I will not allow anyone to force her to drink.*

His sire obviously read the determination etched on his face and conceded defeat. *As you wish. Perhaps she will be more reasonable when she wakes tomorrow.*

Marcus reached deeper into Christina's mind finding fear, confusion…and of course her pain. She was starving, but her fear of anyone other than Marcus sharing his blood with her kept her from accepting what others offered. He knew she would only feed from him. And as a result, there was no reason for the Council members to remain. She wouldn't feed tonight, and their presence caused her discomfort.

"Please leave us," Marcus requested, wanting to calm his heartmate.

"As you wish." Stephan gave a weighted glance at the other two Council members.

The Alphas left one by one, each wishing him well before crossing the room. Silently the Alphas made their way to the door, as Marcus added, "Thank you for helping us this night."

Stephan closed the door behind them, shutting Marcus and Christina into the suite. Relieved to finally be alone with his mate, Marcus turned back to Christina. "We need to rest now. If you will not feed, I want you to sleep to take the hunger pangs away. May I help you sleep deeply?"

Christina snuggled into his side. "If you help me sleep, will it keep me from having nightmares?"

"Yes," was all Marcus could reply as emotion constricted his throat. His heart broke for her and the trauma she'd been put through. If he had been the one to convert her, he would have made sure Stephan attended the conversion to ease the pain with his unique ability to heal. She would have suffered but not nearly to the extent she had been forced to endure by Michael. She certainly would not have nightmares.

Christina's sigh brought him out of his rumination. "Then do it."

Needing no further invitation, Marcus sent her into a deep, dreamless sleep, then closed his eyes and let sleep come to take him away from the horrors of the evening.

****

Demetri walked through the doorway of the plantation. His awkward gait caught Nicholai's eyes.

"You hurt, cousin?" Nicholai's worry furrowed his brow.

"I'm fine. Don't concern yourself." Demetri leaned heavily against the door after he closed it.

"Where's Tatiana?" asked Stephan.

"She left," Demetri replied curtly. "I don't know where she went."

You sure you are all right, cousin?

I said I was fine, didn't I?

Yes, but you aren't standing straight. You are a little hunched over. Did something happen after you dropped off Tatiana?

I don't want to talk about it. I'll be fine.

But I can tell your groin is injured. Who did this to you?

No one. I don't want to discuss it.

Demetri's pain flowed across their mindlink, and Nicholai had a good idea who probably caused it. *Perhaps, if you do not want to share I could just look at your memories. I just want to be sure you do not need medical attention.*

The corner of Nicholai's mouth twitched at the horrified look that crossed Demetri's face when he accessed a memory of him telling Tatiana women didn't belong in combat. Nicholai wasn't shocked to discover she didn't take the news well.

I'm fine. Drop it! Demetri sent along the mindlink before shutting the private channel of communication down, keeping Nicholai from his mind with no way of accessing his memory.

Stephan moved toward the door, taking command, as was his way. "I think we should all feed then retire for the evening. It has been a long night, and we all need to rest.

"Marcus has a few bags of blood in the kitchen. We can drink that tonight to get by, but since we have all donated, we will need to drink from a vein to replenish our strength. Tomorrow we will hunt to replenish the blood lost tonight."

Alex padded down the stairs, his steps silent as he approached them. "Kat is doing well," the blond Alpha informed the group. "She took another bag and fell asleep."

"Thank you for staying with her while I saw to Marcus."

"Of course, Stephan. Anything I can do to help. You know that."

The leader put a hand on Alex's shoulder. "I know. But you have my thanks just the same."

Nicholai turned, taking in each member of the group with a steady sweep of his eyes. These were good men. Men you could count on to have your back. They were tight, a great team. Good friends that Nicholai felt honored to fight with.

"Did I hear you say Marcus has some blood in the kitchen?" Alexander asked. "I could use a fill up."

"Me, too," Demetri agreed, the timbre of his voice

a little higher than usual. He cleared his throat before continuing. "Lead the way, Stephan."

Chapter 35

During the next two nights, Marcus awakened Christina and asked her to feed from another. Each time the scene played out in the same way. She awoke screaming and pulled the sheets tightly to her chin, then refused to feed from anyone but Marcus. Even Kat and Tatiana offered to let her feed from them, thinking perhaps she might be scared to feed from a male, but she still refused.

Since Marcus had been healing and unable to feed her, Christina was sent back to sleep until the next time they tried. So it went for forty-eight hours, different vampires coming to their room to take turns giving Marcus their blood and offering to feed Christina. Christina awoke only long enough to refuse to feed.

Tonight it was Alexander who walked into the suite as Marcus came out of the bathroom, one towel wrapped around his waist while he used another to rub his brown hair dry.

"Hello, Marcus. I see you are up and moving tonight. Feeling better?"

"Yeah, I'm feeling great, thanks to you and the others. Look, I'm almost completely healed." Marcus stretched his arms and showed Alex the two fine, pink welts indicating where his cuts had been. "I'll be completely healed by daybreak."

"Do you need to feed?"

Having toweled most of the water from his hair, Marcus tossed the terry cloth on a chair. "No, I had some bagged blood earlier. That was enough. I'm feeling good."

"That's great, man. I'm glad to hear it. I guess I'll leave you then."

Alex headed for the door. His gaze fell on the petite redhead sleeping peacefully in their bed. The Alpha stilled. With a flick of his thumb, he gestured toward Christina.

"You gonna feed her tonight, Marcus?"

"I was planning on it."

Alex smiled. "Good luck. Call if you need any help."

"What's that supposed to mean?"

"Well, she was converted three days ago and hasn't fed since, right?"

"Right."

Alex let out a long whistle from between his teeth. "Don't you remember what it felt like when you came through the conversion? How the hunger for blood and your lust hit hard? As for me, I couldn't tell where one started and the other stopped. I've never felt either urge that intense since the first night."

Though it had been over two hundred and fifty years, Marcus still remembered those first sensations as a vampire. He'd awoken after the conversion with a burn in his belly and his shaft throbbing, the pain in both unbearable. Stephan had arranged for his first feeding to be with a female vampire who had satisfied both hungers for him.

"Imagine, Marcus, what it would be like if you'd

waited three days to satisfy those cravings. Man, she is going to be a whirlwind when you wake her. So again, good luck." Alexander gave him a knowing smile and a wag of his brows before he walked out the door, closing it discreetly behind him as he started to whistle.

Marcus rubbed his body dry while he contemplated what Alex said. Alex was right. Christina would wake very hungry and not just for blood. This would take a little planning on his part, and luckily he knew exactly what to do.

After taking the gown from her body, Marcus, in all his naked glory, joined his heartmate on their bed. He blanketed Christina's body with his own, bearing his weight on his forearms. He sent a gentle command into her mind for her to wake and smoothed her hair away from her face as her eyes fluttered open. He captured her lips in a searing kiss and thrust his tongue into her mouth, taking control quickly. Remaining a shadow in her mind, Marcus monitored the sensations consuming his mate's flushed body.

Desire burned through her, bringing Christina out of her torpor. Lust flowed in her veins with fiery fingers. Her arms folded around Marcus' back, fingers tracing the contours of his muscles. She softened beneath him, and her legs wrapped around his waist to cradle his hips against her feminine core. Christina ground against his groin in a sinuous slide that moistened his shaft.

"Easy," he whispered against her mouth.

Christina scoffed at the command. Easy? No way she wanted easy. She wanted hard, passionate, sex. Now. And Marcus would be more than happy to provide her with what she wanted, but first, she needed something other than his shaft.

"I want you to feed first. Come with me."

Marcus slowly lifted off her, testing her self-control. Lifting her in his arms, he carried her to the shower he'd already turned on.

The steam filled the bathroom, thick as soup. The water washed over her sensitive skin, causing goose bumps to pepper her flesh.

"It feels different," Christina whispered and rubbed her arms.

Marcus ran his hands down her arms. "Your skin is more sensitive now. Everything is more sensitive."

He slid one hand down her stomach to the juncture between her legs, cupping her sex in his palm. She moaned, opened for him, and took a deep breath to take the scent of him deep into her lungs. She thought he smelled wonderful. Fresh. Spicy. Masculine.

Images of the two of them in the throes of passion played in her mind for Marcus to see. His shaft jumped against his stomach in response, more than willing to help make those fantasies come true. Her nostrils flared as she registered the musk of his arousal. Her beautiful eyes darkened with hunger for him, and her fangs lengthened from her gums.

Her hand flew to her mouth at the strange sensation.

Marcus took her hand in his. "It's okay. That's natural. Your hunger brought down your fangs."

"I'm so...so..."

"I know, sweetheart. You are in need, and I can do no other but see you are well taken care of," Marcus assured her, lathering his hands with the soap.

Christina looked at him with voracious eyes. He

worked slowly, trying not to trigger her predatory instincts. His soapy hands glided over her skin and sent a burning heat to coil in her stomach. Dampness pooled low between her legs.

He turned his mate away from him and positioned her under the jets of water. Marcus' hands snaked around her waist, glided up her ribs to cup the weight of each breast. He kneaded the creamy mounds. Her nipples pebbled under the pads of his fingers as she arched her back and rested her head against his chest.

One large hand traveled down her body, blazing a fiery trail over her skin as it headed south. She leaned fully against him, the heavy weight of his erection pressed against her bottom, branding her with its heat. Smooth velvet over steel jumped as she ground against his hand when it cupped her sex. He worked two fingers into her folds, timing the thrusts of his digits with the movement of her hips so they touched the sensitive spot within her channel. A moan rewarded his efforts and a rush of cream coated his thick fingers.

"I can't stand it anymore, Marcus. I need you! Please!" Christina pleaded, her voice husky as she turned to face him.

Marcus swept her into his arms, handling her as if she weighed no more than a small child. After carrying Christina from the bath, he lay with her on their bed, not caring that they both remained wet.

"You need to feed, *cara*. Come here to me." Marcus brought her on top of him, her legs straddled his hips. "Let the instinct take you. Find the vein in my neck. Can you see it pulsing? Hear my heart calling to you?"

"Yes," she squeaked, staring at the base of his neck

where the blood pulsed in time with his heartbeat. She watched in fascination as it throbbed, calling to her with its siren song, begging her to take what her body so desperately needed to ease her pain. And Fates above, how he longed for her to fulfill that need.

"That's the vein you want. Bite it! Now!" Marcus' cock jerked in anticipation.

Christina leaned over, brought her lips to his neck. He felt her breath on his skin and moved his head to one side to accommodate her. He wanted this as much as she did, needed to provide her what she desired. He sucked in an anticipatory breath and held it, waiting for her strike.

She hesitated, unsure as she heard him inhale.

"Do it," he coaxed with a whisper.

Christina bit, deeper than needed, and drew a large gulp. Marcus shuddered. The erotic sensation of his heartmate sinking her fangs into his neck pushed the air from his lungs. A low moan rumbled against his throat while she succumbed to the sensuous sensation and began rocking her hips against his hardness.

As Marcus' blood nourished her cells, he felt her lust rise. The pain in her stomach eased, subsiding with each draw while conversely the ache in her core increased. His blood was powerful. She could feel it pour into her, through her, warming her from the inside out until she burned for him.

Without taking her fangs from his neck, Christina eased her hips up and slid her hand between their bodies. She took him in her hand, stroking from the base to the tip. Her grip tightened, urgency spurring her on. And wasn't that just the most amazing feeling in the world.

She felt achy, needy and only one thing would satisfy her. She slid his shaft inside of her, seating herself fully on this thickness.

Marcus moaned in ecstasy. He'd never tire of how she felt, all creamy heat and velvety slick folds. She rode him while she continued to take from his vein. Marcus allowed her to take the lead, set their pace. Tonight he would follow, giving her what she wanted. Letting her take him.

He pumped his hips, matching her pace. Their pace quickened as she geared up for the first explosion. Her orgasm hit hard. Christina threw back her head and screamed, "Marcus!"

An answering growl pushed from his throat, and her eyes snapped to his. Her hunger for him showed in the intensity of her dark emerald stare.

Christina planted her hands on his pectorals to brace her ride as she gyrated her hips against him in wanton abandonment. Blood ran down his neck from the puncture wounds she forgot to seal, tickling his flesh. The red streams drew her gaze, and she paused, stone still atop him.

Marcus' breath hitched when she bent down and licked the wound closed with her tongue, swirling around the small punctures. Her red mane cascaded around his head, concealing them from the world. He wrapped one arm around her back, drew her tightly against him, and flipped them over without separating from her.

She arched, lifting her breasts to his chest as he took control and set their pace with a gentle sway of his hips. He took one of the creamy swells with his hand, cupping the full weight into his palm. He drew the other one into his mouth, teasing the nipple into a hard peak with his tongue. His mouth switched back and forth between the two globes, driving her mad with the contrast between his warm, moist mouth and the cool, dry air.

As he suckled, she shifted her body beneath him, planting her heels in the mattress, and arched her hips to drive him deeper inside of her. With every breath, a small mewling sound escaped her throat, making Marcus wild. An erotic moan flowed over her lips that he matched as he released her breasts to look down into her flushed face.

"You're beautiful," he breathed, lowering his lips to take her mouth with a fierce, bruising kiss.

Their bodies came together in a quick pace. The sound of their skin slapping together filled the room, music to their ears. The steady rhythm increased tempo as he brought them to the crescendo. Their desire flowed between their mindlink, feeding, building, until it became a fierce storm. It spurred him on, feeding his body's reactions, her reactions. His pace quickened. Blood pounded in his ears. His balls tightened against his body when the pressure within built. His undoing was feeling her velvet muscles grip him in a satiny fist. They tumbled over the precipice together, his roar of ecstasy rivaling her own.

Heaven.

He now knew what Heaven must be like. Marcus marveled at the sight of her. Christina glowed with vitality and health from everything he'd given her. He collapsed on top of her and exhaled in a shudder, wondering in the miracle of her.

Too soon he shifted off her, separating his shaft

from her beautiful sheath. They lay holding each other as he answered the questions she asked about being a vampire.

"I'm not going to be able to take the job in Atlanta now am I?"

"I'm afraid not, *cara*. It would be too difficult as a new convert to be around the blood."

Christina turned in his arms. "What will I do now?" she asked.

"I have an idea of what you could do now." Marcus smiled and feathered kisses down her body.

His hard shaft pressed against her thigh. "You're ready to go again? So soon?"

Marcus smiled a sheepish grin, "Just one of the benefits of being a vampire, my dear. You aren't tired of me already, are you?"

Christina looked at him from under hooded eyes. "I'll never tire of you, lover."

"Good answer," he remarked, blanketing her with his muscular body.

****

After two more rounds of making love, Christina felt sated, her body deliciously sore. Marcus held her to him, looking deep into her emerald eyes.

I've never seen anyone look more beautiful, Marcus thought to himself.

I heard that, heartmate, Christina sent along their private channel.

You're getting good at using the mindlink.

It's not the only thing you think I'm getting good at. A sexy smile played over her pretty face.

Marcus raised a questioning brow. *Oh really? And just what do you think I think you are good at?*

Christina gave him a playful slap on his chest. *Maybe I should show you what you think I'm good at.*

You're insatiable, you little minx!

You made me that way.

Marcus' arms expanded with Christina's back when she yawned.

I think you should show me later. You are tired, cara. *You need your rest.*

But I don't want to sleep. I want to stay awake with you.

We have forever, my dear. We can afford to get a little sleep.

The meaning of that statement hit Christina squarely. They really did have forever. She and Marcus had centuries together, and she was determined to make them the happiest centuries two people ever shared.

Sure, there would be struggles, and she wasn't exactly sure how she felt about not taking the job in Atlanta, but with Marcus by her side, she knew she could get through anything. She loved this man with all her heart and soul. In a short time, he had become her life, her reason for existing, and from their mindlink she knew he felt the same way toward her.

"I love you, Marcus," she murmured and snuggled sleepily against his bare chest.

When he wrapped his arm tightly around her in a bracing hug, his warmth soaked into her body to create a lassitude that pulled her under.

"I'll love you forever," he breathed as they drifted off to sleep.

Epilogue

Marcus strolled up to the glass door of the counseling center. He sauntered through and greeted the receptionist sitting behind the partition. "Good evening, Catherine. How are you doing?"

Catherine, formerly given the nick name Food by Michael, gave him a shy smile. "Hi, handsome. I'm doing okay."

"You're looking good. How's the family doing?"

"I think my parents have finally gotten used to the idea of me living here."

"I'm sure it wasn't easy deciding not to go back to Virginia, but Christina is sure glad you decided to stay. She says you are invaluable here."

A sad smile came to Catherine's face. "I just didn't feel like I could say no to a chance to help her get this center up and running. It gave me a chance to help others like she helped me." She shifted in her chair as if the memories made her uncomfortable. "I'll buzz you in."

Marcus flashed her a sexy smile in an effort to alleviate her unease. "Thanks."

With the buzzer sounding, Marcus turned the handle of the door separating the lobby from the rest of the building. He walked down the hallway toward his destination. As he passed one of the meeting rooms, he glanced in. The sight warmed his heart.

Tammy and Anne led the support group session. Anne held the hand of the woman sitting beside her, while the woman relayed the story of how she came to be at the counseling center. Tammy crossed the room to get the woman a tissue. She looked up, noticed Marcus, then gave him a small smile and raised her hand to gesture hello. Marcus waved, before resuming his stroll.

At the end of the hallway stood an unassuming door. The lettering on the frosted glass said, "Christina Prescott: Director."

Christina looked up from the desk she sat behind when he pushed through the door. The deadbolt clicked into place behind him, as Marcus subtly locked the office door. As always, he monitored her thoughts and found she rather liked the sight of her mate. The way he looked in his suit sent a flood of heat through her body that flowed over their link and right to his groin.

"Hello, my love." He glided toward her. "You're working late tonight."

Christina stretched in the chair. "Tatiana came by to talk. She wants me to start a vampire support group for female vampires who have been abused. Apparently the victim from her latest case needs our help. After talking to her, I got busy creating a new group and completely lost track of time."

The pretty redhead glanced down at her watch, noting the time. "I missed our date didn't I? I'm so sorry."

Marcus sat on the corner of her desk and stretched out his legs, crossing them at the ankles. "Forget it. We can go to dinner any time. I see Anne and Tammy are leading a session tonight."

"Their fifth, this week."

"You know, they amaze me. In only a year, they have gone from Michael's victims, who by the way, were not able to speak of the trauma they suffered, to women who not only regained their lives but are now helping others who have been traumatized."

Tears welled in Christina's beautiful green eyes. "I know. They are a real inspiration to the women who come here for help. Did I tell you Catherine has gone back to school? She is studying to be a psychiatrist. I offered her a job here when she graduates."

Marcus pulled his mate to him and kissed the tears from her cheeks. "You amaze me too. You felt a need to help Michael's victims, and look what that has turned into. Hundreds of women have been helped by the counseling center you opened. I only see one problem."

"What's that?"

"The name on your door. Shouldn't it read Christina Botticelli?"

"Technically no, we still haven't married."

"Well I think it is about time we rectify that. I planned to do this over a romantic candle-lit dinner, complete with violins and roses, but you stood me up, so you've left me little choice." Marcus dropped to one knee in front of her and pulled a red velvet box from his pocket.

"Will you marry me, Christina Prescott?" He opened the box to reveal the three-carat, pear-shaped solitaire inside.

"Yes, yes!" she squealed, jumping up and down.

Marcus stood, removed the ring from the delicate velvet box and slipped it on her finger. It fit perfectly.

Christina threw her arms around her heartmate and

hugged him tightly, examining the ring behind his back.

"We'll have to set a date soon. I want a big wedding. I want all our friends there and the girls from work…. Oh, the girls from work, I have to go tell them."

Marcus tightened his hug, keeping her to him when she tried to pull away. "There will be time for that later, *cara*."

Christina gazed up into his deep brown eyes and smiled. "Thank you."

A grin tugged at the corners of Marcus' full lips. "You're thanking me for marrying you?'

"No, not just for that. Thank you for everything: marrying me, making me the happiest woman in the world, helping me with this counseling center. I couldn't have done it without your support and love, my heartmate."

Christina gave Marcus a kiss that said what her words did not. He reached behind them and swept the items from her desk with one grand motion. He then lowered her down on the desk and covered her with his body. Marcus gazed down into her emerald eyes, luxuriating in the love visible within.

"You will always have my support and love, Christina. Always."

He sealed his pledge by loving her with his body and soul.

A word about the author…

Born in Virginia, Brenda Sparks now resides in the Sunshine State. Balancing her professional commitment to the local school district with her writing is challenging at times, but writing suspenseful paranormal romances is a passion that won't be denied.

Her idea of a perfect day is one spent in front of a computer with a hot cup of coffee, her fingers flying over the keys to send her characters off on their latest adventure.

Brenda loves to connect with readers. Please visit her at www.brenda-sparks.com.